"You'll not have him. I heard you say it."

His hand inched its way down her spine and splayed across the small of her back.

"I didna mean it," she said, and tried to look away. He wouldn't let her.

"Aye, you did." He kissed her, hard.

Her lips parted of their own accord, her arms slipped 'round his waist. Mairi closed her eyes and lost herself in his scent, a heady fusion of sweat and leather.

His tongue mated with hers, then plundered her mouth as if it were a treasure trove. She knew she should stop him. Why didn't she?

Heat consumed her as his hands kneaded her backside. What was happening? She let out a whimper. Conall groaned in response.

Her eyes went wide. "Nay," she breathed, and tried to pull away.

"What's wrong?" Conall nuzzled her cheek, his eyes catlike slits.

"Ye must stop. I...I must—" She spun out of his arms....

DEBRA LEE BROWN

A ROGUE'S HEART

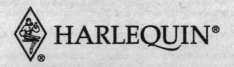

HARLEQUIN®

TORONTO • NEW YORK • LONDON
AMSTERDAM • PARIS • SYDNEY • HAMBURG
STOCKHOLM • ATHENS • TOKYO • MILAN • MADRID
PRAGUE • WARSAW • BUDAPEST • AUCKLAND

ISBN 0-373-29225-2

A ROGUE'S HEART

Visit us at www.eHarlequin.com

Printed in U.S.A.

Please address questions and book requests to:
Harlequin Reader Service
U.S.: 3010 Walden Ave., P.O. Box 1325, Buffalo, NY 14269
Canadian: P.O. Box 609, Fort Erie, Ont. L2A 5X3

For Mark and Ken and Steve and Greg
Rogues one and all

Chapter One

The Highlands of Scotland, 1213

Conall Mackintosh hated water.

Perhaps 'twas the ill-fated sea voyage he'd barely survived the year before, or the memory of being dunked in the horse trough once too often as a lad. Whatever the reason, he had a bad feeling about his brother's proposal.

"Why me?" He shot Iain a disgruntled look. "Why not Gilchrist? He's always splashing about in that bloody spring of his."

"Ye know well his clan canna spare him for such a task. Nor can ours spare me. That leaves you."

Conall swore silently under his breath.

"Negotiate the terms with Dunbar, build out the docks, and make ready for the first trade boats." Iain nodded as if Conall had already agreed.

Boats. Docks and boats. His skin prickled at the mere mention of such things.

"Och, what are ye worried about?" Iain said. "'Tis no' the western sea, just a wee loch. Ye'll be done with the task and off to wherever the devil it is this time—''

''Glenmore. To hunt with your wife's cousin.''

''—long before the winter sets in.''

Conall smirked. '''Tis easy enough for you to say, here at home.'' He swept his gaze over Findhorn Castle, their birthplace and seat of Clan Mackintosh.

''So the adventurer tires of his lifestyle, eh?''

''That's not what I meant.''

''What was it ye said last spring when the MacBains proposed a match for ye?''

Saint Columba, not this again.

'''I'm no' one for settling down' is what ye said. 'I prefer travel, adventure.'''

Conall rolled his eyes at Iain's perfect but painful imitation of him.

''Well then, brother, here's the adventure of a lifetime.''

Jupiter's deep bark echoed behind them off the stone battlement where they stood overlooking Findhorn's bailey.

''See?'' Iain said. ''Even your mangy partner agrees with me.''

Conall glared at the mastiff. ''Traitor.''

''Och, come now.'' Iain mustered what Conall knew was his most serious expression.

Here it comes. He waited for the inevitable lecture.

''Ye are third son and, as such, ye've been left with damned little to make a start of your own. Ye'll always have a place here with us at Findhorn or at Monadhliath with Gilchrist, but—''

''A lifetime of domestic boredom doesna suit me? Aye, well, that's the God's truth.''

''That's no' what—'' Iain closed his eyes and exhaled. Conall watched, amused, as his brother silently counted to ten.

"Hmm? You were saying?"

"I was *saying,* ye've traveled the bluidy world. Can ye no' tarry long enough to do this one thing for us?" Iain clapped a hand on his shoulder in that annoyingly paternal way Conall hated. "For the Chattan?"

The Chattan. The five. Mackintosh, Davidson, Macgillivray and the rest. Five Highland clans aligned in peace. Well, most of the time. It had been their father's dream, God rest his soul.

Iain had seen it through, forged the bond some ten years ago, with Gilchrist's help. Conall had been a reckless youth at the time, more concerned with horses and women than with politics. In fact, he preferred them still.

"We need the trade," Iain said. "Three hard winters in a row—we canna abide a fourth. Last year many died."

Conall shrugged out of his brother's grasp and stepped to the edge of the battlement. Jupiter nudged his hand. "Good boy," he whispered, and patted the mastiff's enormous head.

The bailey was alive with the shouts and laughter of their kinsmen: stable lads, fletchers, farriers, women with baskets scurrying between the timber cottages hugging the curtain wall.

"Will ye do it, Conall?" Iain asked. "If no' for the Chattan, then for Gilchrist and for me?"

God knows, he'd done damned little for family or clan these last years. He wasn't like his brothers, content to stay in one place with one woman. The wanderlust was in his blood. 'Twas part of him, the best part.

Perhaps he was being selfish. On the other hand, 'twas just like Iain to draw him into exactly the kind of life he didn't want to live, one small task at a time.

"O' course he'll do it! He's a good lad."

Conall bit off a curse and turned toward the familiar voice.

"Rob," Iain said. "Convince my brother here to pay Alwin Dunbar a wee visit."

"Dunbar of Loch Drurie?" Rob cocked a tawny brow and fisted chubby hands on hips.

Conall crushed his conscience long enough to fight the smile tugging at the edge of his mouth. His short, balding friend Rob oft reminded him of the rotund gnomes of boyhood tales.

"Aye," Iain said. "The same."

"'Tis a fair piece o' land he holds, The Dunbar," Rob said.

Iain nodded. "Aye, and well situated for our purpose. We shall trade game and furs for grain."

"And a bit o' drink if we're lucky, eh?" Rob winked, his blue eyes flashing mirth.

"'Tis a good plan," Conall said warily. "I'll admit that. But how do you know Dunbar will agree?"

Iain shrugged. "I don't. 'Tis your job to convince him."

Conall snorted. The only convincing he'd done lately had resulted in a thrashing from a village lass's father.

"Och, come on," Rob said. "Ye know ye love a challenge."

Iain crossed his arms over his chest. "So he says."

They had him on that, and they both knew it, damn them. "Whoresons," he muttered.

Rob grinned. "I told ye he'd do it."

Iain grunted satisfaction.

"I'll not miss that hunt with Grant, mind you." His words fell on deaf ears.

"'Twill be good for him to shoulder a bit o' responsibility on behalf of the Chattan, eh?" Rob said.

Responsibility. Even the word made him itch. His coarse woolen shirt suddenly felt too tight about the neck.

His brothers' responsibilities over the years had grown tenfold, their successes spawning only more work, not less, and staggering obligations. The years of hardship and struggle, a thousand forgone pleasures. And for what? He shuddered to think of what he would have missed of the world had he succumbed at an early age and followed in their footsteps.

Nay, 'twas not for him.

"There's a fair reward for the service," Iain said. He studied his fingernails in a way that made Conall instantly suspicious. "I nearly forgot to mention it."

"What reward?"

"Oh, no' much," Iain said, not looking at him. "Some land, a bit o' cattle—" he paused and met Conall's gaze "—a bride, mayhap."

"What the—"

"Only if ye wish it," Iain said quickly. "She's a bonny lass, the youngest daughter of one o' the Chattan lairds."

Conall shot toward him. "Bloody matchmaker. I'll have none of it, d'ye hear?"

Rob—who was supposed to be his friend, the blackguard—dissolved into laughter.

"Suit yourself." Iain shrugged. "'Twas just a thought. About the bride, I mean."

"Aye, and by the new year you'd have me bound

to some simpering virgin. A bairn on the way by Easter.''

"Och, surely sooner than that, eh?" Rob winked, and Conall shot him a murderous glance.

"All right," Iain said. "Forget the lass, but ye'd be damned stupid to refuse the land and the cattle. 'Tis meant as a reward, no' a millstone around your neck."

"Hmph." His gaze was drawn again to the bailey, where a group of children played in sight of their young mothers. He felt overwarm and sweaty, and pulled at the leather ties of his shirt. "I dunno."

Jupiter let out a small whimper and licked his hand.

"Och, hang the reward," Rob said. "We'll do it for the fun, for the challenge, won't we, Conall laddie?"

"We?" Conall looked his short friend up and down. "So you think to come with me?"

"O' course. Why wouldn't I?" Rob grinned. "Someone's got to keep ye out o' trouble."

"Take Dougal and Harry with ye as well," Iain said. "They're good scouts and in need of a change." Iain slapped him on the back.

Out of the corner of his eye, he caught Iain's grin of satisfaction and Rob's dancing eyes. "The two of you are thick as thieves. Did I ever have a choice?"

Jupiter barked and wagged his monstrous tail.

"And you." He swatted the dog's rump. "I suppose you were in on it, too?"

The mastiff cocked his head, looking up at him with huge liquid eyes. Iain and Rob grinned.

"Boats," he muttered. "Docks and boats." Already his stomach grew queasy.

"Mairi Dunbar!"

She froze at the rich, familiar timbre of Geoffrey Symon's voice. The ax she wielded hung in midair, poised over the felled larch.

''What in God's name are ye doing?'' Geoffrey bellowed from behind her.

Dora looked up from her work gathering kindling, and rolled her eyes. Mairi glared at her, then dropped the ax and quickly wiped the perspiration from her face.

'''Tis his second visit in as many weeks,'' Dora hissed, and shot her one of those I-told-ye-so looks Mairi hated.

Mairi ignored her, squared her shoulders and turned to greet their visitor. ''Geoffrey, what a surprise.''

He was alone, which was unusual, and dressed in some of the finest garments she'd e'er seen him wear. Hmm, even more unusual. His plaid was newly woven, laced with rich colors—nothing like the common hunting plaids most everyone wore.

Atop his dappled gelding he sat tall, chin high, more like a prince than the lesser chieftain he was. His jet hair was tied back, as always, with a leather thong, accentuating his fair features and crystalline blue eyes.

She would think him handsome if she had a mind to notice such things, but she did not. Geoffrey was just like her father. She mustn't forget that, not ever.

He slid easily from the horse's saddle and smiled at her—a bold, disarming smile that made her blush involuntarily. Of all the stupid responses.

She fisted handfuls of her gown, soiled from a morning of hard labor, and boldly returned his gaze. ''What brings ye to Loch Drurie again so soon, Geoffrey?''

''Ye know why…Mairi.''

The way her name rolled off his lips caused a small

shiver to course through her. She wasn't certain if she liked it or not.

Dora snorted behind her. Mairi glanced back in time to see the older woman pick up the ax and hack at the felled tree with renewed vigor. Dora shot them both a disgusted look.

Geoffrey laughed. "Your friend doesna like me much."

Dora hated him, in fact.

"No matter," Geoffrey said. "She'll come 'round, as will ye, Mairi Dunbar."

"Geoffrey, I told ye I—"

"Hush." He crossed the tiny clearing and put a finger to her lips.

She drew back, bristling. No one told her to be quiet. No one. "I've work to do, so state your business."

He laughed again. "Ah, that spirit o' yours is as fiery as your red head. 'Twill get ye into trouble yet."

A smart retort burned on her lips, but she clenched her teeth against it.

Geoffrey's expression sobered. "Mairi, I would speak to ye alone." His eyes darted behind her to Dora, who, from the sound of it, was hacking the larch to splinters.

The chopping abruptly stopped.

"Dora is clan," Mairi said. "There is naught fit for my ears that she may no' hear." She arched a brow, her terms set.

The edge of Geoffrey's mouth twitched. He studied her for a moment, then said, "All right, then. Ye know of what I wish to speak."

Mairi's pulse quickened. The chopping recommenced. She knew all too well why Geoffrey was here. "My father's debt."

"Aye."

"Well, what of it? I told ye I'd pay by the new year. 'Tis two months away yet."

Geoffrey grasped her hand, and she tensed. "Why d'ye fight me, lass? It doesna have to be this way."

"I dinna know what ye mean," she lied, and pulled her hand away.

"This." He pointed past her to the tiny, ramshackle village lining the shore of the loch. "And this." He lifted the skirt of her filthy gown.

Dora grunted with another stroke of the ax.

"Women shouldna be forced to such labor," he said. "If ye were my wife, Mairi, 'twould no' be so."

"Wife?" The word made her cringe.

"Aye. I'm willing to forgive the debt." He paused. "And what's passed between us."

She crossed her arms over her chest, a derisive sound escaping her throat. Perhaps he was willing, but she was not.

"Come now, ye know 'tis the best thing for ye and what's left of your clan. Just look at the place."

She did look, and hardened her heart against what she saw. Rickety timber cottages, leaky boats, docks mildewed and rotting. Her father had done this to them, the negligent clod. She bristled at the memory of his sloth and gambling.

Her gaze lit on two women scrubbing dirty clothes on a rock at the water's edge. Children played in the mud with makeshift toys. Most of the men were dead or gone, all but the old and infirm. Driven out by her father's oppression, or their own disgust.

"Ye canna survive another winter like the last,"

Geoffrey said. "Women and children, alone, with but a handful of ragtag clansmen to protect and provide for ye."

Mairi clenched her teeth. He was right, but she'd never admit it. She'd find a way to pay the debt and get them through the winter without starving. She had to.

"We're doing just...fine," she stammered, and nodded once for emphasis, more to convince herself than him.

Geoffrey mouthed a silent curse and kicked at a pile of wood shavings near his feet. "Ye'll be paying me a visit afore the winter's e'en here. Methinks ye'll change your mind. Ye need me, Mairi, admit it." She tipped her chin at him, and he grabbed her wrist. "Mark me, Mairi Dunbar. I'd have ye willing, but I'll have ye—one way or another."

"Presumptuous lout!" She jerked her hand away and shot him a murderous look. "Think ye to control me, as did my father? Think again."

He had the nerve to smile at her.

"Get off my land! And dinna return till 'tis time to collect your payment."

Geoffrey shook his head, and his expression softened. "I love ye, lass, don't ye know that?"

"Aye, ye love my land. Now go!"

He looked her up and down as if he were appraising a sheep. Another smile curved at the edge of his mouth and his eyes danced like bright blue flames.

Her blood boiled.

He mounted the dappled gelding and raised a hand in farewell. "And when I break ye of that wild spirit and no'-so-comely boldness, ye'll make a fine, obedient wife."

"Obedient wife?" Mairi repeated, and fisted her hands on her hips.

Dora dropped the ax and stepped to her side, breathing hard, her face sheened with sweat. "Aye," she wheezed. "When pigs fly."

Jupiter bounded ahead along the well-worn forest path, making occasional detours into the brush to ferret out hares and other small game.

"Does the beast never tire?" Dougal asked.

Conall grinned. "He'll be plenty tired tonight."

"Aye," Rob said. "Mind, Dougal, he doesna curl up in your plaid with ye."

Dougal smirked at them.

"Dinna laugh," Conall said. "He's kept me from freezing on many a winter's night in the rough."

Harry urged his mount even with Conall's and leaned in close to whisper. "Dougal's afraid of him, is all."

"Who, Jupiter?" This surprised him.

"Aye, and who wouldna be?" Harry's gaze followed the mastiff as he burst from a tangle of gorse and spooked Dougal's mount. "Look at the size of him. What does he weigh, ye reckon, ten or twelve stone?"

"Fifteen," Conall said.

"The devil, you say! That's more than a man." Harry lifted a brow in appreciation.

"More than most. I'm heavier, but not by much."

Rob spurred his white gelding up beside them. "Aye, but ye're no' a man, Conall laddie, ye're a giant."

"Nay," Conall said. "'Tis just that you're a dwarf."

Rob tipped his bearded chin high. "No' where it counts."

The three of them melted into laughter. Indeed, over the years Rob had proved quite the ladies' man in spite of his diminutive size.

"What are ye yappin' about back there?" Dougal called over his shoulder.

"The usual topics," Harry said. "Dogs and women."

"Aye, ye can hang the one," Rob said, "but I'll take some o' the other."

Harry and Dougal snorted in unison.

Conall was pleased Iain had suggested he take the lads along. They were young and eager, two of the Chattan's finest scouts. Dougal was a Mackintosh, and Harry a Davidson, but the two clans had lived amongst each other for so long it hardly mattered. The two youths were close as blood kin.

They rode for a time in silence, snaking their way south through the Highland wood. The day was warm for so late in the year, and Conall was glad he'd worn a sleeveless tunic instead of the woolen shirt Iain's old housemaid had bade him don for the journey.

Their mounts kicked up a firestorm of brightly colored leaves as they cantered along the path. Gold and green and cinnabar—autumn's palette. The sky changed as morning gave way to afternoon, startling blue against the thick canopy of larch, laurel and the occasional pine. After a time the trees thinned, and they came upon a crossroad leading west. Conall reined his black stallion to a halt.

"Monadhliath lies that way," Rob said.

Conall nodded and let his gaze drift along the path. Monadhliath Castle, seat of Clan Davidson, his mother's people. His brother Gilchrist was laird there now—had been these five years past.

"Shall we pay them a visit?" Rob asked. "'Tis but a day's ride out of our way."

It had been nearly a year since Conall had seen Gilchrist and his wife. Too long. They'd had another child, so Iain had told him. All the same...

"Nay," he said, and urged the black onward. "We'd best keep moving. 'Twill be nearly dark by the time we reach Loch Drurie."

Rob shrugged. "Suit yourself. I just thought—"

Not waiting for Rob to finish, Conall spurred the black into a gallop, outdistancing the rest of their party. He was more than ready for something new, something dangerous, perhaps, and exciting. There'd be plenty of time for family and domestic obligations later.

Much later.

Two hours hence they broke out of the trees onto a rocky ridge. Loch Drurie lay below them, stretched out like a lazy cat warming itself in the afternoon sun. The placid water glimmered a deep, mysterious blue—the color of a woman's eyes. Not any woman Conall had ever seen, but it reminded him of one all the same.

Rob drew up beside him and nodded to the loch below. "'Tis no' so big."

"That's only the tip of it. The rest is around that bend there." Conall pointed to what appeared to be the far end of the loch.

"Oh," Rob said, clearly disappointed. "Well, then, we'd best get down there, eh?"

They rode on as the sun dipped low in the sky, transforming the loch's surface into a golden looking-glass. He'd seen one once in France, in a lady's bedchamber. The lady he could not recall, but the glass, now that was something special.

"Ah, here it is," Dougal said, wresting Conall from his thoughts.

"Aye, I see it now," Harry added.

Conall peered ahead through the trees, narrowing his eyes as if that would allow him to see better. He turned to Rob and arched a brow in question.

Rob shook his head. "I canna see a bluidy thing."

Conall laughed. "Aye, that's precisely why Harry and Dougal are the scouts."

They stepped up their pace and followed the two younger men, who seemed to know exactly where they were going. The trees thinned, and then he saw it.

"Saint Columba, will ye look at that!" Dougal said.

Rob let out a long, low whistle.

"This is it?" Harry looked to Conall for confirmation.

Conall shrugged and let his gaze drift over the ramshackle grouping of timber cottages and sheds, rotting docks, and twisted, sunken piers. A good-size fortified house stood on the hill above them. It had seen better days and looked all but abandoned.

Few people were about—women and children mostly, and a few old men. Jupiter barked and bounded ahead, kicking up clods of mud and rocks along the water's edge. When the villagers caught sight of the huge dog and Conall's party of mounted warriors, they fled to the safety of their cottages.

"Where are all the men?" Rob asked.

"I know not," Conall said. "But 'tis clear something's amiss. We'll dismount here. I dinna wish to frighten them." He slipped from the black's saddle and his men followed suit. They tethered their horses at the edge of the wood and waited for further instruction.

"Rob, come with me," he said. "Dougal, Harry, wait here with the men. I'll call if I've need of you."

The two scouts nodded.

Conall and Rob approached the village on foot. Sets of eyes peered out at them from windows draped in tattered furs and bits of dingy plaid. Children's squeals and women's hushed censures drifted from behind tight-shut cottage doors.

"Charming place, eh?" Rob whispered.

Conall cast him a cool look.

A branch snapped up the hill to their left, and they whirled toward the sound. Conall's hand flew to the hilt of his dirk, Rob's to his bow.

An old man stood in the open doorway of the fortified house, a bucket in each hand. His brows shot up when he saw them. "Ho, visitors!"

"I am Conall Mackintosh," he called up the hill to the man. "I have business with your laird."

The old man set the buckets on the ground. "Ye do?"

"Aye, we do," Rob said.

They climbed the short, steep hill to the run-down house. Conall nodded to the old man. "This is Alwin Dunbar's clan?"

"Aye, what's left of it."

"Is the laird about?"

"Oh, aye, he's here all right." The old man looked him over. "Conall Mackintosh, ye say—of the Chattan?"

"Ye know us, then," Rob said.

"I've heard o' the alliance. 'Tis a good thing, methinks.'' The old man continued to scrutinize Conall, who quickly grew impatient with the chitchat.

''Where's your laird?'' he demanded.

''Oh, Alwin? Over there.'' The old man nodded to a small, overgrown garden at the far end of the house.

Conall made for it, and Rob followed. The so-called garden was a tangled mass of weeds and dead summer flowers. No one was there. No one alive, at any rate. A pile of stones covering what looked to be a shallow grave dominated the center of the weedy enclosure.

''Where is he?'' Conall asked.

The old man appeared behind him, buckets in hand. ''Who, Alwin?''

Conall's patience was at an end. ''Nay, the bloody King of England.''

''Testy, ain't ye?'' the man said to Rob.

Conall had had enough. He reached out and grabbed the old man by his shirt.

''Ho, wait—he's there!'' Conall instantly released him. The old man set the buckets down and pointed to the grave. ''Alwin Sedgewick Dunbar, laird.''

''What?'' Conall snapped. ''You mean he's dead?''

''Oh, aye, nearly a month now.'' The old man matter-of-factly dumped the contents of the buckets at the foot of the grave. Ear-shattering squeals pierced the air as two sows raced from the back of the house and devoured the stinking pile.

''God's blood.'' Conall wrinkled his nose in disgust as he sidestepped the pigs. ''Who the devil is in charge then?''

''Oh, down there.'' The old man nodded toward the loch below.

Conall turned and immediately stopped breathing. His eyes widened as they followed the length of a narrow pier he'd missed earlier. The floating timbers began at the far end of the village and extended a hundred feet or so out into the loch. A radial raft of logs floated tethered to its endpoint, topped by the strangest-looking house he'd e'er seen.

"What do you make of that?" he asked. "'Tis… round."

"Aye, 'tis a *crannog*," Rob said. "A lake house. Did ye no' see them in Ireland?"

Conall shook his head.

"Oh, they make fine lodgings—if ye like the water."

Conall smirked at him.

"Well, we'd best get out there and see the man in charge."

"What, you mean…out there?" Conall stared at the rickety pier.

"Ye wish to cull the deal, do ye no'?" Rob didn't wait for an answer. He grabbed Conall's arm and pulled him down the hill. "Come on, it should be fair easy, given the state o' this place. I expect they'd take any offer ye make them."

"If 'tis dealing ye've come to do, have a care," the old man called after them.

Conall wondered what the elder meant by that, but had no time to think. His stomach was already churning at the thought of merely negotiating that pier, let alone the deal.

As they passed through the village, Rob tugged on his arm and let out a low whistle. Conall followed his friend's gaze to an open cottage window where two blushing maidens leaned on the sill, gawking at them. Conall glared back and they giggled.

"Cloying virgins," he muttered under his breath.

"Ye dinna fancy them?" Rob asked as he steered Conall toward the pier.

"Nay, I prefer women of substance."

Jupiter's high-pitched yelp cut the air. Conall froze.

"What, ye mean like that?" Rob pointed to the lake house at the end of the pier.

Jupiter stumbled on the rickety timbers in a tug of war over what appeared to be a ham. His rival for the savory loin was— Why, 'twas a woman! A barefoot woman with wild red hair and skirts rucked up to her knees.

Jesu, he breathed, and took in the fine curve of her calf silhouetted against the setting sun.

Her hair was a brilliant fusion of cinnabar and sunlight, whipping in the wind off the loch. The huge mastiff cowered as she thumped him squarely on the nose, but he did not release the meat. Conall grinned.

"He'll take her hand off!" Rob cried, and pushed him toward the pier.

Conall's grin widened, his gaze fixed on the woman. "If he wanted to, he'd have already done it."

Conall stepped out onto the pier— "Whoa...w-wait" —and instantly tried to step back again as the unanchored timbers rolled under his weight. Rob moved behind him, a short but solid wall barring his retreat.

"Is this your dog?" the woman shouted at them.

"A-aye, he's mine," Conall called back.

"Well, come and get him!" She thumped Jupiter again with the flat of her hand. Jupiter let out a low whine, but did not let go the meat.

Conall drew a breath, fixed his gaze on them and put one foot in front of the other. "Bloody hell." The pier rocked, but not so violently he couldn't maintain his balance.

"Come on, come on." Rob prodded him in the back.

Halfway there. Keep moving. The water was all around them now, and Conall's stomach tightened.

"Hurry it up," Rob said.

"Aye, before I decide to butcher the dog instead o' the ham!" the woman shouted.

Just a…few…more…steps. Conall grabbed the mastiff by his thick leather collar. "Jupiter, drop it!"

The dog obeyed instantly, releasing the ham.

"He's ruint it!" the woman cried. "Ye'll pay me for this in kind, d'ye hear?"

Conall stared at her, transfixed. Her face was flushed from her struggle with the dog, and her eyes flashed anger. Blue eyes, deep as the still waters of Loch Drurie.

"Well, are ye dumb? What say ye, will ye pay or no'?"

She was tall for a woman, much taller than Rob, but she still had to tilt her chin upward to look Conall in the eye. He fought to keep his gaze from drifting to her breasts, then smiled at her. She glared back at him, her eyes jeweled daggers.

"Who's in charge here?" he finally had the presence of mind to ask, ignoring her question.

"I am." She redoubled her grip on the ham and tipped her chin higher.

"I see. Hmm…"

He liked her. She was bold. His gaze was drawn to her mouth and he found himself wondering if her lips were soft, if she'd taste of honey and wine.

"I'll have my payment now," she quipped, and arched a delicate, fiery brow.

Conall ignored her demand. "Where is your husband, madam?"

"Husband, indeed. I have none. Now, my payment if ye please."

"Payment?" What payment? "Oh, aye, for the ham." On impulse he grabbed her and kissed her hard on the mouth. Rob wasn't the only one who had a way with women. Mmm, her lips were indeed soft and her breath sweet. "There, paid in full." He released her, and she staggered backward on the pier.

For a moment she seemed dazed, then recovered herself. Her eyes blazed murder. "Of all the—"

"Watch out!" Rob cried.

She swung the ham and it caught Conall full in the gut, knocking the breath from him. He grunted, his arms closing over the smoked loin as the force of the blow knocked him clear off his feet.

The next thing he knew he was in the water, flapping arms and legs madly in an attempt to stay afloat. He went under and came up choking. The woman stood at the edge of the pier, hands on hips, smirking at him. Impudent wench!

Jupiter barked frantically and ran back and forth along the rickety timbers. Conall couldn't tell if the dog was alarmed over his master's plight or merely upset at the loss of the ham, which had sunk like a rock.

He slipped under a second time, paddling furiously to no avail. His eyes widened in panic.

"What's wrong with him?" The woman's smirk melted quickly into a frown.

Rob shook his head. "He canna swim."

Chapter Two

She was tempted to let him drown.

Mairi tapped her foot impatiently on the pier and waited for the rogue to come up for air. "Waste of a perfectly good ham. He'll pay for it, the cheeky lout."

"No' if he's dead."

She glanced at his short companion. "I hadna thought of that." A flurry of bubbles broke the surface. The dog began to whine. She supposed they ought not let him drown. 'Twould be un-Christian. "Well, dinna stand there gawkin'—fish him out."

"Who, me?"

"Aye, go on." She thumped the diminutive warrior on the shoulder.

"'Twill do no good," he said, eyeing the bubbles.

"Why not?"

"I canna swim, neither."

"God's blood! Are all the Mackintoshes this helpless?"

"Aye, where water's concerned." He narrowed his eyes. "How did ye know who we are?"

"The clan badge in your bonnet." She quickly unlaced her gown and pulled it off over her head.

"Aye, a cat with—" His eyes nearly popped from his head at the sight of her in her shift. "What are ye doin'?"

"Savin' his life, though he doesna deserve it. Bluidy bother." She took a deep breath and dove headfirst into the chill water.

He was dead easy to find. She merely followed the telltale trail of bubbles to the bottom. He was still struggling. Good. At least she'd not have to revive him. She grabbed him by the leather strap belting his broadsword to his back. Men and their weapons. No wonder the idiot nearly drowned. The sword alone had to weigh more than a stone.

She kicked toward the surface with the warrior in tow. He was heavy as sin. Weapons, garments, boots—what a load. Too bad he hadn't held on to the ham. She'd remember to send Kip in for it later. The water was barely a dozen feet deep here. 'Twould be easy to recover.

As soon as they broke the surface, the warrior began to thrash about, his arms and legs flailing.

"Be still or I'll let ye sink." She pulled him to the pier.

The blasted dog started barking again. The short man patted the mongrel's head, then knelt to help them from the water. "Is he all right?"

"He'll live." She let go of the warrior when his shaking hands grabbed hold of the timbers. "The bluidy fool." He coughed up another lungful of water, then turned to look at her, breathing hard. 'Twas then she noticed his eyes. They were green. Nay, brown. Hmm…perhaps he—wait a minute! She didn't give a whit about his eyes. What nonsense.

"I...dinna...know—" he coughed again "—whether to thank you or strangle you."

She ignored his comment and started to pull herself onto the pier.

"Y-your name," he sputtered.

For a moment she thought not to give it, then changed her mind. They *were* green, at least in this light. "Mairi. Mairi Dunbar." He studied her face, and her cheeks warmed under his scrutiny. She'd rather die than blush, she thought, and bit off a curse.

"I'm...Conall...Mackintosh," he said between huge gulps of air. He started to shiver, and she realized she was trembling, as well. 'Twas the cold water, nothing more.

The little man on the pier cleared his throat. "And I seem to be a bluidy fisherman. Now get yer arse out o' that water."

"Oh, this is R-R-Rob," Conall said, teeth chattering, as he grabbed his friend's extended hand.

Mairi pulled herself easily onto the pier and came face-to-face with the huge mastiff. "This is your fault, ye ill-mannered mongrel."

Jupiter flattened his ears back and looked at her with plaintive brown eyes.

"That's his way of apologizing." The warrior struggled to his feet and offered her a hand. She eyed it suspiciously and drew her knees up close to her chin. "Come," he said, "I'll help you up."

"I need no help, especially from you." She was shivering now, soaking wet, and the sun nearly set. What foolery. She struggled to her feet. "What d'ye want? Why have ye come here?"

He stared at her, silent. What a trio they made: the huge, sodden warrior—plaid twisted and dripping, weapons askew—his short, bright-eyed companion, who seemed vastly amused by the whole ordeal, and then there was the bloody dog.

She was suddenly aware of the warrior's mouth. He chewed on his lip as his eyes drank her in. No man had ever looked at her that way. Not even Geoffrey. A flush of heat consumed her, and she was at once conscious of her breasts beneath her wet shift.

Her shift! She snatched her gown from the pier and held it protectively in front of her. She wasn't used to having men around. Her eyes darted to the shoreline. There were more of them! Twenty warriors at least, and horses laden with goods. Why hadn't she noticed before?

Not one of her clan was about. Where in God's name was Dora? Even Kip, who usually trailed after her like an orphaned pup, was nowhere in sight.

She backed toward the lake house, her thoughts racing as she tried desperately to recall where she'd left her father's sword. Conall stepped toward her. Her pulse quickened and she clutched the gown tighter to her body.

"We mean you no harm," he said. "Dinna be afraid."

There was one thing she'd learned from her dealings with both Geoffrey and her father—never show fear. Never. She tipped her chin at him and arched a brow. "Afraid? Of you?"

The corner of his mouth turned up in a boyish half smile. In truth, he looked more drowned sheep than warrior.

She mustered her courage. "What d'ye want here? State your business, I've work to do."

He glanced at the ramshackle cottages lining the

shore and the sunken, rotting timbers of the ancient docks. "I can see that."

Cheeky sod. She pursed her lips and waited for him to continue.

"I wish to see the man in charge. I've come to propose a business arrangement."

This she did not expect. News of her father's death must have spread far. 'Twas not every day a Mackintosh appeared on Dunbar's doorstep offering business arrangements.

He was after the land. She was sure of it.

"I'm in charge. Just what kind of arrangement?"

"Ha!" The warrior shot his companion an amused look that set her blood to boil.

Something flashed in the water behind them. The dog noticed it, too, and his ears pricked. Sweet God, 'twas Kip! The reckless lad must have swum from the shore, undetected, under the pier. Mairi watched, transfixed, as he grabbed the edge of the timbers and drew himself out of the water, a short dagger between his teeth.

Before she could react, Conall Mackintosh whirled and grabbed the boy by his shirt. Kip went for the dagger, but the warrior was too quick. He sent the weapon flying, then hauled the boy, dripping, from the loch. Kip kicked and struggled, but 'twas no use. Conall was too big. He held him aloft like a drowned kitten, and grinned.

"What have we here, your bodyguard?" The warrior flashed her a smile.

"Let me go, ye bluidy whoreson!" Kip flailed madly in midair.

"Kip, that's enough," she said. "Put him down, Mackintosh, he's just a boy."

"I'm no' a boy, I'm a man! A Dunbar warrior." To Mairi's horror, Kip drew his fist back and landed a solid blow to Conall's tautly muscled abdomen.

"Unh!" Conall winced, and sucked a breath. "Christ, laddie, that's the second time today a Dunbar's tried to deck me."

Mairi dropped her gown and reached for Kip as Conall released him into her arms. She shot the boy a hard look, then drew him back protectively against her chest. She'd save the scolding for later. Conall stepped toward them, and her heart leaped to her throat.

"Dinna hurt him," she said. "Please."

Conall snapped his fingers, and Jupiter bounded forward, Kip's small dagger dwarfed between huge canine teeth. "I would return this to him." To her astonishment, he took the weapon from the dog and offered it to Kip. "Go on, lad, take it."

Kip ripped it from Conall's hand and brandished it in front of him.

"Put it away now," Conall said, "and later, if you promise not to slit my throat, I'll show you how to use it."

Mairi was stunned. She felt the tension in Kip's small shoulders ease a bit. "D'ye mean it?" he asked.

"Aye. Now off with you, I've got business with your mother, here."

"Oh, she's no'—"

"Kip, hush! Go on now. Find Dora and send her to me, quickly." She pushed him toward the shore, and he took off running.

"I thought ye didna like bairns, particularly?" Rob said. He crossed his arms over his chest and eyed Conall.

"I don't, particularly," Conall said as his gaze strayed over her body. "Now, where were we?"

Mairi retrieved her gown and pulled it quickly over her head. She smoothed it as best she could over the wet shift. Instantly the water began to soak through. "Blast! The gown'll be ruint as well." She glared at the warrior. "What is it ye want then? Be quick about it."

He arched a brow. Like his hair, and hers, 'twas fiery copper in the setting sun, and made his eyes look all the more green. She pushed the thought from her mind and waited for his reply.

"I've come on behalf of the Chattan."

"Aye, the alliance. I've heard of it. What of it?"

"We've arranged for trade boats to bring supplies from the south. We'd like to borrow a bit of your land for docking—loading and unloading—and for storage, too."

'Twas as she'd suspected. He wanted the land. Hmph. They were all the same. Her father. Geoffrey. Now this one. Greedy cads without a thought for her or her people. "And what makes ye think I'd allow such a thing?"

He glanced back at the dilapidated collection of cottages along the shoreline. "It seems to me you could profit from the enterprise."

Several of the younger Dunbar women had ventured outside to speak with Conall's men. Mairi watched in alarm as one of them allowed a young warrior to take her hand. Idiots! What were they thinking?

"And there might be other, well…benefits I hadna considered." Conall grinned at her.

"Bluidy men! Go on, get out of here." She turned on her heel, but he grabbed her wrist.

"'Twas the kiss made you save me," he said. "Admit it."

She jerked her hand away, her pulse racing.

"I expect you want another."

"I'd as soon kiss the dog!"

Rob snorted in the background.

Conall stepped closer. "Methinks Jupiter would like that. He's not been 'round many women."

She fisted her hands at her sides and shot him a cautionary look. "Touch me again and ye'll get another dunkin'." He stood there dripping, grinning like a bloody fool. Her nose twitched as she caught his feral scent. "'Twould do ye some good, too."

"What do you mean?"

She blinked and crinkled her nose. "Ye smell worse than that mastiff."

"What?" The smile slid from his face.

Jupiter let out a low whine, and Rob dissolved into laughter.

"Go on. Get off my land." She backed toward the lake house, then nodded toward the men on the shore. "And take that roguish lot with ye."

Before he could answer, she ducked inside the house and bolted the door behind her. Her heart thrummed in her chest as she leaned back against the cool timbers.

"Now there's a fine-lookin' man."

At the sound of Dora's voice, Mairi jumped nearly out of her skin. When her eyes adjusted to the dim light, she focused on her friend crouched at the small front window. "Who, that big, sodden lout?"

"Nay, no' him." Dora giggled like a bride and flashed her a toothy smile. "The short one!"

* * *

Conall rubbed himself down with a dry plaid, sniffed tentatively at his underarms and frowned.

"She's right, ye know," Rob said, and thumped him on the shoulder as he passed, on his way to the camp they'd made at the edge of the wood.

Conall smirked in the dark and finished dressing.

He couldn't recall the last time he'd bathed. Summer, most likely. Aye. He'd just arrived home, and Iain's old housemaid refused to allow him at table until she'd had him up to his ears in a tub of hot water. He shivered at the memory of the old woman's scrub brush.

"Come and eat," Dougal called out from the campfire, "afore there's nothing left."

Conall pulled on his wet boots and squished over to the fire ring. Most of his men had already eaten and were bedded down for the night. Rob and Dougal sat cross-legged by the fire, picking at the remains of some roasted meat. He joined them.

"Where's Jupiter?" He scanned the camp for signs of the dog.

"Over there." Rob nodded to a small copse just outside the bright ring of firelight.

Jupiter lay on his side, snoring lightly, surrounded by a scattering of picked-clean bones.

"Aye, he's had quite the day."

"Haven't we all," Rob said, and arched a brow at him.

Dougal poked at the fire, then settled back against a tree.

"So, what will ye do now?" Rob asked.

"What do you mean? We'll build out the docks, of course."

Rob and Dougal swapped glances.

"Why the look? What are you thinking?"

"Well, she didna agree, if memory serves," Rob said.

Conall snorted. "Aye, but she will. She has no choice. Look around you, man." He nodded toward the group of dilapidated cottages just beyond the fire's comforting glow. "They've little enough to eat now. When winter's full on them, they'll likely starve."

"I hear there's a fine ham lyin' at the bottom o' the loch," Dougal said, straight-faced. After a second of silence, during which Conall was tempted to slug him, Dougal and Rob burst into laughter.

Conall smirked at them. "Aye, verra funny. I've not seen a man fit to bear arms amongst the lot. What do you make of it?"

Dougal's expression darkened. "Ye're right about that. Some of them died, but most just up and left. The old man told me. Dunbar drove them off—gambled away what little they all had."

"Aye, well whatever the reason, the result is in our favor. Mairi Dunbar will take what I give her, and be grateful for it."

His spirits brightened. Iain had been right, after all. 'Twould be an easy task, this dock-building. One he was determined to complete quickly, and move on.

"She's damn vulnerable," Dougal said. "Any man with a mind to could take the land."

"And her," Rob added.

An image of Mairi Dunbar, cheeks flushed and eyes blazing as she fought Jupiter for the ham, flashed in Conall's mind.

"'Tis a fair piece o' land," Dougal said. "The right man could make something of it, what with the loch trade and all."

"No' to mention the lass." Rob arched a tawny brow. "Mairi Dunbar, no simpering virgin there."

Conall shot him a hard look, but recalled how Mairi's wet shift had clung to the lithe curves of her body. His gaze drifted across the water to the lake house. 'Twas eerily dark. He could almost feel her watching him from the window.

"All the same," Rob said, "she needs a man's protection—whether she'll admit it or no'."

Conall grunted and tossed another fagot onto the fire. So what if she did? What was it to him? He was charged with securing the land and building out the docks. Nothing more. The last thing he needed was to get involved with a ragtag band of Dunbars. Women and children and old men.

A branch snapped in the wood behind him. Conall's hand shot to the hilt of his dirk.

"She's got a man's protection," a thin voice called out. "Mine." The boy Kip stepped from behind a stout larch, his small hands fisted on narrow hips. His eyes bore into Conall's.

Dougal started to laugh, but Conall silenced him with a look. "Come here, then," he said to the lad. "Let's have a look at your weapons."

Kip approached the fire cautiously, his dark eyes darting to the small clearing where their horses were tethered and where twenty-odd Mackintosh warriors slept. He unsheathed his small dirk and waved it in front of him.

The boy had courage. Conall sized him up as he would a rival, then nodded approval. "Aye, you'll do." He held out his hand. "Let's have a look at that wicked dagger."

Kip's eyes met his and, for a moment, neither of

them moved a muscle. Then, slowly, the boy placed the weapon into Conall's open palm.

"'Tis fine, if a bit dull." Conall ran a finger over the notched and pitted blade. "Rob can hone it for you, if you like." The boy frowned. Without waiting for his agreement, Conall tossed the dirk across the fire ring. Rob caught it and nodded.

"Now, 'tis late…Kip, is it?"

The boy squared his shoulders. "Kelvin Francis Dunbar. But aye, most call me Kip."

"Well, Kelvin Francis Dunbar, find your bed and on the morrow I'll show you some tricks with that dagger you'll not learn from women and old men."

Kip held his gaze, and Conall could tell the boy struggled to repress a smile.

"Off with you," he said, and watched as Kip disappeared into the cover of the trees, as quiet as he'd come.

Rob weighed the small dagger in his hand. "If ye wish to win a widow's heart, win her bairn's first." He grinned and pocketed the weapon. "Ye're smarter than I thought, Conall laddie."

Mairi frowned and let the deerskin cover fall back into place over the window.

"I told ye they'd no' leave." Dora arched a brow at her in the dark.

"Hmph."

"Strike the bargain. After all, what choice d'ye have?"

Mairi peeked out again and her eyes fixed on the Mackintosh warrior. He sat cross-legged before the campfire his men had built earlier that evening. The fire's glow lit up the angular features of his face and sparked gold from his hair. She could almost make out the curve of his smile as he laughed at some remark.

"I saw how he looked at ye," Dora whispered as she knelt beside her.

"What d'ye mean?" Mairi slapped the deerskin cover back in place.

"Och, dinna go pretendin', now. Ye know exactly what I mean. Strike the bargain while ye still can."

"While I still can?"

Dora snorted. "Are ye as big a fool as all that? The man's made ye an offer of business, and God knows he didna have to. What's stopping him from just taking what he wants—the land and you?"

Mairi frowned again. She hadn't thought of that. Well, she had, but… "Nay, he's no' that kind of man."

"They're all that kind of man."

Dora was right. In her limited experience, Mairi had known few men well—her father, Geoffrey, a few of her kinsmen. But there was something different about Conall Mackintosh. She read it in his eyes when he thanked her for saving his life, and again when he returned Kip's dagger and allowed the boy to go free.

"Consider the alternative, is all I'm saying." Dora rose stiffly and started for the door.

"What alternative?"

"Wedding Geoffrey Symon, o' course." Dora shot her a pointed glance then tripped the latch. "I'm off. My bairns will be wantin' their supper."

Dora closed the door behind her, and Mairi watched from the window as her friend made her way along the pier in the dark. They'd been through hard times together, she and Dora. 'Twas not the first time, nor the last, Mairi would think on the older woman's advice.

When Dora reached the shore, Rob called out to her from the campfire set just outside the village. Dora curtsied briefly in the little man's direction, then bolted toward her cottage. The sound of men's laughter drifted across the water. One man's in particular.

Strike the bargain, indeed. Hmph. If she did, 'twould be on her terms. Mairi turned from the window and stared into the comforting glow of the hearth fire. She was certain of one thing—she'd never marry Geoffrey, or any man, not as long as there was another way to pay the debt and keep her land. Dora was right. 'Twas the smartest choice.

Later, as she burrowed under the thick pile of furs that made up her bed, Mairi recalled more of Dora's words…

I saw how he looked at ye.

Conall Mackintosh, indeed.

She would see what he was made of on the morrow. He'd come looking for a business arrangement, and that's exactly what she'd give him. Nothing more.

Her eyes closed and she hovered a while at the edge of sleep, listening to the warrior's laughter floating across the water in the dark.

"Get up." Mairi kicked at the pile of plaids.

Jupiter barked, then tugged on the laces of his master's boots, which stuck out from the bottom of the pile.

"People die in bed," she said.

"Huh?" Conall stirred and poked his head out from beneath the plaids. His sleepy eyes focused on her. "Who so says?"

"My father. He was right, too." A vision of the great Alwin Dunbar flashed in her mind: sprawled fat and naked in his bed, quite dead, drowned in his own vomit. Her nose twitched as she recalled the stink of spirits, and worse things, wafting from his bloated body.

Conall sat up and surveyed the camp in the half-light of dawn. His men still slept, but that seemed not to concern him.

She crossed her arms in front of her and arched a brow at him. "Ye'll no' finish till the spring at this pace."

"Finish what?" He blinked the sleep from his eyes and stared at her dumbly.

"The docks, ye fool. And the village must be rebuilt as well. If we're to house boatsmen and traders, we'll do it proper."

Conall frowned, then all at once his face lit up, much as Kip's did when she allowed him a rare sweet. He threw back the plaids and scrambled to his feet. "You agree then? You'll give up the land?"

"I'll do no such thing." She narrowed her eyes and tipped her chin at him. "I'll allow the building, aye, but I give up nothing. And in exchange for the use of my land, I'll take a fourth of the goods which pass this way."

"Ha! A tenth, and we'll start tomorrow." He smiled at her, and she felt a strange tingling.

She ignored the sensation and tipped her chin higher. "A fifth, and we start today."

He regarded her for a moment with what she thought was no small amount of amusement. Her anger surged. She ground her teeth together to stop herself from commenting. Her sharp tongue and stubborn pride had ruined many of her father's arrangements, and she was not about to lose this chance for her clan. She held his gaze and her breath.

"Done," he said.

She exhaled.

"I'll rouse the men and, after they've broken their fast, I'll direct them where to begin."

"No' so fast," she said. "Aye, ye may rouse them, but I shall do the directing."

"You?" He looked her over again and laughed. 'Twas the same look he'd had in his eyes after he'd kissed her on the dock.

Her cheeks blazed against her will. She dug her bare feet into the loamy soil. "'Tis my land and my docks. I shall oversee the work."

"That's ridiculous."

"No' as ridiculous as a man who canna swim." Aye, that got him. He started to speak, but she cut him off. "A man who canna swim is of no use here."

"I can learn," he said flatly.

"Hmph. Seeing's believing." She turned to leave.

"Swimming's one thing, but what do you know of engineering and construction?"

That stopped her. In truth, she knew little. The ancient docks and the *crannog* had been built long before her birth. 'Twas by sheer luck, and Dora's handiwork, that the crannog still stood. The docks had fared less well. But her mind was made up; she'd not relinquish her land to a stranger. She faced him. "I know enough. I shall direct the work."

"Fine."

Fine? His acquiescence stunned her.

"And for every day past the feast of Saint Catherine's 'tis not finished, you shall forgo your share of one shipment of goods.''

"What? For each day? That's larceny!'' She should have known better than to think him honorable.

"Perhaps, but those are my terms. I plan to be out of this godforsaken place before the snows come. Well, what say you, woman? Being in charge is not so attractive now, is it?''

Dora was right. All men *were* the same.

The corner of his mouth curled in a smile. It drove her over the edge. "''Tis more attractive now than ever,'' she said. "Rouse your men. We begin at once.'' She extended her hand to him, as she'd seen her father do many times upon sealing a bargain.

His eyes widened. "But, I thought…surely—''

She grabbed his hand and shook it awkwardly. Somewhere amongst the sleeping piles of plaids dotting their makeshift camp, she heard Rob's unmistakable laughter. "There, 'tis done,'' she said. "Now if ye'll kindly—''

Jupiter let out a deep, short bellow—a warning—jolting the Chattan warriors from their slumber. They shot to their feet, scrambling for cast-off garments and weapons. Conall continued to grip her hand while he looked past her into the wood.

"What is it? What d'ye see?'' Mairi followed his narrowed gaze. She was acutely aware of his strength as his fingers tightened over hers.

"Are you expecting someone?'' he whispered, his green eyes fixed on the hillock above the camp.

"Nay.''

"Well, it seems you've some uninvited guests, then.'' He pulled her behind him, and her heart skipped a beat.

Mairi yanked her hand from his as her eyes focused on the object of his attention—a warrior astride a dappled gelding, flanked by a score of clansmen.

Blue eyes burned into her.

"Geoffrey," she breathed.

Chapter Three

Conall disliked the man immediately.

'Twas plain Mairi knew him. She called for the Chattan to sheathe their weapons as the warrior guided his dappled mount down the hill toward the camp. Conall nodded, and his men complied. His own hand twitched on the hilt of his dirk.

Rob materialized at his side. "What d'ye make of them?"

"Frasers, likely. The one has a sprig of yew leaves tucked in his bonnet."

"Aye, and they're a damn sight far from home."

Jupiter positioned himself in front of Mairi and let out a low, ominous growl. To Conall's surprise, she thumped the dog squarely on the head. "Hush now," she said as she brushed past him. "They're neighbors."

Neighbors. Her voice betrayed a familiarity Conall didn't like. He locked gazes with their leader, a dark-haired warrior who glanced briefly at Mairi and frowned at her obvious acceptance of Conall's company.

Just short of the camp he reined in his mount, and

his men fanned out beside him. "Who are ye? What d'ye want here?"

"I am Conall Mackintosh, third son of Colum Mackintosh, here on behalf of the Chattan."

A wary recognition crept into the warrior's expression. "The alliance?"

"The same. And who are you?"

"I am Geoffrey Symon, laird and master of the lands to the west." He drew himself up in his saddle.

"Symon," Conall repeated.

"A sept of Fraser," Rob whispered.

"Aye, though a small one," Harry breathed in his other ear. "Less than a hundred men." The two young scouts had moved quietly to Conall's side.

"What's your business here?" Symon asked. "Ye didna say."

"Aye, I didna."

"Geoffrey, I—"

Symon silenced Mairi with an upraised hand. He and his men remained mounted, livery creaking, horses restless. The neighboring chieftain was sizing him up, Conall knew, and while Symon's escort equaled his own, Symon had a clear advantage on horseback. Nonetheless, a hint of uncertainty clouded the chieftain's eyes, enough to buoy Conall's confidence.

"The lady has struck a bargain with the Chattan," he said.

"What bargain?" The dappled gelding stirred in response to Symon's obvious surprise. "This lady is under my protection. Her father, Alwin Dunbar, was my lifelong friend and ally."

"Under your protection?" The bloody fool. She

could have been dead by now, or worse, had Conall wished it.

Symon narrowed his eyes at Mairi, who stood still as a stone. "What bargain, Mairi?"

"Mackintosh shall build out my docks," she said, "so trade boats from the south might harbor here."

"What?" Symon threw a leg over his horse and dropped to the ground.

"In return, Clan Dunbar shall receive a quarter of all goods that come and go."

Rob snorted, and it took Conall a full five seconds to comprehend what she'd just said. "A fifth," he blurted out.

Mairi arched a brow at him and, after a moment, conceded. "Aye, a fifth." His eyes were drawn to her mouth for the second time in as many days. A catlike smile bloomed there.

"There is no bargain." Symon closed the distance between them in a half-dozen strides. "If there are bargains to be made for the lake trade, then I shall make them." The chieftain was tall, as tall as Conall, and not many men could boast that.

He met Symon's angry gaze. "So be it. I'd prefer to deal with a man." He was about to continue when a red-gold flurry elbowed her way between them.

"Ye shall do no such thing!" Mairi pushed them apart, her cobalt eyes afire. "'Tis Dunbar land. No' yours, Geoffrey Symon. I've struck a bargain, and it shall hold."

"Mairi, ye dinna know what ye're doing."

"I've struck a bargain!"

"Aye, she has." Dora marched from the edge of the camp's clearing to Mairi's side. Rob grinned at the fair, middle-aged woman who stood nearly a head taller than he. She pretended not to notice.

"As for you, Mackintosh—" Mairi whirled on him. "Ye shall deal with me alone on this."

"It shall be my pleasure, lady," he said, and held her fiery gaze. Her eyes widened just enough so that he knew his response had unnerved her. It pleased him.

"I...I would speak with Geoffrey alone now." Before he could answer, she turned and took Symon's arm. "Come, there are things we must discuss."

Symon's eyes never left Conall's as he allowed Mairi to lead him from the camp. She stopped at the edge of the clearing, near the first dilapidated shack marking the boundary of the village, out of earshot but within sight.

Conall watched them with a growing impatience. She seemed to know Symon well—too well. Why the devil did it annoy him?

After a few minutes the Dunbar women, all save Dora, strolled down from the village and welcomed Symon's men. One by one, the warriors dismounted and tethered their horses. With a nod, Conall instructed his own men to stay out of their way. Jupiter plunked himself down at last with a sigh, but never took his eyes off the strangers.

"What are they discussin', d'ye suppose?" Rob said, eyeing Mairi and Symon.

"I know not. I care not." Conall turned away and pretended to study Jupiter's seemingly bored expression.

"His plans for the wedding, no doubt," Dora said casually.

"What?" Conall spun on his heel. "She is betrothed to him?"

"Aye. Well...she was." Dora nodded toward them.
"They make a bonny pair, do they no'?"

"Oh, aye," Rob said. "Verra bonny."

"What do you mean, she *was?*" Conall asked, ignoring their comments.

"Och, that's quite a tale," Dora said.

Rob stepped closer and invited her to tell it. Conall
ignored his better judgment and inched closer to listen.

"Well," Dora began, "about a year ago, Alwin lost
her to Geoffrey."

"Lost her?" Conall said. "How?"

"Oh, 'twas on a wager."

His eyes widened of their own accord. What kind
of a man would risk his daughter on a wager?

"So they were to wed?" Rob said.

Dora nodded. "But Mairi'd have none of it."

Conall fixed his gaze on Mairi Dunbar and caught
himself smiling. "Smart woman."

Dora and Rob exchanged a glance, the meaning of
which did not escape him. Suddenly his collar felt too
tight. He pulled at his shirt laces. Why the devil did
he care how she felt about Symon?

"So she wouldna have him," Rob said.

"The wedding day came," Dora continued, "and
Geoffrey strutted in here like a royal peacock, dressed
to the nines."

"And Mairi?" Rob prodded.

"She didna show up."

"What?" Conall couldn't help himself.

Dora smiled slyly. "Aye, she hid herself, miles
away in the wood. Alwin was furious."

"She jilted him!" Rob cackled loud enough to draw

Symon's attention. The chieftain glared at him, then returned to his conversation.

A conversation that had gone on long enough, Conall decided. He had docks to build, and the morning was half over. He took off across the clearing toward them, Jupiter tagging behind.

"Ye dinna want to hear the rest?" Dora called after him.

He ignored her and kept walking.

Kip appeared out of nowhere. 'Twas beginning to be a habit. Conall stopped and watched as the lad approached Symon. The two exchanged words Conall couldn't hear, then the warrior laughed. Not *with* the lad, but at him.

Kip went for his blade. In three strides Conall was there. "Ho, laddie!" He stopped himself just short of catching Kip's hand.

"Idiot bairn," Symon said. "Think ye to challenge me? Come on, then."

"Geoffrey, stop it," Mairi said. "Kip, sheathe your dirk."

Kip wavered, his gaze fixed on Symon. Conall recognized hate when he saw it. So did Mairi.

"A man must choose his battles and his opponents wisely," Conall said evenly. The message was meant for all three of them. After a strained moment, Kip lowered the blade. "Come, lad. Your mother has business with her neighbor." He shot Mairi a loaded glance, then turned and strode toward camp, Kip and Jupiter in his wake.

Mairi stood at the window and let the breeze off the loch cool her anger.

"May I sit?" Geoffrey asked.

She nodded at a bench flanking the wooden table dominating the interior of the lake house. "Suit yourself."

"Mairi, I—"

"That was no way to treat the boy."

"Who, Kip? I was simply—"

"'Twas cruel, and ye know it. He's at a difficult age—no longer a child, but no' yet a man."

Geoffrey reached for her hand, and she snatched it away. "Mairi, I...I'm sorry," he said. "Truly." She heard the creak of the bench as he sat at the table.

"He needs a man's encouragement and guidance, no' ridicule."

"Aye, and that's exactly my point," Geoffrey said.

"What d'ye mean?" She turned toward him, and in that moment the morning light caught the seriousness of his expression. 'Twas not like him, and she'd known him many years.

"Sit down, Mairi," he said.

She obeyed, not because he asked her, but because of the way he looked at her. His eyes were tired, as if he carried the weight of the world on his shoulders. She'd never seen him so.

"Ye both need a man to guide ye, you and the lad," he said.

"Hmph." She started to rise, but he clutched her hand.

"Mairi, ye know I'm right."

He was wrong. She needed no one. Least of all a callous, domineering husband. The memory of her father's tyranny over her after her mother died burned bright in her mind.

"I'm fine on my own," she said. "'Tis barely a month since my father's death and already I've secured an arrangement that will feed the clan through the winter—and for years to come.''

"Aye, an *arrangement*.'' The way he said it annoyed her, as if 'twas something wicked. "And how d'ye know this Mackintosh will keep his word?''

"He shall.''

"But how d'ye know?'' Geoffrey leveled his gaze at her. "What d'ye really know about him?''

In truth, she knew nothing—only what Conall Mackintosh had told her of himself and the Chattan, and that was fair little.

"What will stop him from taking the land and paying ye nothing?''

"He'd never do that.'' Would he? She glanced out the window and let her gaze drift along the pier leading to the village. All was quiet.

"Let me protect ye, Mairi, and what's left of your clan.'' He squeezed her hand gently. "Ye know I love ye. I always have.''

She looked at him and what she read in his eyes disarmed her. This was a new Geoffrey—tender, persuasive—not the vain, demanding chieftain who, together with her father, drank and gambled and made sport at other's expense.

"N-nay. I've told ye.''

Geoffrey rose and skirted the table until he stood beside her, then drew her close and willed her look up. She did, and before she could protest, he bestowed the gentlest of kisses on her surprised lips.

"I love ye, Mairi,'' he whispered. "Think of it…together our lands will span the whole of the southern wood, and nearly all of Loch Drurie. Fraser will be forced to reckon with me, then.''

"What?'' She pushed him away.

He smiled. "I was saying I love ye."

"Trickster, ye love my land!"

"Nay, 'tis *you* I desire." He reached for her again, but she stopped him with a look.

"I dinna doubt it, Geoffrey. Ye desire me as ye do a prize. Something to be won and owned."

"But—"

"Ye hate to lose, admit it." Mairi turned toward the open window and looked out across the loch.

"Come now, ye deal too harshly with me."

She felt his powerful hands on her shoulders, his breath in her hair. Perhaps she was too harsh. 'Twas true, Geoffrey had goaded her father into offering their land as collateral in his wager—and who knew he'd die so suddenly? Not that she mourned him, the drunken sod. But she also knew Geoffrey could have taken both her and the land, had he a mind to.

But he hadn't. Why?

She looked up suddenly and recognized Conall Mackintosh lounging against a timber cottage, staring at her from across the water. Autumn breezes lifted his fine red-gold hair and played at the hem of his plaid, revealing powerful thighs. A shiver coursed through her as she recalled his relishing kiss.

"Cad," she breathed.

"What?" Geoffrey whispered, jarring her back to the moment.

"Oh." She turned quickly into his arms. "Nothing. I was just—"

"Marry me, Mairi."

"Geoffrey, I—"

"Say ye'll consider it." He grasped her hands. "Please consider it."

Flustered, she freed herself from his embrace and moved to the door.

"Mairi," he entreated.

"All right." She tripped the door latch, anxious to be rid of him. "I'll think on it, but dinna press me further."

His face beamed, blue eyes dancing. "I've brought meat. We shall celebrate."

"We will do nothing of the kind." Now she was sorry she'd acquiesced. She threw open the door and the wind blasted her. "Ye may stay to supper, along with your men, but then ye must go. I've work to do." She drew a sobering breath and looked again to the spot Conall Mackintosh had occupied not moments before.

He was gone.

Geoffrey burst onto the pier like a cock o' the walk and strutted toward the village. "'Tis venison," he called back to her. "The finest to be found in this part o' the wood."

Mairi leaned back against the open door and let the wind rush over her. She must protect what remained of her clan. Her goal was unequivocal, yet the means of attaining it uncertain. All she knew was that she must act now.

Whom should she trust?

A man she'd known her whole life, or one she'd only just met?

"'Tis no Findhorn Castle," Rob said, surveying the shabby hall of Dunbar's fortified house.

"Nay," Conall agreed, "but 'twill do well enough."

His men had spent the afternoon cleaning and repairing the place, with the help of the Dunbar women. Mairi and Dora were conspicuously absent. Tonight they would feast there. Symon had brought meat, provisions enough for all of them.

Conall studied the thick wattle-and-daub walls. The house would provide them a dry place to sleep, and would do as a headquarters for the construction.

"I'm surprised she agreed to let us stay here," Rob said.

"Aye. I canna imagine why she chooses to live on that floating pile of timber, when she could occupy the house."

A cackle echoed off the walls of the empty hall.

"Who's there?" Conall whirled in the direction of the sound.

"Och, 'tis just me." The old man who'd directed them to Dunbar's grave appeared in the doorway leading to the kitchen. "Walter. Walter Dunbar. I dinna believe we were properly introduced."

They hadn't been. Conall had been too preoccupied. He waved the old man closer.

"She'll ne'er live here, ye know," Walter said.

"Why not?" he asked.

"'Twas her father's domain."

"I see." But he didn't see. 'Twas a perfectly good house, or could be with some fixing up.

"Well, he didna keep verra good care of it," Rob said, wrinkling his nose at the chipped and battered furniture.

Conall's eyes were drawn to the red-stained walls. "Blood?"

"Wine," the old man said. "Alwin loved the drink."

"Ah." He was beginning to understand Mairi Dunbar a little better.

"Speaking o' which," Rob said. "How soon's supper? I could use a pint o' something, myself."

All of them stopped to savor the delicious smells wafting from the kitchen.

"Soon," Walter said, "by the smell o' things. Ye'd best call your men, Mackintosh. I'll go round up the Symons."

Symon.

Conall wasn't pleased that Mairi had asked the chieftain to stay. Symon had a stake in their plans Conall hadn't counted on, and Conall knew he wasn't going to give up without a fight. "I wouldn't," he breathed, recalling Mairi's kiss.

"Eh?" Rob said.

"Never mind," he muttered, pushing the thought from his mind. "Go on, then, gather up the men."

An hour later they were seated in the hall, as many of them as would fit. There had been a tense moment when 'twas clear some would have to eat outside. Neither Conall nor Symon would yield. In the end, Mairi had settled it. She counted off an equal number of Dunbars, Symons and Chattan warriors, and shooed them all out. Dougal and Harry were among them, as was Kip. Jupiter had been banned from the house altogether.

"Methinks the lads were pleased to go," Rob said, his blue eyes flashing mirth.

Conall glanced out the window at the two scouts. Each was engaged in flirtatious banter with a pretty Dunbar lass.

"Harry and Dougal have taken a fancy to our women," Dora said from across the table.

"That wouldna be hard to do," Rob replied, catching her eye.

"Nonsense," Mairi muttered. "Pass the salt."

Conall reached for the small wooden box Symon had brought with him at the same time the chieftain did. Their hands collided, sending the salt box flying. Both men cursed and locked gazes.

"Never mind," Mairi said, pretending not to notice. "The meat's fine without it."

Symon edged closer to her on the bench, then whispered something in her ear that made her blush. Conall bristled and continued to glare at him from across the table.

"What's the matter wi' ye?" Rob muttered under his breath. "D'ye see something ye like that belongs to someone else?"

"Shut it," Conall said between clenched teeth.

Rob chuckled, then resumed his animated conversation with Dora.

The mood at table was light, for the most part. The Chattan and the Symons appeared to enjoy each other's company. Conall suspected 'twas not often either had the chance to break bread with any but neighboring clans. As for the Dunbar women...all but one seemed thrilled at the abundance of male attention.

Mairi remained silent, reserved, and though Conall had known her barely a day and a night, he suspected 'twas unlike her. He thought to stir the pot a bit for amusement.

"So, Mairi Dunbar," he said, "what plans do you have for my men on the morrow?"

She met his gaze but did not return his smile.

"What has she to do with your men?" Symon was clearly agitated by his question.

Conall grinned. "Ask her."

Mairi speared a small piece of roasted venison from the trencher she shared with Symon, then paused. Without looking at either of them, she said, "I'm directing the construction of the new docks."

Symon's eyes widened. "You?"

"Aye, me," she said, and devoured the bit of meat hanging from her dirk.

"What d'ye know of building?" Symon laughed, and she delivered a look that would stop a Spanish bull in mid-charge. The smile slid from his face. "I only meant…'tis just that…Mairi, ye are no' thinking clearly."

She slammed the point of her dirk into the splintery wood of the table. All conversation ceased. "I'm thinking quite clearly, thank ye." Her face flushed with color, setting off dark-sapphire eyes that burned first into Symon, then him.

By God, she was intoxicating when she was angry. Conall became aroused as he continued to study her. She fascinated him. A woman alone, yet not lonely. Nothing like the spoiled, insipid maidens he'd so easily conquered in the past.

Symon continued to question her plans, angering her more. Conall felt a strange satisfaction in her prompt dismissal of the chieftain's advice. Symon wanted the land, 'twas plain, and Mairi Dunbar was not about to give it up.

He admired her spirit and found himself wondering how spirited she might be between cool linen sheets. A man could get lost in that tumble of fiery hair.

"Don't ye agree, Mackintosh?" she said.

"W-what?" Good God, she was speaking to him.

"About the barrels floating 'neath the timber piers.

They must be caulked with fat, all the way 'round, so they willna leak.''

"Oh, aye, the barrels. And…and fat." He wrenched his unfocused gaze from her and fixed on Symon. "She's right. About the barrels, I mean."

"I still say it willna work." Symon inhaled an oat-cake.

"It will," she said.

Conall felt her eyes on him and, after a moment, met her gaze. She cast him a tiny smile that caused his pulse to quicken. Geoffrey saw it and renewed his icy glare. Conall recalled the two of them together in the lake house that afternoon. Geoffrey had kissed her, and she'd allowed it. Conall had watched them from the shore, his gut knotting.

'Twas ridiculous. What did he care if they were lovers?

He drained his ale cup and reminded himself he was here to do a job, nothing more. The last thing he needed was to get involved with the locals. Especially one who was pledged to a Fraser—to an ally of Fraser, at any rate.

His gaze drifted to Mairi's mouth, along the fine curve of her neck and collarbone. Mmm. Perhaps 'twould be all right to play at love—for sport. After all, it wasn't as if she were some unskilled virgin. Conall knew women, and Mairi Dunbar was a woman of experience.

She frowned suddenly. He followed her gaze first to Rob, then to Dora, both of whom, after only a day's brief acquaintance, appeared quite smitten.

"He's taken with her," Conall whispered across the table to Mairi.

"She's a widow with six bairns."

"Rob prefers experienced women." He paused and cast her a devilish look. "So do I."

Symon shot to his feet. "Ye'll find none here, Mackintosh. Mairi Dunbar is mine."

Somehow Conall didn't think so. His suspicion was made fact when Mairi's hand closed over the hilt of her dirk. She rose and yanked it out of the table. "I most certainly am not!"

"We're to be wed," Symon said matter-of-factly.

"What?" Dora snapped to attention. "Who's to be wed?"

"Mairi and I." Symon turned to her. "Mairi, ye said ye'd consider it. Just today, ye said it."

Conall watched her tremble, not with fear but rage. Her face flushed red as her wild hair.

"Aye, Geoffrey Symon, and I'm done considering."

"Then—"

She pointed her dirk at him. "I'll never wed ye. D'ye hear? Never!"

Symon was stunned. Dora nodded in apparent satisfaction. To his surprise, Conall shared her sentiment.

"And the debt?" Symon bellowed.

What debt? Conall hadn't heard anything about a—

"I've told ye already," Mairi snapped. "'Twill be paid by the new year. That was the term ye and my father set."

Ah, there was more here than met the eye, after all. He was beginning to understand Mairi Dunbar very well, indeed.

In an unexpected rage Symon kicked the bench backward, nearly knocking Dora to the floor. "And how on God's green earth d'ye expect to pay it?"

Conall gripped the table's edge, waiting.

"With my share of the goods traded between the Chattan and the boatsmen from the south."

The veins in Symon's neck pulsed like a butchered cock's. Without warning, he grabbed her. Conall shot to his feet. In a flash he leaped over the table, upending ale cups and scattering the remains of their feast.

Before he knew what he was doing, he had wrenched Symon by his shirt and slammed him into the wall. Women screamed, and two dozen warriors were on their feet, scrambling for their weapons.

"Enough!" Mairi yelled. "Ye will stop this now!"

Conall ordered his men to hold as Dougal and Harry burst through the door, Symons and Chattans pressing at their backs. Jupiter barked at the window, his huge paws draped on the sill.

"'Tis finished!" Mairi said to them. "Go back to your feasting." The scouts looked to Conall for confirmation. He nodded, and they backed out into the courtyard, sheathing their swords.

Then, to his astonishment, Mairi rushed to Symon's side. "Geoffrey, are ye all right?"

Is *he* all right? God's blood, the woman should be thanking *him*, not fawning over that—

"Aye, fine." Symon picked himself up off the straw-strewn floor and dusted off his plaid.

"Well, get on with ye, then. 'Tis nearly dark and ye've a long ride home."

Symon exchanged a look with her that Conall couldn't discern, then faced him. "This is no' the last time we shall meet, Mackintosh."

Conall expected 'twas not.

"And you!" Mairi finally turned her attention to him, but 'twas not the reaction he'd expected. "Ye'll be startin' no wars in this house, d'ye hear?"

He nodded, silent, unsure of what had just happened or what to do next.

"Go on, Geoffrey." Mairi pushed him firmly toward the door.

The Chattan gave the Symons as wide a berth as they might, given the smallness of the hall. Geoffrey Symon's blue eyes remained riveted to Conall's until he was out the door and halfway down the hill to where their mounts were tethered.

Mairi, too, glared at him as she passed, then stormed off to the village. Symon mounted, and his men followed him out of the camp and into the wood bordering the loch.

"Of all the bloody—" The events of the past day whirred in Conall's head till it throbbed. "I've just broken rule number one."

"Never get involved," Rob said, and joined him in the doorway.

They watched as Mairi Dunbar marched out onto the pier leading to the lake house. The sun, a fireball in the west, crashed softly on Loch Drurie's placid surface, drenching her in its radiance.

"Ye're up to your neck in it now, Conall laddie."

"Aye," he breathed, "it seems that I am."

Chapter Four

She'd show them. Both of them.

Mairi hacked at the last of the rotting pilings with an ax whose blade had dulled days ago. *"Mairi belongs to me,"* she mimicked, and pictured Geoffrey's neck as she landed another stroke. Waist-deep in water, she nearly lost her footing as the piling gave way. She pushed it with a grunt, and it floated toward the heap of debris Conall's men had piled at the shoreline. *"I'd prefer to deal with a man,"* she quipped, then flung the ax onto the rocky beach.

"'No' a bad imitation. Methinks Conall laddie would find it fair amusin'."

She whirled in the direction of the voice. Rob sat in a rowboat not ten feet from her, silhouetted against the rising sun.

"Dinna sneak up on me like that, little man."

"Och, I didna mean to." He rowed closer. "Ye were so caught up in your work there—" he nodded at the fruits of three days' demolition "—ye didna notice me."

She eyed him and wondered whether or not he was

lying. What did it matter? She waded to shore and watched as he beached the boat.

"Where's your friend?" she asked. She'd purposefully avoided Conall the past few days.

Rob hopped onto the rocks and secured the craft. "Off with Kip, I expect."

"What?" She'd seen the two of them together on several occasions, and was suspicious of the easy camaraderie growing between them. "What's he doing with Kip?"

Rob arched a tawny brow. "Swimmin' lessons."

"I'd pay to see that."

"Go on, then." He nodded at the boat. "They're in the cove just south o' here."

"I think not," she said, and snatched a dry plaid from the beach.

Rob eyed her up and down. "Well, I wouldna go like that, if ye take my meaning."

"Like what?"

"Half dressed."

She ignored him and began to towel her hair. "I'm fair decent." She had, in fact, taken great care to ensure modesty while working in the water. She'd worn a dark wool tunic over her shift. 'Twas bloody ridiculous and made swimming near impossible, but it served to keep the eyes of the workmen off her.

"Suit yourself," Rob said, and started up the beach toward the village.

As soon as he was out of sight, Mairi untethered the rowboat and pushed it out onto the loch. Conall's men were busy dragging rotted timbers from the debris pile higher onto the beach. After the wood dried, they'd burn it. 'Twould take hours. She planned to be back long before they were done.

The men had labored three days under her direction, and hadn't made near the progress she'd expected. Only half the Chattan warriors could swim. Bloody idiots.

She waved at Dougal, whom she left in charge each time she left the work site. At least the scout could dog-paddle. He waved back as she rowed the small boat out onto the loch.

Conall had stayed away, as she'd bade him, but he watched them—and her—from her father's house on the hill. She wondered at his all-too-easy relinquishment of power. Geoffrey would have never let her direct his men.

She reminded herself that her management would exact a price should the work not be completed in time to receive the first trade boats from the south. She glanced at the sun's position in the sky, and noted the forest's brilliant autumn palette. Saint Catherine's Day was barely a month hence.

She rowed faster and fought the anger simmering inside her. She would finish on time, pay the debt and be done with Geoffrey. And with Conall Mackintosh. "Bluidy swindlers, the both o' them."

A shout echoed off the loch's placid surface. Mairi stiffened, then steered the boat quickly toward the thickly forested shoreline. She'd reached her destination. 'Twas a well-hidden spot two furlongs from the village.

She stepped into the shallow water and beached the rowboat. She'd steal quietly on foot from here, across the small wooded peninsula jutting out into the loch forming the cove on the other side.

As she approached, she heard laughter—a boy's and a man's. Pausing at the top of a small rise, she crouched low behind a stand of gorse. *Slowly, slowly now.* She crept closer on hands and knees until the pair of them came into view.

"God's blood!"

Conall stood on a flat rock at the water's edge, stripped. Kip stood beside him, a stick in hand, while the dog Jupiter waited patiently for him to throw it. Unknowingly, Kip aimed right at her and flung the stick.

"Blast!" she whispered, and ducked.

Jupiter crashed into the brush. She could hear the mastiff's lumbering footfalls and wheezy pants directly below her hiding place. She dove under a bush, held her breath and waited for him to pass.

Conall and Kip continued their conversation, seemingly oblivious to her presence. After a few minutes, she couldn't hear the dog anymore. Thank the stars.

She backed out of the shrubbery into— "Ouch!" A rock? She recalled no rock. Mairi turned, and her heart skipped a beat. Jupiter crouched behind her, the stick dwarfed between huge white teeth.

"Easy, boy," she whispered, edging toward him. "Easy."

Jupiter dropped the stick. Before he could bark, Mairi grabbed his muzzle. "Dinna make a peep, now, and I'll see to it ye get a nice, fat hare for your supper." She held the dog's gaze until she saw compliance, then removed her hands.

Jupiter nudged closer as Mairi maneuvered herself into a comfortable position overlooking the cove. She smiled. Kip was demonstrating how to make a modest swimming costume of his shirt.

"Ye tie it this way," he said, and grabbed the long

tails of his shirt and tied them in a knot between spindly legs.

Conall laughed. "I'll not look like some swaddled bairn, thank you. I prefer to swim in the raw."

"Och, 'tis fine here," Kip said, "but at the village ye might wish to wear it, to spare the ladies the sight."

"Ah, but methinks some of them dinna wish to be spared."

"Rogue," Mairi muttered. She turned to Jupiter. "Is he always so base?" The dog cocked his head.

Her eyes widened as Conall turned slowly on the rock, affording her an excellent view of those attributes Kip thought she ought to be spared.

Mairi sucked in a breath. She'd seen men unclothed before—lots of them—but mostly elders and youths. Never had she seen a man quite like Conall Mackintosh.

She wet her lips unconsciously.

His hair was loose and rested about his shoulders like a lion's mane, red-gold, like hers, in the morning light. Her gaze was drawn to his chest—'twas lightly furred—then lower.

"Jesu," she breathed.

"Come on," Kip shouted and splashed into the shallows.

She watched as Conall followed him, caution in every step. He inched into the loch waist deep, then stopped.

"All right," Kip called. "''Tis far enough." He dove under the water and came up with a larch wood branch in hand. "Here, grab on to this and I'll tow ye around the shallows."

"Are you sure about this?" Conall asked.

"Oh, aye. I've taught dozens o' bairns to swim."

"Aye, well, I'm no bairn." He grabbed the end of the branch and allowed Kip to lead him deeper into the loch.

When Conall was chest deep, Kip said, "Now let your legs drift off the bottom, and just…well, float."

"Float," Conall repeated.

"Aye, float."

Mairi debated about whether or not to move closer. Should Conall go under, she doubted Kip had the strength to pull him to the surface.

"Bluidy nuisance," she whispered to Jupiter. "I should have let him drown the first time." The dog remained silent, his gaze riveted to his master.

In one fluid motion Conall pushed off the bottom and propelled himself into deeper water. He sank like a rock, a thrashing dervish of arms and legs.

"Damn the idiot!" Mairi sprinted from her hiding place, then stopped short at the edge of the wood, surprised by Kip's swift and capable rescue.

The boy was smart. Pride surged within her. Instead of grabbing Conall and risking a dunking, Kip pushed him with the branch toward shallower water. In less than a minute Conall was sputtering and coughing on the beach.

Kip slapped him on the back to aid his recovery. "Dinna fash," he said. "We'll try again as soon as ye're ready."

Conall nodded at him between huge gulps of air.

Mairi hid herself in a thicket and marveled at the strange kinship sprouting between the warrior and the fatherless lad. Conall treated Kip as if he were a man, an equal, and with something she'd experienced damn little of from her father or from Geoffrey—respect.

Last night she'd barely slept, worrying she'd been

wrong to dismiss Geoffrey's proposal, that she'd done her clan a great disservice merely to protect her own independence.

Now, watching Conall and Kip together, she felt more confident in her decision. The docks would be built, the trade boats would come, she would pay the debt and be free of any man's dominion.

She watched as Conall sprang to his feet, water sluicing off his muscled back.

Or would she?

The woman clearly needed his help.

Conall shook his head as Mairi surfaced for the third time, the heavy piling chain still in her hand. "She'll ne'er anchor it alone."

"Perhaps not," Rob said. "But she's no' givin' up, that's for certain."

Mairi took a deep breath and dove again. This time Kip followed her under. Harry and Dougal continued to tread water beside the construction raft. The scouts could swim well enough, but neither proved able to hold his breath for the time required to secure the piling chain to the bottom.

"She's doing it all wrong to begin with," Conall said, and started toward the water.

"Ye mean she's doin' it her way, and no' yours."

He ignored Rob's comment and marched out onto the rocky beach. "Harry, Dougal," he called, "what the devil is she doing down there?"

Harry drew a breath and somersaulted under the water. Conall waited. And waited. And—

Harry shot from the water, sputtering. Dougal grabbed his arm and guided him to the raft.

"Well?" Conall said, his patience at an end. "What's happening?"

"She's...she's still down there," Harry gasped.

"I can see that, you fool." He pushed the small, beached rowboat into the water and shoved off before Rob could jump in beside him.

Kip surfaced as Conall pulled up alongside the construction raft. "She's nearly got it," Kip said. "I'm to fetch a length of rope."

"Up at the house," Harry said. "The women are working it up now. Come on, I'll go wi' ye." The two of them swam for shore.

"I'll go as well," Dougal said.

Conall grabbed the back of the scout's soaking shirt before he could get a stroke off. "You'll stay here with me, Dougal."

"But—"

"I know well enough why you want to go." He bid Dougal steady the raft as he climbed awkwardly out of the boat. "'Tis the women, one in particular, methinks." He eyed Dougal and recalled the young lass he'd seen him mooning over at supper three nights running. She was a wisp of a thing with pale, fragile looks.

Dougal shrugged and grinned.

"Stay away from her, lad. We've a job to do here, and then we're off."

Dougal nodded toward the water. "Ye'd leave her, then?"

"Who?"

"Mairi. I thought ye fancied her."

"You're daft, lad. I have no such—" His heart stalled. He scanned the surface of the water for bubbles. "Where in God's name is she?" He thumped Dougal on the head. "Go after her!"

Dougal arched a dripping brow. "Ye do fancy her."

"I don't, I just—" He stood at the edge of the raft, gripped by an absurd sense of panic. "Damn the minx!"

Mairi broke the surface, causing barely a ripple.

"Thank Christ," he breathed.

She swam toward him. "Dinna stand there like a fool! Take this." She was hauling something heavy, and he knelt to grab it.

'Twas the ham.

Conall smiled, recalling their kiss, as he hefted the waterlogged loin onto the raft.

"What are ye grinnin' at?" she snapped.

Dougal guided her to a handhold on the raft. "He was worried ye was drowned," he said.

She flashed both of them an incredulous look. "When hell freezes. Where's Kip with that rope?"

Dougal answered that and a dozen other questions she had concerning the men's progress cutting timber in the wood.

Conall studied her as water dripped from her hair and ran in tiny rivulets down her face and throat. Sunlight shimmered from the wet tendrils framing her face.

"Did ye no' hear me?" she said to him.

"What?" He snapped to attention.

"Give me a hand up." She reached for him, and he grasped her hand, pulling her onto the raft. "The chain's anchored and will hold the pier in place once the floating timbers are set." Mairi pointed to a spot halfway back to shore. "We'll set another one just there."

"Nay, 'tis not necessary," he said. "Besides, we're running behind schedule. I think we should—"

"*'Tis* necessary. Dougal, have Dora show ye the shed where the rest of the chain is stored. We'll need three yard at the least."

"Nay," Conall insisted. "Dougal, have the men assemble the timbers on the beach. We'll start setting them today."

Mairi shot to her feet and glared at him. "The chain, Dougal."

"Nay, the timbers." Conall glared back.

"'Tis my land and my docks, and I'll direct the work. Ye agreed, or did ye forget?"

An overwhelming urge to kiss her possessed him. At the least 'twould shut her up. Out of the corner of his eye he saw the ham, lying well within her reach, and thought better of it.

"Perhaps we might do both," Dougal said. They'd forgotten him, floating there in the water next to the raft.

"Both?" she said.

"Aye." Dougal nodded toward shore. "Nearly half the timbers are cut. Surely 'twould no' hurt to begin to join them on the beach."

Conall nodded, pleased Dougal saw things his way.

"But Mairi's right," Dougal added. "We'll need another anchor point. Just there—" he pointed "—like she said."

Mairi crossed her arms over her chest and arched a brow at him.

Conall scowled. "All right, then. At the least we'll lose no more time."

"Fine. Dougal shall help me with the chain."

The hell he would. "Nay," he said. "Dougal shall

oversee the timber work, along with Harry. I shall help you with the chain.''

"You?" She smirked at him. "Ye canna swim a stroke.''

"I can. I've been practicing.''

"Oh, aye, ye call that swimmin'? Why if Kip hadna been there, ye'd have sunk like—" Her mouth snapped shut.

He knew it!

She'd been there, at the cove! He'd felt someone watching him, and when Jupiter had disappeared, he'd known. Had it been anyone but her, the mastiff would have alerted him. For some unfathomable reason the dog liked her.

He was beginning to like her, himself.

He smiled, and a flash of color bloomed on her cheeks. She quickly looked away.

"I wasna worried," he said to her. "You would have saved me, had I been in any real trouble.''

"Dinna be so sure of it." She brushed past him and fiddled with the raft's anchor line.

"Here, let me." One sharp tug, and the rope was freed.

She eyed him with suspicion.

"I'm good at knots," he said.

"Aye, well we'll see what kind of a knot ye can make with that." She pointed toward the shore, where Rob and Dora were busy stretching out a long length of anchor chain.

Dora's children, all six of them, buzzed around Rob like bees to the honey. To Conall's surprise, Rob stopped what he was doing and chased them along the beach. Even at this distance, he read the unmistakable joy in Dora's expression.

"Now there's a pair," Dougal said, as he pulled himself onto the raft.

Conall snorted. He'd never seen Rob behave so. The two of them had wenched together for years, across the whole of Scotland and abroad. Rob's interest in a woman rarely lasted much beyond one night. If he couldn't bed her after a single evening of wooing, he'd move on to the next willing lass.

And now, his friend was rolling in the sand with a half-dozen squealing bairns as their mother looked on in delight.

"Hmph." Mairi grabbed a long pole and shoved it into the water. "I'll be speaking with her this evening."

"And I with him," Conall said.

She grunted as she poled the raft toward shore and the second anchor point. Conall now wished he'd not volunteered to help her set the chain.

"Aye," Dougal said, eyeing them both. "A pair."

Mairi spent the better part of the next day with the rest of her kinswomen in the wood above the village, braiding lengths of boiled wool into rope. Dora did not let up the entire time.

"Dinna even think it," Mairi said, and shot her friend a hard look.

"I was only sayin' how much better your father's house looks since the Chattan have come to stay."

Mairi snorted.

"Aye, and the village," Judith said. The girl's gaze was fixed on a small group of men repairing one of the cottages.

Mairi recognized Dougal's tall, lean figure among them. "I've told ye both, they're no' stayin'."

"But Dougal said—"

Mairi arched a brow, and Judith clamped her mouth shut.

"When the docks are finished, they'll return home."

"No' all of them, surely," Dora said, and reached for another pile of wool. "Some will have to stay—permanent, I mean."

"Permanent? What for?"

"To manage the trade," Judith said.

Mairi noticed the girl's cheeks had taken on an uncharacteristic bloom. She seemed livelier of late. Prettier, if that were possible. She watched as Judith fashioned the rope, her eyes glued to Dougal's every move in the village below them. The two had been meeting in secret, Mairi was sure of it.

"We can manage the trade ourselves," she said. "We've no need of the Chattan. They can come for their goods once a month."

Dora snorted. "Oh, aye. As if any man in his right mind would agree to that."

"What's wrong with it? 'Tis a fine plan. I'll propose it to Conall on the morrow."

"I'll tell ye what's wrong with it, ye ninny." Dora dropped her work in her lap. "We are what? Thirty at most, and nearly all of us women and children."

"There's Walter," Mairi said.

"Aye, and he can barely lift a bucket o' pig slop these days, what with his bones ailing him. Mairi—" Dora reached for her hand, and Mairi let her take it. "Whether ye want to admit it or no', ye need him."

"Who?"

"Ye know verra well who." Mairi tried to pull her

hand away, but Dora held it fast. "And make no mistake, lass. Geoffrey will come for what's owed him."

"Aye, but no' until the new year." Mairi looked away. She and Dora both knew Geoffrey would be back long before then.

"He'll come soon, and for more than the debt. He'll come for *you.*"

She yanked her hand from Dora's grasp. "Aye, let him try."

"Just what d'ye think ye'd do? And all of us alone."

"Conall's men would stay and protect us," Judith said. "I've heard them talking, and—"

"Who was talking?" Mairi demanded. "When?"

"Why…nay, I…"

"Spit it out, girl!"

"'Tis just that…well—" Judith wrung her thin hands "—Dougal said that—"

"Dougal again," Mairi snapped.

"And Rob as well." Dora pursed her lips. "They'd all stay if we'd but ask them."

Mairi threw down a half-braided length of rope. "They'll none stay, if I have anything to say about it."

"Ye need him, Mairi," Dora said.

"I need no one. Least of all that…that…" The image of Conall's muscled body, wet and naked, leapt unbidden to her mind.

"A woman needs a man," Judith said, "to protect her."

Mairi beat the image away and replaced it with one more familiar, one easy to despise. "Oh, like my father protected my mother, ye mean."

"Sorry," Judith breathed.

"'Twas no' his fault, Mairi," Dora said. "Will ye ne'er stop blaming him?"

"Never." Mairi slowly shook her head. "Alwin Sedgewick Dunbar, may ye burn in hell for your sins."

Judith gasped.

"Stop it, now," Dora said.

Mairi ground her teeth and fisted handfuls of her gown in her lap.

Dora's hand lit on her shoulder. "I know, lass," she whispered, "I know."

Mairi drew a controlled breath of autumn air and buried her pain deep where no one could touch it, where she couldn't feel it. She shrugged Dora's hand away. "I need no man, and neither do you. Just look at ye—six bairns and all of them fine and strong."

"Aye, and I'm half-dead from the work of it."

"Ye've managed fine on your own, and so shall I."

A quaking boom shook the ground. Judith yelped. Mairi shot to her feet as a thousand spent leaves rained down on them from the trees above. "What was that?"

"Some o' your fine management, methinks."

She followed the line of Dora's pointed finger, down through the woods and onto the beach. "Oh no."

"Is that no' the huge pine ye ordered felled?" Dora asked.

Her stomach tightened as she watched a dozen men struggle to move the downed tree. "Aye, 'tis."

"The very tree Conall Mackintosh told ye no' to touch?"

"Why, it smashed all the new piers the men fashioned on the beach," Judith said.

Mairi's face burned.

"'Twill put us behind a week," Dora said.

"Look!" Judith cried.

Mairi sucked in a breath as Conall and Rob rode into the camp at a near gallop. She hadn't even known they'd been gone. She watched as Conall dismounted and marched onto the beach. Even at this distance, she could hear him swearing.

"He's wicked angry," Judith said.

"Aye, as he should be." Dora arched a brow at her, but Mairi ignored it.

Conall spun on his heel and shaded his eyes with a hand.

"He's looking this way!" Judith cried.

Mairi ducked behind a fat larch.

"Ye should have listened to him from the start," Dora said.

Conall started up the hill, heading directly for them. Fine. Let him come. Mairi stepped out into the open and prepared herself to face him.

"Ye'd best do as he says from now on," Dora said, "if ye want to finish the docks on time."

Mairi balled her hands tightly on her hips. "I'll be hanged if I'm going to let him, or any man, tell me what to do and how to do it." She dug her heels into the soft earth, fixed her gaze on his and waited.

Chapter Five

"I'll do exactly as ye say," Mairi said. "Without question."

Conall eyed her with no small amount of suspicion, and 'twas all she could do to keep from smiling. She'd complied with his request to speak somewhere more private, and though she loathed her father's house, she sat there now with Conall and Rob.

"Why would you do that," Conall said, "after you've been so much..."

"Trouble?"

"Aye."

She shrugged. "Ye said it yourself. I know naught of engineering and construction. Evidently, ye know much."

"So he says." Rob took another swig of ale, and Conall glared at him.

"Fine," she said. "Tell my people what to do, and we'll do it."

"Exactly as I say?"

"Exactly as ye say." She mustered her most compliant smile.

Conall snorted, then stood to leave.

"By the way," she said. "For each day past the feast of Saint Catherine's the construction is no' finished, the Chattan shall allow the Dunbars double their share of as many shipments as days."

"What?"

She fought the grin of satisfaction about to bloom on her lips.

Rob cackled.

"That willna do," Conall said. "We've already lost time with you in charge."

"Perhaps, but ye shall make it up because ye are so skilled." She arched a brow at him. "Are ye no'?"

"So he says," Rob repeated.

"What's good for the goose, Dora always says…" She rose from the table and started for the door.

"Smart woman, that Dora," Rob called after her.

As soon as Mairi was outside, she put her hands to her mouth to stifle her laughter. Raised voices drifted from the house. She stood still as stone and tried to make out Conall's words.

Out of the corner of her eye she saw Kip round the corner from the garden, skipping and waving a stick. Jupiter nipped at it as he jogged along beside him. Mairi caught the boy's attention and pressed a finger to her lips. "Shh." She nodded toward the open door of the house.

Kip stopped in mid-skip, and Jupiter crashed into him from behind.

"Quiet," she whispered.

Kip tiptoed closer. "What's goin' on?" His eyes widened at the litany of curses echoing from the hall.

Mairi smiled. "Conall Mackintosh is in charge of the construction now."

"Oh?" Kip said. "Good. Men should be in charge o' things, not women."

"Who told ye that?"

"He did." Kip glanced at the doorway, which was suddenly filled with Conall's imposing frame.

Green eyes burned into her.

"Ye told him that?" Of all the nerve.

"Aye." Conall brushed past her.

"I would appreciate it if, in the future, ye didna—"

"Have your clan assembled on the beach within the hour," Conall said as he strode down the hill.

"But I'm no' fini—"

"An hour!"

Hmph. Mairi crossed her arms over her chest and watched him until he disappeared into the village.

Jupiter looked up at her expectantly.

"Ye'd best do as he says," Kip said.

"Oh, I intend to." She smiled. "*Exactly* as he says."

Nothing had gone as he'd expected.

Conall swore under his breath as the timber pier swayed and teetered on the water. They'd worked for days and had made damned little progress.

"She was right, ye know," Rob said. "About the third piling anchor. Ye should have listened to her."

"It sways something wicked, don't it?" Harry jumped up and down on the newly constructed pier.

"Christ!" Conall grabbed Rob's shoulder to steady himself as water lapped over the timbers onto his boots.

"Oh, sorry," Harry said, and stopped. "I forgot."

Rob grinned. "Aye, his swimmin' lessons have no' been as fruitful as he'd hoped."

"All right, that's enough. What do you mean I should have listened to her?"

"I heard her plainly say the first pier should be anchored at three points, no' two."

"Three points? What the—? Did you know about this?" He turned to Harry, and the scout nodded.

The bloody wench!

He'd helped her set the second anchor and got naught for it save sharp-tongued gibes and nasty looks. She'd said nothing to him of a third.

He inched his way back along the unstable pier to the shore where Mairi stood waiting.

"We did exactly as ye told us." She pursed her lips and tipped her chin at him.

So help him, if she did that one more time, he was going to throttle her.

"Are ye pleased?"

"Nay, I am not." His blood boiled just looking at her.

"Well, I must say I told ye—"

Conall grabbed her arm. For a second he read panic in those deep-blue eyes, then her expression cooled to stone. She was fearless, he'd grant her that. He released her.

"Ye knew this would happen," he said, and pointed to the unsteady pier.

Mairi shrugged.

"Why the devil did ye no' speak up, woman?"

"I thought ye said to do exa—"

"Ye spiteful little vixen! Have ye no concern for anyone save your—"

"Ye talk more like us when ye're mad. Did ye know that?"

"What? What are ye blabbering about?"

"See. Ye did it again." She grinned, and he was tempted to slap her. "Your accent. 'Tis fair strange. No' like the rest of us, or even your own kinsmen."

One. Two. He breathed deep and resisted the urge to…to…Christ, the woman was maddening! At the moment, all he could think about was throwing her down on the beach and shagging her senseless.

"Did ye no' grow up here?"

"What?" What the devil was she talking about?

"The Highlands. Are ye no' from here?"

"Aye, I am." His anger cooled. "Born at Findhorn and raised nearby at Braedûn Lodge."

"I've heard tell of those places. So why d'ye talk so strange?"

His gaze drifted to her mouth, the sun in her hair, the breeze playing at the neckline of her gown. "I…I was fostered abroad, in France, with my brother's wife's family. I was ten and five when I left home, twenty when I returned."

"Ah, well, that explains it."

He licked his lips and felt suddenly overwarm. "I didna rest long anywhere after that."

"Why not?"

"I…we traveled a lot, Rob and I."

She studied him for a moment, then said, "And your wife? She abides this…travel?"

He held her gaze and marveled again at how her eyes reminded him of Loch Drurie's still waters. "I have no wife," he said, and walked past her toward his mount.

Mairi didn't follow.

A moment later, Rob's light footfalls sounded behind him. "Where are ye off to?"

Conall untethered the black and pulled himself into the saddle. "To the place we scouted four days ago."

"Where ye thought ye saw some of Symon's men?"

"Aye." He patted the stallion's supple neck and reined him toward the wood.

Jupiter's enormous head poked from the thicket that served as his favorite sleeping spot. He crashed out of the bushes and lumbered after him.

"I'll go wi' ye, too," Rob said, and started toward his mount.

"Nay. Stay here and see to it that third anchor is set."

"But—"

"And keep the dog with you." He snared Jupiter's attention. "Stay, boy. Stay with Rob."

Jupiter ignored him and kept coming.

"Tie him up. I dinna want him following."

Rob grabbed the mastiff's collar. "Come on, laddie. Stay here with me, and I'll ask Dora to spare ye a bone."

"And send Harry along after me. I'll need a scout's good eye to find what I seek."

"Ye suspect Symon's up to something."

"I do, and he is." Conall kicked the stallion lightly and they shot forward into the wood. "Send Harry," he called back over his shoulder. "I'll wait up on the ridge."

But he did not wait.

All along the ridge line he saw signs that someone had been there—muddled hoofprints, a dozen broken tree limbs, piles of fallen leaves. "To hide behind," he said to himself.

Someone had been watching them.

And that someone was Geoffrey Symon.

Conall spurred the black down the far side of the ridge and skirted the northeast edge of the loch. Harry would pick up his trail easily. He needed some time alone, time to think.

Certain things began to make sense.

Each night the men had left stacks of newly cut timbers for the piers just inside the cover of the trees. Most of the Chattan slept at the house, but a few still made their beds in the camp. Two mornings in a row they'd awoken to find some of the timbers missing. Conall had thought they'd simply miscounted.

Other things had happened that no one could explain. A length of anchor chain went missing, along with a whole day's work's worth of rope. And then there was the felled tree. He couldn't blame that on Symon. "That blasted woman!"

He chastised himself for having left Mairi alone with his men, without clear instructions for them to follow. 'Twould never happen again.

As for the breach of security, that had been his fault alone. "Damn it," he breathed, and scanned the leaf-littered ground for Symon's trail.

'Twas foolish, perhaps, to pursue him without a full escort. But he couldn't spare the men. The weather had turned noticeably colder, and the construction was just beginning.

He studied the scattering of clouds and the wind in the trees. Brittle leaves danced and blustered overhead, raining down on him in showers of russet and gold.

The first trade boat would arrive from the south a fortnight before Christmas. They must be ready. The Chattan's livelihood depended on it, and the Dunbars'. 'Twould be an early winter, and a hard one, if he was any judge of the signs.

The Dunbars. What in God's name was he to do with them? Nothing, if he was thinking straight. Their share of the goods would feed them through the winter. Christ, 'twould feed them all year. What else mattered?

Alwin Dunbar's debt.

Rob had filled him in on the details, which he'd heard in full from Dora. The amusing part was, should Mairi agree to wed Symon, the debt would no longer matter. Their lands and their clans would be joined.

But she'd refused him.

"Ha!" He'd ne'er seen such audacity in a woman before—except in his brothers' wives. He laughed, recalling how Iain and Gilchrist both had lost their hearts.

And risked losing so much more.

He guided the black onto the small but well-worn path skirting the north end of the loch. They'd come this way from Findhorn, and while the landscape was familiar to him, he wished now he'd waited for Harry.

For a warrior's bonnet rested on the standing stone marking the small hunter's camp off the loch. A sprig of yew leaves was twisted into the wool.

"What d'ye mean he's gone?" Mairi snapped. "Gone where?" She patted Jupiter on the head and scowled at Rob.

"Och, just out for a wee ride."

He was lying. She could see it in his eyes.

"Why's the dog tied? That fool practically sleeps with the beast. He'd never tie him."

Rob shrugged. "Uh...he... Well, to be honest..."

"He doesna want him to follow. Why not? Where's he gone?" She scanned the camp to see which of the other mounts were missing. "God's blood, they all look the same to me."

"What?"

"Where is it ye went before? The two of ye, nigh on four days ago?" She stepped toward him, and Rob's eyes widened. "Come on, little man, spill it."

"I…uh, we was just ridin' and—"

"Ho!" Harry came up behind her. "Where's he gone, then? To find Symon?"

"What?" Mairi whirled on him. "What business has he with Geoffrey?" She didn't wait for an answer. "How dare he interfere?"

She started toward one of the tethered horses, but Rob cut her off. "Whoa, lass. Just where d'ye think ye're going?"

"After him. I canna allow his meddling. These are local affairs, of no concern to him."

"Ah, but they do concern him," Rob said.

Harry stepped to his side. "Aye, they do."

She frowned at them and waited for some explanation. Both remained silent.

"Besides," Rob said. "I canna allow ye to ride our steeds."

"Why not?"

"They're far too spirited," Harry said. "For women, I mean."

"Bah!" What a load of pig slop. She marched toward the smallest of the horses and studied it. Hmm, 'twas big, at that. She'd not done much riding. What few mounts the Dunbars had owned had left with the men or were gambled away by her father.

"I said nay, lass." Rob fisted his hands on his hips. His eyes were deadly serious.

"Fine. I'll stay. But ye bring him back this instant," she said to Harry. "I'll no' have the lout stirring the pot more than he already has, d'ye hear?" Geoffrey was mad enough already. There was no telling what he might do if pushed.

"Aye, I'll find him," Harry said, and vaulted onto his horse. He galloped into the wood before she could say anything more.

"Conall's asked me to set a third piling anchor, to steady the pier," Rob said, and smiled. "Just as ye recommended. Would ye care to advise me on the placement?"

Mairi appreciated his gesture. 'Twas rare that any of them had asked for her advice. But she had other plans. "Methinks ye know right well where to place it. Besides, I must meet Judith in the village." She started toward the girl's cottage. "But I thank ye all the same, Rob."

He was buying it. She could tell from his relaxed expression. Her pulse quickened.

"All right, then," he said. "I'd best get to it."

As soon as he disappeared onto the beach, Mairi skirted back through the trees to the camp. Jupiter lay, snoring, tethered to a stout laurel. She prodded him with her foot.

"Wake up, ye lazy beast. We've no' much time."

Jupiter shot to his feet.

"Come on, let's find your master." She untied the rope securing him to the tree and cast it into the wood. "Where's Conall? Where's your laird?"

Jupiter barked, and she clamped her hand over his snout. "Shh, or ye'll alert the whole bluidy village. Come on."

A half hour later the mastiff stopped at the edge of the loch where the forest path first met the water.

"Good boy," Mairi said. 'Twas as she'd suspected. Conall was making for Geoffrey's stronghold on the other side. 'Twould take him hours on horseback. She knew a shortcut, which is why she didn't bother stealing one of the Chattan horses. "Far too spirited, indeed."

Mairi jogged up the path until it crossed a small inlet. "Ah, here's the spot." She cut up a steep hill into the wood and scanned the bushes until she found what she sought.

A boat.

She'd kept one hidden here for years, for just such a purpose. One tug and it slid easily down the hill on a raft of autumn leaves.

In minutes they were on the water rowing toward the northwest shore. Both she and Jupiter were soaked to the skin.

"Ye mangy mutt. 'Tis a wee boat. 'Tis a wonder ye didna sink it climbing in."

Jupiter pasted his ears back and let out a whimper.

"Be still, now. We'll be across in no time. Ye can walk back with Conall."

The dog panted happily at the mention of his master's name.

"Dinna look so pleased."

She'd have more than a word with Conall Mackintosh over this. The nerve of the man. Shivering, she rowed faster, as a strong head wind chilled her to the bone. Only a few more minutes. She put her back into it and fixed her eyes on the water.

"There, we're here." Mairi beached the boat where she always did, next to the standing stone marking a footpath into the wood. Jupiter leaped to shore and his nose began to twitch.

"That's right. Ye'll pick up Conall's scent here, if he had sense enough to keep to the path."

She stepped from the boat and shook out her wet gown. "But the man's got no sense at all, has—"

A hand clamped over her mouth. Another shot 'round her waist. Jesu! She was lifted off her feet and dragged backward into the wood.

Jupiter plodded stupidly along after her. Useless mongrel! Why didn't he do something?

"Who's the one with no sense, eh?" her captor hissed in her ear. "Are you bloody mad?"

She knew that voice, that ridiculous accent. Of all the—

He shook her, then set her on her feet but didn't let go. "Quiet, do you hear? We're not alone."

She nodded, and slowly he removed his hand from her mouth. A hand that smelled of horse. "Unh. 'Tis horrible."

"Shh!" He turned her in his arms, and she was not surprised to find herself staring up into those green eyes.

"What are ye doin' here?" she whispered.

"Me? What are *you* doing here? Shh! Dinna answer." Conall pulled her farther into the cover of the trees.

"Let go of me!"

He gripped her waist tighter. "Nay."

"Of all the stupid—"

"Hush! Look!" He pointed to the standing stone.

Her eyes traveled upward along its mossy surface, and lit on— "That's Geoffrey's bonnet! What have ye done with him?"

"Nothing—yet."

"So help me, Conall Mackintosh, if ye so much as—" He pulled her closer, and she was suddenly aware of his body pressed to hers.

"If I so much as what?" He grabbed her chin and wrenched it upward.

"If ye…if…"

His eyes devoured her, and his breath was hot on her face, his lips dangerously close to hers. Mairi's pulse raced.

"You despise him," Conall whispered.

"Nay."

"You'll not have him, I heard you say it." His hand inched its way down her spine and splayed across the small of her back.

"I…I didna mean it," she said, and tried to look away. He wouldn't let her.

"Aye, you did." He kissed her, hard.

Her lips parted of their own accord, her arms slipped 'round his waist. Mairi closed her eyes and lost herself in his scent, a heady fusion of sweat and leather.

His tongue mated with hers, then plundered her mouth as if it were a treasure trove. She knew she should stop him. Jesu, why didn't she? She was vaguely aware of Jupiter barking. Conall seemed oblivious to the dog's displeasure.

Heat consumed her as his hands kneaded her backside. What was happening? She let out a whimper.

Conall groaned in response and ground his hips against her.

Her eyes went wide. "Nay," she breathed, and tried to pull away.

"What's wrong?" Conall nuzzled her cheek, his eyes catlike slits.

"Ye must stop. I...I must—" She spun out of his arms and crashed headlong into a—

"Good God, Geoffrey!"

Chapter Six

She was right. He had no sense at all.

Conall unsheathed his dirk and locked eyes with Geoffrey Symon. "Let her go."

"Conall, don't," Mairi begged. "Geoffrey—"

"Shut up, ye little whore." Symon eyed Jupiter, then pushed Mairi away.

Conall stepped in front of her and raised his weapon. Jupiter growled low in his throat.

"What did ye call me?" Mairi slipped past him and the dog, and lunged at Symon.

"Mairi!" Conall grabbed her by the only thing within his reach, her hair.

"Ahh! What are ye—"

He yanked her back.

"Ow!"

"I'm trying to protect you," he said. "'Twould be far easier if you helped."

She looked at him as if he were daft.

"Christ," he breathed. He *was* daft. He let go her hair and gripped her firmly around the waist. Jupiter moved in front of her. "Good dog."

"I had wondered at this little arrangement," Symon said. "'Tis clear what's included in the bargain."

"What d'ye mean by that?" Mairi struggled to free herself, but Conall held her fast.

Symon raised a brow in response.

"'Tis no' what ye think, Geoffrey," she said.

"Isn't it?" Symon lowered his own dirk and fixed his gaze on Mairi. He was breathing hard, and Conall knew from experience the chieftain worked to control his rage. "I didna see ye struggle."

"I...I..." Mairi wrestled against Conall's grip. He took a chance and let her go. She shot him a surprised glance, but didn't move from his side.

"No matter. Ye're more trouble than ye're worth." Symon sheathed his weapon. "As for you, Mackintosh, I fear ye've bargained poorly."

Mairi bristled. Conall was tempted to restrain her again.

"Ye dinna know her like I do." Symon grinned at him. "Or do ye?"

"Ye bluidy—" Mairi shot forward and tripped over the dog. Conall grabbed her to keep her from falling.

Symon laughed. "She's a handful, is she no'?"

"I hate you!" Mairi cried.

Symon's expression turned to stone. His eyes, which had burned with rage just moments ago, grew dull and lifeless. "Aye, I can see that," he whispered. "And it cuts me like a knife."

Conall watched her reaction, and didn't like what he saw. Could it be that she loved Symon after all? He reminded himself why he'd ridden out in search of the man. 'Twas the thievery.

Or was it?

An unfamiliar sensation bloomed inside him,

gnawed at his gut as he watched the two of them stare at each other. He gripped his dirk tighter, then abruptly sheathed it.

Christ, he was jealous.

He shrugged it off. "Symon, you and I have business."

"Aye? What business?"

"It concerns an anchor chain."

Mairi frowned. "What anchor chain?"

"Hewn timbers," he continued, "and a goodly length of rope."

"What are ye talkin' about?" Mairi narrowed her eyes at him.

"Your neighbor knows well of what I speak."

Symon grinned. "I canna say that I do, Mackintosh."

Conall flexed the muscles in his back and felt the comforting weight of the broadsword strapped there. In a flash, 'twas in his hand. "Perhaps I need remind you." He pushed Mairi behind him and shot her his most threatening look, a silent warning not to intervene. Jupiter barked.

"Conall, watch out!" she cried.

He whirled. God's blood! Three of Symon's henchmen. Mairi bolted to the safety of a small copse. 'Twas the first sensible thing the bloody woman had done all day.

Two of the warriors unsheathed their swords, but 'twas the third who startled him. He was a Chinese. Conall had seen such men in his travels abroad, yet this man sported Symon's colors. The man pulled an arrow into an intricately carved crossbow and aimed directly at Jupiter. The dog growled but held his ground.

"Loose that arrow, heathen, and 'twill be the last thing ye do," a voice called from behind them.

Dougal!

Conall exhaled in relief as Harry and Dougal stepped out from behind two trees.

"We thought ye could use the help," Dougal said, eyeing Symon's men.

Harry nodded and flicked his sword at the bowman.

A string of curses drifted from the copse beside them. "Ow!" Mairi's red head poked out from the bushes. Her eyes blazed. "Are ye happy now?" she asked, and wrestled herself free of the vegetation.

"Mairi," he said. "Go back."

She ignored him. Why was he not surprised?

"Three against four," she said. "Ye're matched well enough, methinks." She fisted her hands on her hips. "So d'ye want to kill each other now and get it over with?"

No one said a word.

"Fine. Then we'll be gettin' on home. Fare ye well, Geoffrey." She pushed her way past Symon's men, ignoring their weapons, and took Conall's arm.

He was at a complete loss for words.

"Come on," she said. "We've docks to build, or had ye forgotten?"

He hadn't forgotten. Well, not entirely.

"I wish ye luck, Mackintosh." Symon backed toward the hunter's camp from which he'd come. "Ye'll need it." He nodded to his men, and they followed.

As soon as they were out of sight, Mairi jerked her hand from his arm. "Idiots, all of ye. What did ye think ye were doing?" She stormed toward the loch.

Conall had had enough. He grabbed her arm and spun her 'round. "Dinna ever call me that again."

Mairi's eyes sparked fear.

"Where are you going?" he demanded.

"B-back to my boat."

Remorse shot through him. He hadn't meant to frighten her. Controlling his anger, he released her.

"Ah, so that's how she beat us here," Harry said, joining them.

Conall arched a brow at the scout. He'd have words with Rob over this.

Mairi took off. He called to her, but she kept walking. "Damn the woman!"

Five minutes later they were both mounted on his horse, trotting south toward the village. Mairi was not happy about it.

"I dinna…l-like…r-riding," she sputtered, as she bounced up and down in the saddle in front of him. "W-what about m-my boat?"

"I'll send someone back after it," he said.

"I st-still dinna ken why I must r-ride."

"Squeeze your knees together and try to stay put. That bloody bouncing is making me seasick." He wrapped an arm around her waist to still her, and she promptly removed it.

"B-bluidy horses."

He had refused to allow her to take the boat back. 'Twas far too risky. He didn't trust Symon. Jilted lovers were dangerous. Who knew what the chieftain might do to her?

The fact that Conall gave a whit disturbed him greatly.

Mairi bounced along holding on to the pommel and swearing under her breath. Conall grinned. She was unlike any woman he'd e'er known.

He glanced down at her bare feet and golden calves.

Riding astride, as she'd insisted, her wet gown barely covered her knees. "They're freckled," he said absently, "like your face."

"What?" She turned in the saddle and frowned at him. "What are ye talkin' about?"

Conall didn't answer.

As they rode, he recalled their kiss. Her response had both delighted and surprised him. She'd been ardent, more than willing, but it seemed a virgin's kiss all the same. He wondered whether he'd been wrong in his first assessment of her.

"Bluidy swivin' horse," she muttered.

Conall grinned. Nay, he'd been right. Mairi Dunbar was an experienced woman. Symon had alluded to it, as well. He bristled at the thought of them together. If Geoffrey Symon so much as touched her again—

"Did the dog no' alert ye?" Harry called back to him.

"Hmm?"

"Jupiter. He would have known Symon was there long before ye did, aye?"

Mairi snorted. "Aye, he was barkin' up a bluidy storm."

"Then why…ah, well." Harry caught Conall's glare and spurred his white gelding ahead along the path.

Conall swore silently to himself. He'd let his guard down in the most dangerous of situations. 'Twas her fault, the vixen. He stared at the sunlight dancing in Mairi's hair. If she'd not looked so damned tempting.

"What was all that about the anchor chain and the timbers?" she asked.

"Dinna forget the rope," Conall said. "He thieved them in the night."

She glanced back at him. "Geoffrey? Nay, he wouldna steal from me. Ye're wrong, and ye were wrong to go lookin' for him, startin' trouble."

"I'm never wrong. And he's the one who started it, not me."

"Ye sound like a ten-year-old. Methinks ye've been spending too much time with Kip." She turned her back on him again and redoubled her grip on the pommel.

"Mairi, you trust too easily." He chanced resting a hand on her arm. "Geoffrey's not to be—"

"Take your hand off me!" She yanked her arm out of his grasp. "Ye've pawed me once today, already. Is that no' enough?"

Conall recalled the feel of her in his hands.

Nay, it wasn't enough.

"I should trust *you,* a man I dinna know from Adam?" He started to speak, but she cut him off. "A few things go missing and ye blame it on my neighbor without even speakin' to me about it."

"Geoffrey Symon was there, above the village, watching us."

"Ye're jealous is all."

"Ha! Dinna flatter yourself. I've no more interest in ye than—"

Without warning, Mairi grabbed the black's reins and jerked hard. "Ye miserable son of a—" She wrenched her leg over the horse's neck and leaped to the ground.

"Get back on this horse!" he ordered her.

She stormed down the path, thumping Jupiter on the head as she passed him.

"I said, get back on the horse!"

"I'll walk," she said without looking back.

Dougal and Harry nudged their mounts off the path to make way for the hellion bearing down on them. Both looked to him for instruction. He ought to have them strangle her.

"Let her go," he said, and kicked the black forward.

Jealous.

Ridiculous.

She was naught to him but a temporary amusement. Very temporary. The moment they returned to the village, which might not be till Christmas if she was hell-bent on walking the whole bloody way, he'd step up the work schedule.

The sooner she was out of his life, the better.

The sooner he was out of her life, the better.

The cad.

Mairi didn't stop until she reached the camp outside the village. 'Twas nearly dark. Dora's children were on the beach helping Kip collect bits of leftover rope from the construction site. 'Twas strange. Dora usually had them abed by now.

"Kip!" she called to him. "Where's Dora?"

He shrugged. "I dunno."

Blast! Where was the woman when you needed her? She took off toward Dora's cottage, ignoring the fact that Conall had tethered his horse at the camp and was now following her.

Mairi breathed in the familiar smells of the village at twilight—burning peat and wood smoke, and suppers simmering on the hearth. Her stomach growled. Perhaps Dora would ask her to stay and eat.

Even before her hand closed over the door latch, Mairi knew something was amiss. Dora never covered the cottage window this early, yet the deerskin shade was in place. She tripped the latch.

Locked?

'Twas never locked.

Good God, something was wrong. "Dora?" She knocked on the door. No answer. "Dora!" Perhaps she was ill, or... She pounded this time, and jiggled the latch again. "Dora, are ye all right?"

"What is it?" Conall's voice sounded behind her.

She didn't want his help, and bristled at the concern in his expression. All the same, something was terribly wrong, and this one time she'd ask his assistance.

"'Tis Dora," she said. "Something's amiss. The door's locked. 'Tis never locked. She could be hurt or—"

"Stand aside," Conall said. The second she moved, he kicked the door in.

Dora's scream pierced the air.

Mairi flew across the threshold, her heart hammering. "Dora, good God, what—" She stopped short, and Conall crashed into her. She blinked her eyes, trying to adjust her vision to the dim firelight. And blinked again.

"Um...I was just..." Dora stammered. "We just thought..."

"Ye're abed? So early?"

Dora yanked the bedcovers up around her neck, her eyes big as saucers. Perspiration sheened her face.

"Are ye ill?"

Conall started laughing.

Mairi glared at him, and he laughed harder. "I see naught of amusement here," she said.

"Oh, nay?" Tears sprang to the corners of his eyes, and he nearly doubled over cackling. She'd give him something to double over about—her fist. "Me…me-thinks we've interrupted," he sputtered.

"Interrupted what?" The bedcovers shook, seemingly of their own accord. Conall snorted, and this time she elbowed him in the ribs. "What in God's name is going on?"

Rob's head popped from beneath the bedclothes.

All at once, truth dawned.

"Uh…good evening, Mairi, Conall," Rob said, and grinned stupidly.

Her mouth dropped open.

Dora shrugged.

Mairi was vaguely aware of Conall's voice, his hands on her shoulders. "Come on, lass. Let's leave them to their sport."

"But…" Conall guided her to the door. Her feet moved against her better judgment. At the threshold they paused. The moon was up, and in the half-light she spied Conall's devilish smile. "Sport?" she said.

He ran his thumbs lightly down her arms. "Aye, sport."

Her blood ran so hot she thought her head might explode. She burst like a raging bull from the cottage and made for the loch. A torrent of raw emotion bombarded her—fury, embarrassment, confusion. And something else. Something she was not prepared for.

Envy.

Conall's laughter followed her out onto the water. Mairi put her hands to her ears and raced down the pier to her sanctuary, the lake house.

She slammed the door and collapsed on her pallet by the hearth. Tears flowed hot and unbidden from her eyes, only serving to fuel her rage. *Slow, deep breaths.*

Aye, that's it. She wiped at her eyes and tried to get a grip on herself.

Why was she so angry?

She rocked herself on the straw mattress. 'Twas unusually warm. Only then did she notice the crackling fire in the hearth. She moved closer to warm her chilled limbs, and saw it—a covered pot set carefully in a bed of coals. Supper. 'Twas Dora's doing. She'd laid a fire and had brought her food.

Her friend, Dora Dunbar.

Mairi eased back onto the mattress and pulled a fur coverlet over herself. She'd been wrong to be so angry, and felt shame at her reaction. Who was she to judge Dora, a woman who'd been to hell and back?

Dora's husband had up and left two years and some months ago. No great loss there. Like Mairi's father, the man had been a drunkard. He'd beaten Dora on occasion, and the children. She shivered at the memory.

Nay, who was she to begrudge her closest friend a moment of comfort in an otherwise comfortless existence? Dora had been like a mother to her, after her own had died. The least Mairi could do now was rejoice in her happiness. And if Rob Mackintosh was the man responsible for that happiness, Mairi would do everything in her power to see the two of them together.

She closed her eyes, and Conall's laughter still echoed in her mind. ''Sport,'' she hissed. That's all it was to a man like him. She needed his help to preserve her clan, but that was all she needed from him.

He was just like her father—and Geoffrey. Shallow and uncaring. 'Twould not surprise her if he had a weakness for the drink, as well. And for women. Aye, she'd seen it in his eyes in the moonlit doorway of Dora's cottage.

No one had ever treated her so vulgarly. No man had ever dared to kiss her the way he had that afternoon. Certainly not Geoffrey.

She hated him.

And Geoffrey, too, for thinking her a whore.

She drew the furs up around her head and burrowed into their warmth. She wasn't hungry anymore. Just tired. So very tired. Her mind drifted, and she let her anger drift with it, though she could not sleep.

Conall's accusations burned inside her. What if he was right about Geoffrey? She didn't want to believe he'd steal from her. Only a fortnight ago, Geoffrey had told her he loved her. All men say that, though few mean it. That's what Dora had told her.

Mairi smirked under the covers. She could never imagine Conall Mackintosh saying it to any woman. The man didn't have a heart. Though neither did she, not anymore.

And yet he'd kissed her with a desperation that was more than rank desire. He'd kissed her as if she were the only thing in his world. "Aye, he didna even hear the bluidy dog bark, did he?" Mairi rolled over and punched at her pillows.

The odd thing was, he'd been deadly serious about protecting her against Geoffrey's wrath. No man had ever done that before—drawn his weapon in her defense. In truth, it had thrilled her, though she was loath to admit it.

Perhaps she ought to give him another chance. She'd cooperate, for the good of her clan, of course. To speed the construction, nothing more.

Aye, 'twas the right move. She'd tell him on the

morrow. Now she must sleep, and dream of the glorious docks and sparkling new village they'd raise.

But she didn't dream of that at all.

She dreamt of him.

He dreamt of her, and it startled him how real the dream had seemed. They'd been kissing, in the lake house of all places, under the warm furs on her bed.

"Christ," Conall breathed, and rolled toward the cold hearth.

'Twas far past dawn. Wood larks sang in the trees outside Alwin Dunbar's house. He'd overslept. Damn. He threw back his plaid and stretched.

Rob poked his head out of the kitchen. "There's some oatcakes and honey laid out. And some fish, if ye've the stomach for it."

"Rob, I'd speak with you." As soon as Conall opened his mouth, Rob disappeared. Bloody gnome.

What had he said? Fish? Ugh. That's all they ate around here, save for a bit of meat now and again. He recalled with relish Symon's gift of venison his first day at Loch Drurie.

He decided to pass on breakfast.

Ten minutes later he was dressed and standing on the newly reinforced pier. Rob and the men had done a good job. He must remember to compliment him on the work. Aye, and to break his bloody head for allowing Mairi to follow him yesterday.

He glanced at the lake house, but saw no sign Mairi was up and about. Their adventure in the wood had been more than enough to warrant her oversleeping.

He was still annoyed at himself for letting Symon catch him unaware. He'd never forget the look of surprise, and rage, in Symon's eyes when the chieftain had caught them kissing. Nor would he forget the way Mairi and Symon had looked at each other after they'd done with their cursing.

Perhaps he'd been wrong to interfere in whatever was between them. If she truly loved Symon… Christ, he must finish the job and be gone. 'Twas the best thing for him, for all of them.

He strode up and down the new pier, inspecting the workmanship. 'Twas still a bit wobbly, even with three anchor points, but what could one expect from a load of timbers lashed together, floating free on the water's surface? 'Twas a far cry from the great docks he'd seen at Inverness, not to mention those in Brittany. All the same, 'twould have to do.

They'd need two more just like it, with reinforced moorings, and good-size platforms at each end for loading and unloading. Storage buildings, as well, to keep the goods safe from weather.

Time was running out.

He needed to work faster, smarter, and he needed Mairi Dunbar's help. She knew the bottom of the loch like the back of her hand. The pits and holes, rocks and sandbars. He would manage the construction, but she would have to guide him.

They must work together. They would start today.

But how the devil would he gain her compliance? They'd not parted on particularly friendly terms last night. He grinned, recalling her rage over Rob and Dora's tryst. 'Twas only a harmless amusement, was it not? Conall couldn't understand her response. He shrugged it off and scanned the work site.

The elder, Walter, squatted on the beach, trimming the ends off some odd-shaped timbers. Perhaps he'd find some answers there. "Ho! Walter," he called out, and joined him.

"Mackintosh, good morrow."

"Might I help you?" He knelt on the beach next to the old man.

"Why not? Ye've a dirk in your belt. Have at it."

They worked together in silence for a time, shaving timbers, while Conall thought about how to broach the subject. Best to dive right in. "Walter," he said. "I'd like to ask you something about Mairi."

The elder stopped whittling and met his gaze. "Aye, go on, then."

"What happened to her husband?"

"Husband?"

"Aye, Kip's father."

"Kip's father? Oh. He ran off when the lad was just a wee'un." Walter started in on the timber again.

"Ah. I thought as much."

"But he was no' her husband."

"What? They were never married, and she a laird's daughter?" This truly surprised him.

Walter looked at him strangely. "Nay, Mairi barely knew Kip's father. Why d'ye ask?"

Conall didn't know what to say. "I...well, I just had wondered, is all, why she's so..."

"Difficult?"

"Aye."

Walter shrugged. "Och, she's been that way e'er since her mam was killed. She was just a child, ye ken. And after Alwin took to the drink, and things went bad, well...'tis no' so hard to fathom, is it?"

Conall nodded. 'Twas not so hard to fathom at all. His own father had been brutally murdered when he was just a bairn, and he was but ten and four when his mother passed. Conall knew well what 'twas like to be on his own. He'd had his brothers, of course, but they were older and, more often than not, consumed by their own demons.

In the end, he supposed, 'twas all for the best. His independence had become his strength. He had few ties, no one to worry about, no one to lose.

"So what's this, a tea party?"

Conall snapped to attention. Mairi stood over them. Where the devil had she come from? She was almost as good at appearing out of thin air as was Kip.

"Ah, Mairi lass," Walter said. "We're trimmin' these timbers for the second pier."

"Aye, I can see that." She looked at Conall, and he had the strangest feeling she'd heard every word of their conversation. Her expression was completely unlike any he'd seen her pose. 'Twas almost...placid. "I would help ye, today," she said to him. "Only if ye wish it, of course."

Her submissive demeanor stunned him. He frowned at her, instantly on his guard.

"I would apologize, too, about the anchor chain." She nodded to the newly finished pier floating on the water. "I should have told ye 'twould take at least three to steady it."

Walter arched a brow. Clearly, he, too, was surprised at her uncharacteristic behavior.

"I could help ye set the other two," she said. "No one knows the loch as well as I. The work would go much faster if I...if we..."

"If we work together," he said.

Mairi nodded.

A long time ago, Conall's uncle had recounted a Greek tale, The Trojan Horse. He'd never forgotten the whimsical moral: *dinna look a gift horse in the mouth.*

He shot to his feet and dusted the sand from his plaid. If Mairi Dunbar had a mind to assist him, he'd not refuse her help. In truth, her compliance could not be more perfect. 'Twas exactly what he'd hoped for.

He took his leave of Walter, and together he and Mairi walked along the beach, inspecting his men's handiwork. Occasionally, when he thought she wasn't looking, he'd steal a glance at her. Now that he knew more of her history, he saw her with new eyes.

He'd misjudged her, and for that he felt remorse. 'Twas time to put things right between them. "I, too, would apologize," he said.

She stopped at the water's edge. "For what?"

"For yesterday." He shrugged, unsure of what to say next. "My behavior in the wood. I—"

"Och, no matter." She quickly looked away. The water lapped at her bare feet. He thought them lovely—long and slender, and bronzed by the sun. She dug her toes into the wet sand.

"Symon's your neighbor, and your betrothed," he said.

"Nay, he's merely a friend."

"I didna mean to interfere. He sees me as a threat. Aye, 'tis only natural." He paused and willed her to meet his gaze. "A man in love will do desperate things to keep safe what he cherishes."

What had made him say such a thing?

She was silent for a moment, speechless, he thought, then she said, "Och, Geoffrey's no'…'tis no' like that. If ye're thinkin'…"

"He saw us kiss."

She blushed like a maid and looked away. "Oh, that. I...I meant nothing by it."

"Nor did I," he said quickly. He didn't, after all. 'Twas simply for amusement, was it not?

"Ah, well...good."

He nodded vigorously, as if to convince himself.

"'Tis best forgotten, then." She turned and started down the beach.

"Aye," he breathed, but knew as he watched her walk away that he'd never forget it.

Chapter Seven

Never had any of them worked harder.

Mairi wiped her brow on the sleeve of her gown and stood back to admire her handiwork. "Perfect."

Conall ran his hand along the tightly stretched deer-skin covering the timber-framed pontoon. She and the other women had fashioned a dozen of them in the past two days. "Aye," he said at last, "but will it float?"

"Of course 'twill float!"

Rob inspected the lacing with a hawk's eyes. "Ye'll need a bit more grease, just there, to make certain 'tis watertight." He grunted his approval.

"Who taught you to make these?" Conall asked.

The question caught Mairi off guard. "Oh…no one, really." She busied herself clearing up scraps of deer-skin and leather lacings from off the beach.

"Alwin taught her," Dora said, looking up from her work. "When she was a child. I remember they used to—" Mairi narrowed her eyes at her, and Dora stilled her tongue.

"I see ye've set a watch at night," Mairi said to change the subject.

"Aye, and by day as well." Conall lifted the finished pontoon and balanced it on his shoulder.

"I still say ye should have sent Harry back to Monadhliath for more men," Rob said. "'Tis only a day and a night's ride."

"Nay." Conall shook his head. "I'll not bother Gilchrist, or Iain, with trivial matters."

Conall had told her little about his family since he'd arrived. Curiosity ate at her. "Iain and Gilchrist," she said, "they're your brothers?"

He ignored her and started out onto the new pier.

She jogged after him. "Uncles, then? I never knew my uncles. They—"

"Brothers. They're my elder brothers."

"Ah, so ye're the bairn, eh?"

He stopped short, and she nearly ran into the end of the pontoon. "Where does this go?" He planted his awkward burden on the pier.

"The pontoon? No' out here. We'll fasten them to the bottom of the platforms, then float them out." She nodded to where his men labored on the beach.

"Why didn't you say so?" He lifted it again and started back toward shore, but she would not let him pass.

"Surely they're married then, with bairns o' their own, if they're the eldest. Your brothers, I mean."

"Aye, they're married. What of it?"

"And children?"

He dropped the pontoon back onto the pier, sending a shock wave along the whole structure. She didn't flinch, and neither did he, she was surprised to see. He'd become fair comfortable on the water these past weeks. That, or he was so annoyed by her questions, he didn't notice the undulating timbers beneath them.

"Ah, well," she said. "If it bothers ye to talk about it…"

"Talk about what?"

"Marriage—and children." She nodded toward Kip, who romped at the shoreline with Jupiter. The mastiff had fast become the boy's favorite companion.

Conall's gaze fixed on the boy and the dog. "Well, 'tis fine for some…"

"Oh, aye," she said quickly. "For some, but not all." Mairi grabbed the pontoon and idly fiddled with the laces. She'd pegged him right all along. He was a drifter, not cut out for family or clan. 'Twas fine with her. What did she care?

"A man needs his freedom, his—"

"As does a woman." She risked a glance. His mouth was still open, and he reminded her much of a landlocked salmon. He studied her, and she'd be damned if she'd look away.

"Is that the reason you never wed?" he said. "Freedom?"

"Aye." She straightened up and arched a brow at him. "What good's a husband except to tell ye what to do every bluidy minute of the day."

"And what's a wife, but a noose around a man's neck." The words rolled easily off his lips, but she felt no passion behind them.

She wondered at his true reasons for being alone. He was the third son in a family she knew was highly respected in the Highlands. The Chattan was a powerful alliance, four or five clans. Surely there dwelled among them a bevy of suitable brides.

"So you'll ne'er wed?" he asked her bluntly.

"Nay. And you?"

He snorted and lifted the pontoon. "Never."

"Well, at least we agree on the one thing." She turned and started for shore, tired of the whole conversation. His heavy footfalls clomped behind her.

"Aye," he said, "at least there's that."

A week later, Conall stood on the pier and nodded in satisfaction. He was pleased with the progress they'd made working together. The Dunbars and the Chattan, every man, woman, and child, had labored each day from dawn until dusk.

The second pier was nearly complete, and the first of the floating platforms ready to move into place.

But 'twould have to wait until the morrow. The days grew short as autumn wore on, and the weather increasingly cold.

He shaded his eyes against the setting sun. "'Twill be an early winter."

"Aye," Mairi said, as she brushed past him on the pier. "All the more reason to set the landing platform now." She squinted against the sun and waved his men forward. "We've another hour of good light."

"At best. 'Twould be wiser to wait until the morrow." He caught her nasty look and quickly said, "But only if you agree."

It had been like that for days now. Each negotiating with the other in an excruciating display of civility. He'd begrudgingly conceded a number of decisions to her, and she to him, although she'd rather have cut off her arm than comply. He read it in her eyes each time they disagreed.

She sized him up for another battle of wills. "The men are ready, and so am I."

He glanced at Dougal, who stood on the beach with Rob and Harry, ready to give the command to launch the platform. Fine. He'd pick another day to argue with her. "All right, then," he said. "Let's do it."

Her eyes flashed triumph. "Dougal!" she called, and waved him on.

On Dougal's command, a dozen men hefted the pontooned raft to shoulder level and marched into the shallows. If the bloody thing didn't float, he and Mairi Dunbar would have words.

To his surprise, she stripped off her dark, shapeless gown—the one she normally worked in—and flexed her feet at the edge of the pier.

"Dinna look, ye rogue! 'Tis no' proper."

He shrugged, as if the sight of her in her shift was of no concern to him, then turned his head and pretended to watch the men.

"I'll ne'er get deep enough to tether it with that bluidy thing on," she said. A second later, he heard the splash as she dove into the loch.

Rob strode out onto the pier and watched with him as Harry and Dougal maneuvered the platform into deeper water. "Well, I'll be damned," Rob said. "It floats."

"O' course it floats, little man," Mairi called from the water.

Conall was stunned. "You allow her to speak to you like that?"

Rob shrugged. "Why not? You do." Conall couldn't argue with him on that point, could he? "Och, she only does it 'cause she fancies me."

"What? Ye bloody well—"

"No' for herself, ye fool. For Dora." Rob grinned and nodded to where Dora stood on the beach surrounded by her bairns. Rob winked at her, and she gave a little wave.

Conall scowled and loosened the laces of his shirt. 'Twas true. Mairi had been naught but encouraging to both Rob and Dora of late. He wondered at the change in her acceptance of their union. He wasn't certain he liked it, himself. 'Twas far too…serious.

"Now, there's a sight," Rob said.

Conall followed the line of Rob's gaze onto the loch's glassy, sun-drenched surface. Mairi swam in a circle, killing time, while Harry and Dougal guided the platform into position. She moved through the water with an easy grace, and he could not take his eyes off her.

"She's a bluidy fish," Rob said.

"Nay—" Conall wet his lips "—a mermaid."

"What, ye mean a silkie?"

He nodded, his gaze riveted to her every stroke.

"But they're dark, so the legends say, hair black as midnight."

She somersaulted under the water, long slender legs bathed in gold, and emerged like some mystical sea creature, her red hair shimmering in the sun's fire.

"Aye," Conall breathed, "but she's one all the same."

He ignored Rob's open scrutiny of him, barely aware of anything save Mairi's slow, fluid movements. God's truth, she was lovely. He'd thought so from the first time he saw her wrestling with Jupiter on the pier.

These past weeks he'd denied the magnitude of his desire for her. Now it surged like molten steel through his veins. He flexed his hands and recalled the feel of her pressed up against him.

She turned onto her back, and he shaded his eyes against the sun as she moved into its path. Her breasts buoyed upward, dark silhouettes undulating gently in the water.

"Holy God," he breathed.

"Your brother used to do that," Rob said.

"Do what?" he said absently. "Which one?"

"Iain. He'd stare at that bonnie horsewoman o' his and sigh like a youth. Now that was love."

Conall snorted.

"Dinna be so quick to dismiss it, Conall laddie. The right woman can change a man."

"Aye, that's what I fear."

Rob laughed and swatted him affectionately on the back. "I'm off to clear up the beach. Can ye manage here without me?"

Mairi swam farther out into the loch, distracting him, and so he did not answer. Rob's departing footfalls sounded on the pier, then faded.

Conall watched Mairi, rapt, marveling at her fearlessness. She had a strength of character he'd ne'er known in a woman—at least not in any of the women he'd wooed—and an almost foolish independence, which both charmed and exasperated him.

She needed no one, or so she thought.

He knew better.

Mairi Dunbar was in a precarious situation, all the way around, and needed a man's protection whether she chose to admit it or not. Rob had been right about that.

But Conall would be damned if Geoffrey Symon would be that man. A woman like Mairi needed a partner as strong-willed as she, but not one who'd subjugate her and tame her wild ways.

'Twas her wildness that stirred him most.

He watched as she turned another somersault in the

water. God's blood, wasn't she chilled to the bone out there? He waved Dougal and Harry on. They had the platform nearly in place.

Conall was amazed by Mairi's own perception of herself. She saw her actions of the past months as nothing out of the ordinary. He thought them extraordinary. Against all odds, she'd held what remained of her clan together after their laird's death. She'd managed to hold Symon at arm's length—at least he thought she had—and strike a bargain with another clan that would feed her people for, perhaps, a lifetime.

She shamed him, truly. Had he ever done as much for family or clan? He reminded himself that they were different, he and she. Whereas he was a free spirit, a man of the world, Mairi had lived her whole life on Loch Drurie and was as fiercely connected to her clan as his own brothers were to theirs. No service was too daunting to perform, no sacrifice too great, when a kinsman's livelihood was at stake.

He turned toward the beach and let his gaze drift aimlessly over the clan folk assembled there. A Chattan warrior lifted a squalling babe out of its mother's arms and comforted the wee thing. Judith, one of Mairi's young kinswomen, stood transfixed, her attention riveted on Dougal, who maneuvered the floating platform into place.

And then there was Kip.

Conall smiled. God's truth, if the boy didn't remind him of himself when he was just that age. Jupiter rolled in the sand beside him, content, he thought, to remain in one place for a change. To have someone to share with. To know each night where he would sleep, and be greeted each day by the same bonny smile.

Conall drew a breath and held the cool air in his lungs. Would that be so terrible a life? To belong somewhere, at long last? To care for someone, for a whole people, perhaps?

He looked out onto the water as the sun dipped below its brilliant, dappled surface. Mairi swam toward him, smiling. Freedom? Nay, he wasn't free at all. And as he met her gaze, he wondered whether he would ever be so again.

"What's happened?" Mairi pushed her way through the throng of Chattan warriors gathered in front of her father's house. "Why's the work stopped?"

They'd set the first platform the evening before and had been well on their way to finishing the second pier this morning. Now the beach was deserted. 'Twas no doubt some harebrained scheme of Conall's.

Dora nearly collided with her at the door. "He's hurt," she said. "They're waitin' to find out how bad."

"Who's hurt?" A cold fear gripped her. "Kip?" Jesu, she hadn't seen him since sunup. She gripped Dora's shoulders. "Where is he? What's happened?"

"Kip's fine. Calm yourself, lass."

She closed her eyes and exhaled in relief.

"'Tis Conall, and a nastier scrape I've no' seen."

"What?" Her eyes popped open. "Where is he?"

"In there." Dora nodded behind her into the hall. "But he's no' going to be dyin' today," she called out to the men milling around them. "So get yourselves back to work. Dougal and Rob will be out directly.''

Mairi pushed past her into the hall. The first thing she saw when her eyes adjusted to the dim light was the blood. Hers ran cold. She followed its sticky trail across the flagstone floor.

Conall lay on a table surrounded by his kinsmen. All Mairi could see were his bare feet sticking out the end. She elbowed her way between Harry and Rob. ''Good God, let me see him!'' They stepped aside.

''Hello, Mairi.'' Conall smiled brightly up at her.

She gasped. ''Your leg, the blood. What on earth happened?''

Then she took in the rest of him. He was soaked to the skin and dressed in naught but a thin shirt, its long tails tied between his legs in the fashion Kip had showed him that day at the cove.

Judith and her younger sister, Elsbeth, hovered over him, giggling, sponging sand and blood from the long gash that ran from his thigh clear up over his hip. He winked at Elsbeth and the girl blushed crimson.

Mairi saw red. She grabbed the damp rag from Elsbeth's hand and shot both her and her sister a stony look. ''Methinks Dora needs your help—outside.''

''Oh, nay,'' Dora's voice sounded behind her. ''I'm right here, and dinna need any help.''

Conall grinned and shrugged. Mairi dipped the rag into the bowl of wine Judith held, and pressed it into his wound until the smile slid from his face.

''Ow! Bloody hell, Mairi!''

''Aye, 'tis a nasty wound,'' she said. '''Twill need a deep cleansing.''

Rob chuckled.

"Come on, then," Dougal said. He took the bowl from Judith and set it on the table.

"You too, lass." Harry placed persuasive hands on Elsbeth's shoulders and guided her toward the door.

"But—" the sisters protested in unison.

"Methinks Mairi has this well in hand, ladies," Rob called after them.

"Hmph." Mairi rinsed the rag in the bowl of wine and slapped it back on the wound.

"Ow!"

"Good. If ye can feel the pain, it means ye aren't dyin'. Laying there half-naked, flirtin' like a—"

"You're jealous." Conall risked another grin and she ignored it.

"What the devil happened?"

"We was heavin' a load o' timbers from the wood to the beach," Rob said.

Dora moved to his side and absently placed a hand on his shoulder. "Aye, I saw it. Fools, all o' ye, tryin' to move so many at once. What were ye thinkin'?"

Rob shrugged.

"Conall tripped," Dora said, "and they all of them went down. He was at the front, and caught the wicked end of a new-hewn log."

Rob shook his head as he inspected Conall's wound. "Nasty, that."

Conall flinched again as Mairi dabbed at the sand that had worked its way into his flesh. "'Tis no' deep," she said. "'Twill scar, likely, but ye have enough o' them so's one more willna matter." Her gaze drifted along his muscled thigh. She drew a breath when he flexed it.

He tried to sit up, but she stopped him with a glance.

"'Tis naught but a scratch," he said. "I must get back to work."

"Ye'll be doing no more work today." She caught Rob's eye. "Will he?"

"She's right, Conall laddie."

"Rest, now," Dora said, and pulled Rob toward the door.

"I'll see the second pier finished," Rob said. "Dougal's taken to the building like a fish to water."

Conall grunted and again tried to rise. "I must—nay, Mairi, dinna—" She placed her hand squarely on his chest and pushed him back down. "Unh!" He scowled at her, then looked to Rob, resigned. "All right, then. But I'll be out at dusk to check your progress."

Rob nodded, and Dora led him from the hall.

Mairi turned her full attention to the wound.

"You dinna have to do this."

"Lie still." She dipped the rag again, folded it and placed it at the top of his thigh. "Here, make yourself useful. Hold this tight across the wound while I fetch some more rags."

Before she could move away, he covered her hand with his and pressed down. "Thank you for helping my men—and me."

Their gazes locked.

She was conscious of her quickening heartbeat, and his, from the pulse point near to where her hand rested mere inches from his groin. He squeezed her fingers gently. Her mouth went dry. "I…'tis naught but what anyone would do."

"'Tis more than that."

She pulled away and made for the kitchen, taking

deep breaths on the way. Jesu, what were these feelings? She must get a hold of herself.

When she'd thought Kip was the injured one, an instinctive, maternal panic had gripped her. No matter that she was not the child's birth mother. She'd cared for him for so long, 'twas as if he was her own son.

But when she realized Conall was the one who'd been hurt, another kind of fear had seized her, one she'd never before felt. 'Twas as if she were about to lose everything—all that she knew and cherished, unspoken dreams, hope for the future.

She'd never felt vulnerable until that moment, had never allowed herself the luxury, not since her mother's death and her father's decline. Mairi had always been the strong one. Stalwart. Invincible. She'd had to be—for herself and for her clan. All the same, the moment Conall's name had rolled off Dora's lips, all Mairi had felt was fear.

Her fingers closed over the pile of rags on the kitchen table. What if it had been something serious? What if she'd lost him?

"Jesu." Mairi closed her eyes and inhaled.

She refused to contemplate what her feelings meant. 'Twas impossible, absurd. She needed no one. Shaking off the momentary lapse into insanity, she began to tear the rags into strips.

What if she did care for him? Of what consequence was it?

He was an adventurer and a rogue, not suited for family or clan. But if he were, what then? A man like Conall Mackintosh would ne'er rest in a place as small and cheerless as Loch Drurie. He was born in a fine castle amidst wealth and prosperity, not in the ramshackle village of a clan who could barely feed itself.

If she did wed him—and that was as bloody likely as her wedding the King of England—he'd only take her away. Away from Loch Drurie, away from her clan. Nay, that she could never bear.

She ripped at the rags, and her nose wrinkled involuntarily. Aye, even Geoffrey would insist she live on his estate, in the dreary halls of Falmar, should she e'er agree to wed him. She would not. She'd not wed at all. Ever.

Her clan needed her now. In time, they'd be strong again. Kip and the other lads would be grown in but a handful of years. He'd make the Dunbars a fine laird. Until then, she must hold them together as best she could. Dora would help her. Dora and Rob.

Perhaps 'twas a good idea, after all, that some of the Chattan remain. Dora was right. They would need help. 'Twas clear she and Rob were a match. And Dougal and Judith, as well. She must convince them to remain at Loch Drurie. Aye, now there was a plan. She gathered up the rags and marched back into the hall, her mind made up.

"What took you so long?" Conall gazed up at her from the table. "You could have shorn the sheep and spun the wool for the rags in that amount of time."

"Be still." She avoided his inquisitive eyes and finished wrapping the wound. "There. 'Twill heal in no time. Until then, I suggest ye stay out o' the water."

"That could be a bit difficult, seeing as my job is to build docks and piers."

"I can do what needs be done in the water with the help of your men. Like last eve."

"Aye, and you looked wicked fair doing it, too."

She froze in place, her hands poised over his bandaged leg, and looked him in the eyes. Green eyes, with flecks of gold and burnished copper. They reminded her of the change of season. Aye, and this was an autumn like no other.

"Mairi," he whispered. "There's something I need you to know."

He guided her hands to his bandaged hip. 'Twas hot, though she could tell by looking at him that he had no fever. Her breathing grew shallow, her pulse rapid.

"W-what?"

"My bandages," he said, and pulled her closer. "The rags."

"A-aye, what about them?" She was riveted to his gaze, drawn in by those smoldering eyes.

"Closer," he breathed.

Oh, God, he was going to kiss her again. She trembled at the thought. Instinctively she wet her lips and waited.

"They're the same ones old Walter uses to swab out the pig trough."

It took a moment for his words to sink in. "What?" She jumped back and yanked her hands away.

Conall laughed, and she was tempted to slap him. He rose up on the table, spreading his hands in front of him in a defensive gesture. "Och, now, you wouldna hit an injured man, would you?"

Bloody trickster! Of all the—

She turned on her heel and headed for the door. Halfway there, she stopped and whirled on him. "I'll send Dora back to change the rags, though if they're good enough for the pigs, they ought to suit ye just fine."

"Aye," he said, still laughing. "Wicked fair."

Chapter Eight

They'd finished, and with nearly a fortnight to spare.

Conall strolled the length of the third and final pier, determined not to favor his right leg. The wound had closed nicely over the past week, but his bruised flesh still ached.

He ignored it and fixed his mind on Dougal's workmanship. The scout had done a fine job. Conall stooped and ran a hand along the timber ends, then checked the tightness of the ropes that lashed them together.

"What think ye?" a voice called from shore.

He looked up and saw Harry and Dougal hefting a barrel across the beach. "'Twill do fine," he shouted back at them. He must remember to thank Iain for sending the lads with him.

Both scouts grinned.

"What's that you're carrying?" Whatever was inside the barrel, 'twas heavy. Dougal stumbled, and they nearly dropped it.

"Ale," Harry called back. "For the feast."

What feast? Ah, he'd forgotten. The lads had in mind a small revelry, to celebrate the completion of the new docks. Why not? They'd earned it. Besides, a little merrymaking could do none of them harm.

Tomorrow was the feast of Saint Catherine's. He grinned, recalling the terms he'd set with Mairi, and how she'd turned the tables on him. 'Twas all for naught. They'd finished in plenty of time to receive the first trade boats.

All they need do now was wait.

He rose and continued along the pier to the floating dock at the end. The day was clear and the sun brilliant, though a chill breeze nipped at his bare legs. He'd taken to going barefoot of late, as did the Dunbars.

God knows what they did in winter to keep warm. Whatever it was, he wouldn't be here to see it. He'd stay through the first shipment of goods, then leave.

Dougal and Harry lowered the ale cask onto the beach and collapsed on the sand. Conall decided to do the same, and dropped, cross-legged, onto the dock. 'Twas beautiful here, really, much more so than first he'd thought nigh on a month ago.

The water danced in the afternoon light. Rooks and crossbills winged their way overhead, entertaining him with acrobatics and bits of song. He breathed in the crisp air. Mmm…'twas never this bracing at Findhorn, nor at Braedûn.

He'd miss it, and other things, as well, he supposed.

Kip tore across the sand like a banshee, Jupiter nipping at his heels.

Conall smiled.

Indeed, the lad was a hellion. "Like his mother," he whispered.

"Conall!" Kip charged onto the pier at a full run. The timbers rolled a slow wave under his lightning feet. Jupiter lumbered after him, spit flying from his enormous jowls.

"Slow down, lad! You'll sink all our fine work."

Kip ignored him and flew onto the dock, gasping, then collapsed beside him in a heap.

"What's the hurry?" He laughed and rumpled the boy's hair. His own father had done that to him often when he was just a sprite, half Kip's age at most. The memory struck a bittersweet nerve inside, and he pushed it from his mind.

"Dora says if we're good, we may get a special treat for Christmas." Kip tugged at his plaid. "The boats will have arrived, full of things to eat."

"Aye, they will have." Conall shook his head at the boy's perpetually dirty face and ragged garments. He imagined Mairi to have looked much the same as a child, though the two didn't share similar features. Kip had not a freckle on him, while Mairi was covered in them. Well, what he'd seen of her had been freckled, at any rate.

"I'll share mine with ye, if ye like."

"Share what?" Kip had been rambling on about the new year, and Conall had not been listening.

"My Christmas treat. Whatever it is that I get, I'll give ye half." Kip stared up at him, expectantly, waiting for his response.

In truth, he didn't know how to respond. Kip had grown overfond of him these past weeks. Conall had enjoyed their friendship, but it must end. "I willna be here at Christmas, Kip. I must move on."

"On where?" The boy frowned, then just as quickly his face brightened. "Can I go with ye?"

"Nay, lad."

Kip's face fell. He pulled his small dirk from its

scabbard and started to hack at the timbers on which they sat. Conall ignored the remorse ripping his gut. He grabbed Kip's wrist before the boy could land another blow, and stuffed the dirk under his own belt.

"My work here is finished," he said evenly.

Kip wouldn't look at him.

"I must leave. My brothers expect me home." 'Twas the truth, though he didn't expect to tarry long at Findhorn, either. An infusion of travel and excitement would do him good. Aye, 'twas exactly what he needed.

"Ye promised to teach me to fight with a sword." Kip's lower lip trembled, and as Conall watched the boy fight back tears, a wave of emotion welled inside him.

"Christ." He inhaled slowly and hardened his heart. "Dougal will teach you, when you're older."

He suspected both scouts would jump at the chance to stay. Judith's and Elsbeth's charms had bewitched them both beyond all reason. 'Twas for the best, after all. He'd need to leave someone in charge here after he was gone.

"I dinna want Dougal," Kip said, and tugged on Conall's plaid. "I want you."

He gritted his teeth and yanked himself out of the boy's grasp. Kip's eyes widened in pain. Saint Columba, he'd done it now. He should have never allowed himself to get so involved with the lad.

"What about Jupiter, then?" The mastiff had lain down beside them, and now Kip grabbed him around the neck and hugged him tight. "Let him stay with me. I'll take good care of him, I promise!" Jupiter panted happily as Kip climbed all over him.

"Aye, I dinna doubt it, lad, but methinks your mother wouldna like it much."

Jupiter rolled onto his side and Kip scratched the mastiff's huge belly. "She's dead, she wouldna care."

Conall's heart stopped.

"And Mairi likes him. Please say he can stay."

He blinked a couple of times.

"She's over there." Kip pointed to the lake house pier. "Ye can ask her."

Mairi stood on the pier, barefoot as usual and skirts rucked up, one hand fisted on her hip, the other shading her eyes against the sun. She watched them.

The truth hit him like a brick. "She's not your mother, is she?" He was a fool not to have seen it before. Her chaste kisses, that virginal blush she fought so hard to control.

"Who?" Kip asked.

"Mairi." He fixed his eyes on her.

"Nay, o' course not. Me mam's dead. Now I take care of Mairi. She needs me."

Conall nodded absently. "Aye, she does."

"She needs a husband, too, o' course."

He snapped to attention and met the boy's innocent gaze. "A husband?"

"Aye," Kip said, "like you."

Geoffrey slammed his fist on the table and leveled his gaze at the Chinese. "So soon?"

Tang nodded. "I have seen it with my own eyes. The piers are complete, the docks in place."

"Damn them! The both o' them."

"Their work is easily destroyed." Tang pressed his brown leathered hands together in a gesture that betrayed his eagerness.

"Aye, but that doesna serve my purpose. The trade boats shall come whether or not there are docks to receive them. What Mackintosh has built is only a convenience, no' a necessity."

"The boats, then."

Geoffrey smiled at the wisdom of the Chinese. "Exactly. Docks or no docks, if she canna get the goods, she canna pay the debt. That's that, then. The land shall be forfeit to me." He rose and paced the floor, his thoughts racing.

Tang arched a brow.

"What?" He stopped and studied the tiny man's ever-cryptic expression. "What is it?"

"My father once said, 'There are often many ways to skin a cat.'"

Geoffrey snorted but caught his meaning. "Mackintosh. Aye. If Mairi asks him to help her, he will."

She'd kissed him. She'd liked it.

He fisted his hands so tight his nails dug into his palms. Mackintosh had pawed her, crushed her body to his. He only wanted the land. Couldn't Mairi see that? She was a fool to trust him.

"Kill him, lord, and all his kinsmen."

"Aye, 'twould be something Fraser would notice, would it not? A thousand Chattan warriors defeated by my hand."

"A thousand?" Tang frowned. "Lord, they are but a score."

Geoffrey shot him the kind of look he reserved for weaklings and fools. "A score at Loch Drurie, and a thousand more just like them, no' two days' ride from Falmar."

Aye, that's all he needed. If he so much as touched a hair of Mackintosh's red head, every bloody clan in the alliance would beat a path to his door. He'd not live to see the end of the week, let alone the new year. "'Tis folly," he said, and gnashed his teeth in frustration.

Tang rose from his seat. "If I may be so bold, lord."

"Go on."

"Perhaps it would be better for everyone if the Mackintosh warrior simply…disappeared."

"Aye, but that's no' likely, now is it?" He saw how Mackintosh had looked at Mairi. The man wasn't going anywhere.

Tang shrugged. "Many things are likely. They feast tonight, with Alwin's ale. 'Tis easy for a man to forget himself and have too much to drink."

Aye, and well Geoffrey knew it. How many times had he awoken with his head splitting, his gut roiling from a night in Alwin Dunbar's house?

"Such a man would be unsteady, dull witted. Any number of things might befall him." Tang fixed black eyes on him. "An accident, perhaps."

Geoffrey grinned. He knew there was a reason he kept the Chinese in his employ. "Aye, an accident." 'Twould solve all his problems. With Conall Mackintosh out of the picture, and the trade boats diverted, Mairi would have no recourse but to submit. "Arrange it."

"Consider it done." Tang smiled and turned to leave.

Geoffrey could barely contain his elation. He strode to the window and looked out on his demesne. The sky was a brilliant blue, the air crisp as an autumn apple.

'Twould be a boon, would it not, to bring Fraser

the lake trade? The Symons would become powerful again, respected—feared even. Aye, and there was a bonus. A terrible accident would befall Conall Mackintosh. Mairi would be his again. His. As she should have been from the start. Alwin had lost her to him. He'd won her fair and square.

Geoffrey bit back a curse, bristling at the memory of his wedding day. He'd waited for hours with the priest, who'd come all the way from Inverness to hear their vows. Mairi had never shown up. The embarrassment it had cost him, the ridicule.

"Bitch," he breathed. She deserved what would happen. She'd had plenty of chances to come to him willing. His patience was at an end. "Tang!"

The Chinese paused at the door.

"What d'ye plan? How will ye do it?" He wanted Mackintosh dead so badly he tasted blood.

"Something sudden, spectacular, perhaps." Tang had a flair for murder. "Have you a preference, lord?"

"Nay." He waved him on. "Just kill him." The sooner 'twas done the better. Tonight was perfect. They'd be in their cups, the lot of them. Mairi would be... "Tang, wait."

"Lord?"

"Ye willna harm Mairi." Remorse licked at him. Aye, the vixen had treated him outrageously. No man in his position would have put up with it, but he loved her all the same. "If she's touched, I'll have your head."

"Aye, lord." Tang bowed low, hands clasped together at his chest, then slipped through the door and closed it soundlessly behind him.

The smells of pitch and wood smoke and roasting meat drew him from the house long before he intended to join the celebration. Conall angled his way down the forested hillside toward the beach, allowing his eyes to adjust to the moonless night. Torches winked at him like stars through the trees, and the sounds of merrymaking waxed on the wind as he approached.

He stepped out onto the sand and blinked. "What the devil…?"

Children ran laughing along the brightly lit shoreline, snaking their way through small knots of revelers—Dunbar women and elders, Mackintosh and Davidson warriors—who sang and ate and lifted their overflowing cups skyward.

Dozens of torches blazed a path of gold along each of the three new piers, casting waves of fiery light to dance on the black waters of Loch Drurie.

"Ho, laddie!" Rob called to him from one of the bonfires crackling on the beach. "Come and sample a bit o' Alwin Dunbar's special brew."

He grinned and walked toward Rob's beckoning wave. The elfin warrior lounged in Dora's lap on the sand, cradling the largest cup of ale Conall had e'er seen. And he'd seen a few.

"What's all this?" he said, and arched a brow at each of his kinsmen in turn.

Rob hiccuped in response. Dora squeezed him and giggled. Dougal sat beside them, draped in Judith, whose once-pale cheeks blazed hot as the bonfire. Elsbeth sat beside her, Harry's head lolling comfortably in her lap.

"What fine warriors I've chosen to accompany me on this most important of missions," he said.

"Aye," Judith and Elsbeth breathed in unison.

"Ye didna choose us," Rob said, and swallowed another hiccup. "We just came."

Dougal nodded dreamily, his dark eyes wide and unfocused. Harry began to snore.

Conall laughed and felt the weight of the past weeks slip from his shoulders. They were good men, all, and deserved to celebrate their success.

His grin broadened as he recognized old Walter kneeling before another of the bonfires, bathed in sweat, his sinewy muscles straining to turn a huge spit. Roast pork, from the look and smell of it. Conall had wondered whether the elder would ever butcher those pigs. Aye, they'd all have full bellies tonight.

His gaze drifted from face to face, up and down the beach, but Mairi's was not among them. He glanced at the lake house and its darkened pier, black and cold as the night. 'Twas just as well.

"She's there." Dora's voice rose over the throng. "Ye just canna see her." When he met the older woman's eyes, all the hairs pricked on his neck. 'Twas as if she read his thoughts a moment before he had them. It unnerved him, and he looked away. "Aye, she's there," Dora said, "sittin' on the pier in the dark, watchin' ye."

His bare feet moved toward the lake house pier, though he willed them not to. One step, another, scrunching the cool, damp sand between his toes. He stood at the end of the floating timbers and gazed into the blackness.

"I thought ye might not come," a voice called out from the dark.

Her voice.

He stepped onto the pier and started toward her. The night swallowed him in pitch. Timbers rolled gently under his weight, but he paid them no mind. He stopped when he sensed her near, though he couldn't see her, so black was the night.

"'Tis like a faeryland, is it no'?" she said.

He gazed at the flickering reflections of the torches on the water, and the eerily illuminated faces of the revelers on the beach. "Aye," he said, "anything might happen on such a night." He dropped cross-legged beside her, accidentally brushing her bare knee with his. Mairi repositioned herself, but the sensation of her skin against his stayed with him.

"Ye've had naught to drink as yet," she said.

"How do you know?" He could just make out the features of her face contrasting against the blackness surrounding them.

"If ye had, I'd smell it on ye."

"Ah. Is your nose so good, then?"

"For the drink, aye, 'tis."

He considered what Rob and Walter had told him of her history. "So that's how it was with your father."

She didn't respond, and he wished he hadn't broached the topic.

"My father," she said. "Alwin Dunbar." She snorted. "Aye, that's exactly how it was."

"Is that why you won't live in his house?"

"Nay." She shot to her feet, and he felt the pier undulate beneath them. "Aye. 'Tis just…I have my reasons." She brushed past him and he blindly grabbed for her hand.

"Mairi, stay."

"Nay." She eluded his grasp. "I must join my kinsmen."

He scrambled to his feet and dogged her steps.

"Why, then? Why will you not live in his house? Has it to do with your mother? Her death?"

She stopped short at the end of the pier, and he nearly crashed into her. She whirled on him, and for the first time that night he could see her eyes. Tiny bonfires blazed in their centers, gold against midnight-blue.

"And what of you?" she snapped. "Why are ye no' wed? No wife, no bairns, no home. The wealth and comfort of the Chattan lie at your feet, yet ye choose to drift from place to place."

He shrugged. "I do as I wish. I'm a free man. Besides, how I live is not your concern."

She arched a fire-gold brow at him and smirked. "So, prying and prodding 'tis good for the goose but no' the gander, eh?"

She was right. He'd had no business asking her such personal questions. Besides, what did he care? He shrugged it off and followed her along the beach.

She moved with an air of power and determination. A woman with a plan. Did she ne'er relax and just enjoy the moment?

He noticed her hair was tied back between her shoulder blades with a strip of plaid, dark blue flecked with ocher. It stood out against her wild red tresses. She had on a gown he'd ne'er seen her wear before. It, too, was blue, and belted at the waist. Her feet were bare, as always. He grinned as he marched along behind her.

She greeted her kinsmen and his as she passed them, stopping briefly to inspect Walter's culinary masterpiece roasting on the spit. When she spoke to his men, she had an easy grace about her he'd not seen in many women. She did not fear them in the least, as would

other maids. 'Twas as if she were completely uncon-
scious of her sex, and what effect she might have on
them.

Or him.

He wanted her, even more so now.

He was fascinated by her innocence, which flew in
the face of her hard-edged demeanor and outrageous
behavior. He shook his head, as if to snap himself out
of it.

All at once, the sound of the pipes and a drum rose
over the raucous din. His men, Gerald and John. Nary
a night passed that the duo didn't make music. 'Twas
a dance they played, and on impulse Conall grabbed
Mairi's hand and spun her into a throng of revelers.

"Let me go!" She tried to pull away, but he held
on tight.

"Give it up, Mairi," he said, "for but a night." She
frowned at him. "You have all day the morrow for
work and more serious pursuits."

She continued to frown, but allowed him to draw
her closer and move her into the dance. She was awkward, uncomfortable in his arms, and her freckled
cheeks blazed.

Her discomfort stirred him, and he grew bold. He
splayed his hand across her back and drew her closer,
spinning her with him. Once, she stepped on his toes,
and he laughed.

"I dinna like this," she said, and glared at him.
"Let me go."

"Nay, Mairi Dunbar." He grinned, enjoying his
physical power over her. "I've no mind to let you
go." The venom rose in her expression. "Just yet,"
he added quickly.

"I…I'm no good at dancing," she said.

"Nay, nor at riding, either." She tried to pull away, and he pressed her body to his. "You're an excellent swimmer, though. Like a silkie on the water."

He risked a quick kiss, and immediately felt her knee jerk upward between his legs. Lightning-fast, he jumped back, narrowly escaping her vengeance.

"Ye're daft!" she said. "Silkie, indeed." He let her wrestle free of his grasp, and she stormed off toward the bonfire where Rob and Dora and the others lounged.

He watched her, laughing to himself. God, if she wasn't the most fetching thing he'd seen in...well, ever.

Without warning, Kip exploded out of the wood and onto the beach, Jupiter right behind him. "Mairi!" he cried. "Mairi, look what I've got!" He spotted her with Rob and the others and bolted toward them, kicking up sand and knocking ale cups from the hands of the revelers in his path. "Mairi, look!"

Conall joined them. Tiny alarms went off in his head when Kip spilled the contents of an unfamiliar saddlebag onto the sand. "What the devil are those?" he said.

"Fireworks," Kip gasped, breathless from running.

"What do you mean? Where did you get them?"

Harry, who'd jolted awake seconds ago, grabbed one of the black sticks and studied it.

"From Tang, no doubt," Mairi said, and arched a brow at Kip. "What were ye doing in the wood alone?"

"Who's Tang?" Conall asked.

"I wasna alone," Kip said. "Jupiter was with me."

Conall shot the mastiff a nasty look, and the dog

dropped his head. "Who's Tang? What kind of a name is that?"

"Chinese," Mairi said. "He's one of Geoffrey's men. He's been with the Symons forever."

Conall recalled the unflinching, steel-cut expression of the Oriental who'd leveled his crossbow at Jupiter in the wood that day.

"I know a bit about black powder," Harry said, fingering the stick. "I've seen it light up the sky in Inverness on feast days and festivals. 'Tis made of saltpeter and other strange things."

Dougal nodded. "Aye, I've seen it, too." He plucked one of the sticks from the pile. "But no' the likes of this. Rob?"

Rob merely hiccuped and grinned from his nest in Dora's lap.

"I dunno," Conall said. He had a bad feeling about this. "They may not be safe." He'd seen fireworks on occasion in Brittany and in Spain. But never up close, and he had to admit, he'd no idea exactly how they worked.

"They're fine," Mairi said. He knew from her expression she disagreed with him just to be difficult. "Tang lights them up for us nearly every celebration."

"Aye, but how did he know we'd have one tonight?" Conall scanned the trees for signs of Symon's men.

"Oh, he didn't," Kip said, catching the worry in Conall's expression. "And he was no' here. I was in the wood, on the forest path. I happened upon him some leagues to the north."

"What were ye doin' so far from home?" Mairi grabbed the boy's narrow shoulders. "How many times have I told ye—"

"Och, I'm sure 'tis fine," Dora said. "'Tis a cele-bration. Let the lad have his fireworks." Conall could tell from her relaxed demeanor she'd had a sip or two from Rob's ale cup.

"All right," Mairi said, though her frown told Con-all she was as suspicious as he was about this chance encounter with the Chinese. "But ye'll no' light them alone. Get Walter to help ye."

"I'll help him," Harry said. "I've seen it done lots of times." He scrambled out of Elsbeth's lap.

"I'll help, too." Dougal rose, pulling Judith with him, and scooped up the saddlebag.

"All right, then," Conall said. He still didn't like it, but perhaps he was being overly cautious. After all, their work was completed, and they deserved some entertainment. And Geoffrey Symon had not shown his face since that day in the wood. Conall dismissed his uneasiness. "Just have a care, do you hear?" He'd heard tales of black powder being used in warfare, but thought it best not to mention it.

Both scouts nodded, then followed a jubilant Kip onto one of the brightly lit piers. Conall helped Rob to his feet, and watched as Dora led him, weaving, toward the steaming trenchers of roasted pork Walter busily assembled on the beach.

When Conall turned 'round, Mairi was gone. "The little vixen," he breathed.

Five minutes later, he was seated beside her again on the darkened lake house pier.

"I didna say ye could join me," she said.

He felt her bristling in the dark beside him. "Nay, but here I am, all the same."

"Hmph."

He suppressed a laugh.

''Do ye always get your way?'' she said.

''Do you?''

She snorted, and he grinned at her in the dark. ''You're a headstrong woman, Mairi Dunbar. I see well why no man has tamed you.''

''No man ever shall.''

''Nay, 'twould be a sin,'' he whispered, and inched closer to her. To his surprise, she didn't move away.

Conall looked heavenward and breathed in the starry night. 'Twas chill and untouchable, like Mairi Dunbar would have him believe of her. He knew better.

A whistle cut the air as the first of the fire sticks shot into the black sky over the water. He could hear Kip's whoops of joy as the missile burst into a thousand shards of light, a green firefall bathing the night in its eerie glow.

He glanced at Mairi and was startled to find her looking not at the display, but at him. A dance of starlight, green lightning, reflected in the dark pools of her eyes.

Slowly—so achingly slow he had time to count his heartbeats and feel her warm breath on his face—he leaned over and kissed her.

She let him, and as her arms slipped 'round his neck, he knew for certain 'twas a night when anything might happen.

Chapter Nine

She planned all along to stop him.

But now that the moment was finally here… "Relax," he breathed, and brushed his lips against hers. One more kiss and she'd end it.

Mairi closed her eyes and brilliant fire falls of red and green flashed across her eyelids. Her lips parted to receive his questing tongue—hot glass darting, probing, melding with her own. She moaned involuntarily, and he groaned in response.

Fire sticks crackling in the sky overhead, their acrid odor, applause from the beach, Kip's laughter drifting across the water—all faded to nothingness as she gave herself up to him.

His hands were everywhere, caressing her, fondling her. His mouth was hot, his scent intoxicating. She felt wild, free, as if nothing could stop them. He bore her back on the rough timbers of the pier, one arm supporting the small of her back, and moved atop her.

She panicked.

Her eyes flew open.

"Get off!" she cried. He ignored her and kissed her again. She pressed her hands against his chest but could not budge him for his weight and his insistence. "Conall—" He kissed her again.

"You like it," he breathed, continuing to trail small kisses over her face. "I can tell." She struggled against him, but he would not relent. In one swift move, he pinioned her arms above her head and held them there with one hand. "Say that you like it," he whispered against her lips.

"Nay, I don't. Stop it!" Her heart beat so madly she was certain he could feel it.

"Aye, you do."

He kissed her again, gently this time. Her lips parted against her will, her tongue mated with his as if it had a mind of its own. And in that moment of submission, her fear waned and her desire surged. She kissed him back with a ferocity that shocked her.

Sparks rained down on them, silver and serpentine and steely red. Like lightning, he spread her legs with powerful thighs and thrust against her.

"Nay!" She struggled against him, and he lifted his weight from her. "Let me go!"

His grip tightened around her wrists. "I dinna wish to."

A burst of light illuminated his face for the barest moment. He was smiling, the lout! He kissed her temple, then her ear. She turned her face away, and her anger melted to fear as his mouth moved lower.

"What are ye doing?" she asked between short, shallow breaths, but knew very well what he was doing. He was going to take her, right here on the darkened pier.

"You're a fine woman, Mairi Dunbar," he said between kisses. "Strong, independent—" He paused and slid his free hand to her breast. She stifled a gasp. "Experienced," he breathed.

He toyed with her nipple through her heavy gown, and she felt it harden beneath his fingers. She was suddenly overwarm, perspiring. She fought to control her breathing, to stay focused, to think of some way to stop him.

God help her, but she didn't want to stop him.

Her face flushed hot with the knowledge of her desire.

"You *are* experienced, are you not?" he said. "After all, you're a mother."

"A-aye." His hand closed over her breast, and she fought for control.

"You've been a long time without a man. I can tell." He kissed her again and kneaded her breast.

Tears stung the corners of her eyes. Why was he doing this? And why did she allow it? Her kinsmen and his were but a hundred yards away. They could not see her in the dark, but if she cried out they would come.

Why didn't she?

"The boy's not yours," he whispered.

She fixed her glassy gaze on his. "Kip? He is most certain."

"Aye, perhaps he's the son of your heart, but he's not of your flesh." She started to protest, but he stilled her with a kiss. "You're a maid, Mairi Dunbar. Why did you let me think you were not?"

She didn't answer, and worked to control her turbulent emotions.

"Admit it," he breathed, and kneaded her breast again.

She struggled against him, but he held her fast. Damn him! Why did he do this?

"Admit it, and I'll stop. No man's touched you. Not even Symon." He trailed his fingers lower, ever so slowly, across each rib and over the soft rise of her abdomen. "Not like this."

Fear and desire fused bright and visceral, an alchemist's creation in the crucible of her heart.

"Admit it, Mairi. Admit it and I'll stop."

A small cry escaped her throat. "Aye, aye 'tis true. I am virgin. No man has ever touched me." He released her, and she lay there beside him, breathless, trembling. "No man save you."

A starburst of color lit the blackness above them, and in that brief moment she read the triumph in his eyes. Out of nowhere and everywhere, rage boiled up inside her. She rolled away from him and scrambled to her feet, rubbing her wrists where he'd held her in his death grip. "Ye are lower than a dog! How dare ye treat me so!"

He had the nerve to smile. She kicked at him, but her foot flailed out in the darkness as he dodged the blow. He shot to his feet, rocking the whole pier, and she pushed past him, shoving him as hard as she could.

"Mairi—" He recovered his footing, much to her disappointment, and followed her toward the lake house. "I meant no dishonor. I only—"

She whirled on him. "Dishonor? Is that what ye call it? Ye would use love to belittle and humiliate me? Ye're more like my father than I had—"

"I'd ne'er do that, and 'twas not meant to belittle."

She breathed a deep draft of night air tinged with the odor of sulfur, and worked to get a grip on her emotions.

"Besides," he said, staring at her in the dark. "'Twas not love…'twas just…"

She fisted her hands until she felt her nails dig into her palms. "Sport," she said flatly.

His silence confirmed her answer.

She turned her back on him and ran to the lake house, slamming the heavy door behind her. His footfalls sounded along the pier, but to her astonishment they grew louder, and she could feel his weight on the water as he approached the door. She bolted it, then threw herself onto her pallet and pulled the furs up around her ears. Whatever pleas he made on the other side of the door, she could not hear them, didn't want to hear them.

He'd reveled in her admission. She'd only felt shame, as if he'd conquered her and stripped her bare. What did it matter to him that she was a maid? It mattered not to her one way or another. Save that it weakened her position in his eyes. She'd read it in his face, felt it in the power of his embrace and in the cruel authority of his kisses.

She traced a finger along the line of her lips. Her face was hot to the touch, more so where the stubble of his beard had raked her. She closed her eyes and recalled the taste of him.

God help her, she'd wanted him to do it, to take her right there on the pier. How could she have been so foolish? Had she submitted, he would have used it against her in some way. Of that she was certain.

Men were like that. Her father had dominated her mother much as a man would a beast, and in turn her mother had cowed to his every whim.

She would never be like that. Never.

No man owned her, least of all Conall Mackintosh.

She peeked over the edge of the covers. 'Twas quiet now outside her door. He'd gone. Good riddance. In less than a fortnight he'd be gone for good and she could get on with her life.

Mairi settled in to sleep, but could not. After a while, the shouts and laughter of the revelers died down. She heard women's voices moving toward the village, and men's toward the house on the hill. No doubt Kip had exhausted his supply of fireworks, and the Chattan warriors her father's ale.

She drifted a bit, at the edge of consciousness. Against the midnight backdrop of her eyelids, bursts of color shot forth in a brilliant storm.

From far away she saw her mother on the beach, screaming, but Mairi couldn't make out her words. She watched as two warriors grabbed her and dragged her, kicking and clawing, toward their boat. Mairi must get to her, was desperate to help her but couldn't. Someone held her back, and no matter how hard she struggled she couldn't free herself. She just watched, a wave of nausea crashing over her, as one of the warriors drew his sword and ran her mother through, right there, on the beach, her blood drifting away on the foaming water. Mairi looked up, tears glassing her eyes, into the stony face of her father. He said not a word, merely took her by the hand and led her back into the house.

Mairi pulled the furs tight around her and rolled onto her stomach, exhausted. She must sleep now. That's what she needed. Sleep. Tomorrow she would check the new piers again, and the docks, and the sheds they'd built to house the—

A deafening boom jolted her from her half sleep.

"What in God's name—?"

Men's screams pierced the air. She shot from her pallet to the window and ripped the deerskin cover clean away.

"Mother of God!"

Another boom sent shock waves across the water, as one side of her father's house exploded into a fireball, raining thatch and timbers and plaster over the entire village.

"Conall," she breathed, and scrambled toward the door.

He was nearly on his feet, broadsword in hand, when the door yanked open behind him. He fell backward across the threshold as Mairi flew from the lake house, and they both went down, cursing.

"Conall!" She tried to right herself, but her gown was caught by the tip of his sword. He jerked it free. "What are ye doing here? I thought ye were...I thought..." Her voice caught.

"I fell asleep, I..."

Together they gawked at Alwin Dunbar's house on the hill. Part of the thatched roof was afire, and over the din he heard Rob calling for water.

"Good God." Conall grabbed her hand and pulled her to her feet. "Come on," he said, and they raced down the pier toward the beach.

By the time they reached the village, men and women had already begun to run buckets of water up the hill from the loch. Light from the fire cast an orange glow upon the sweaty, blackened faces of those men who'd been inside the house when it went up. Conall wrinkled his nose against the acrid odor of sulfur, thick on the night air.

"Oh, God, where's Kip?" Mairi cried, and yanked her hand from his. She ran toward Dora's cottage, where all six bairns gaped wide-eyed from the window. "Michael, where's Kip?" She jerked the biggest of Dora's children across the sill and set him on his feet in front of the cottage. "Where is he?"

"Dunno," the boy said.

She whirled and fixed her eyes on the inferno above them. "He's no' here! Where is he?"

Conall suddenly remembered. "Oh, Christ," he breathed.

"What? What is it?"

"Kip." His stomach did a slow roll. "I...I told him he could sleep in the house from now on, in the hall with the other men."

Her eyes widened in horror. Conall looked up through the trees at the burning house where Rob now directed a small army of water carriers.

In seconds they scaled the hill. The open doorway belched smoke. Men were still coming out. Conall grabbed her before she could bolt past them into the hall.

"Let me go! I must find him!"

"Nay!" He held her fast, and scanned the throng of clansmen for a warrior to take her.

"Conall!" Dougal burst across the threshold, his face and hands black, his plaid singed.

He tossed Mairi into the arms of the nearest warrior. "Dougal, what's happened? Where's Kip? Where's Harry?"

"Harry's inside. John's been hurt. They're carrying him out now."

"And Kip?" Mairi jerked herself free. "Is he in there? Jesu, where is he?"

Dougal shrugged. In the glow of the fire, Conall could see all the color had drained from her face. His gut knotted. He started for the door.

"I'm here!" a small voice cried from behind them. "Here I am, Mairi!" Jupiter's deep bark sounded from the wood below. The boy and the dog jogged, gasping, into the clearing before the house.

Conall thought Mairi would faint dead away, and put a hand on her shoulder to steady her.

"Oh, thank Christ!" she cried, and hugged Kip to her. The boy gawked at the fire over her shoulder.

Harry and two others stumbled out of the house, bearing the blood-black body of his kinsman, John. "He's dead," Harry said. Tears streamed in sooty rivulets down the scout's cheeks. "He was lyin' right there, by the kitchen hearth, when the whole bluidy thing exploded." He choked back a sob. "There was nothin' we could do."

Stunned and speechless, Conall lifted the drummer's body from their arms and laid it gently on a flat rock. This was his fault. He should have been here with them. Instead, he'd fallen asleep against Mairi's door like some smitten youth.

"Thank God ye werena here," Dougal said to him. "Ye would have been killed as well."

"And Kip!" Mairi hugged the boy fiercely to her chest and glared at him. "He might have been in the house."

Guilt crashed over him in dark, bitter waves.

"I was in the camp, with Jupiter," Kip said. "We

have a sleeping spot hidden away in a thicket." He grinned. "'Tis a secret." The smile faded from his face as he fixed his eyes on John's blackened body.

"'Twill be all right," Mairi whispered, and smoothed Kip's ratty hair, her eyes filled with a love that reminded Conall of his own mother before she'd died. "From now on," Mairi said, "ye shall sleep with me. Go on now." She rose and pushed Kip toward the village. "Go down to Dora's cottage and wait there for me."

"Take Jupiter with you," Conall said, and gestured for the dog to follow the boy.

As soon as the duo was out of sight, Mairi fixed blazing eyes on Dougal and Harry. "What in bluidy hell happened? No' that I care about the house. But one man dead, and by the look of it, all o' ye hurt. What the devil caused it?"

Conall already knew. He could smell it in the air. Sulfur and burning copper. "'Twas the fireworks," he said.

Dougal lowered his eyes, and Harry looked away into the distance, his tears still streaming.

"But ye shot them off on the dock o'er the water, like we always do," Mairi said, and Conall could tell her mind worked to comprehend what had occurred. "We watched ye. 'Twas safe."

For a moment no one spoke, and the crackling of the dying fire filled Conall's head with memories of another fire, rich with death and destruction, and memories too painful to contemplate. His brother, Gilchrist, had been terribly injured in the blaze, his aunt and uncle burned to death.

"We had more. More fire sticks." Kip's voice carried from the wood just below them. He stepped out from behind a tree.

"I told ye to get to Dora's!" Mairi cried. "Now go!"

"Let him speak," Conall said.

Kip inched his way back up the hill, Jupiter trailing behind him, and looked with trepidation into Mairi's eyes. "We only set off half. There was a whole other bag full."

"And where did ye put the bag?" Mairi asked. "In a boat on the water, tethered to the pier, like Tang always showed ye?"

Kip looked down and didn't answer.

"Where did you put the bag, lad?" Conall asked.

"He…he gave it to me," Dougal said.

"And Dougal—" the waning fire reflected off the white lump in Harry's throat as he swallowed "—Dougal gave it to me."

Sweet Christ. Conall knew what was coming.

"And what did ye do with it, eh?" Mairi demanded, and stepped toward the scout.

"I…" Harry's voice caught.

"We left the beach after the moon came up, and went back to the house to sleep," Dougal said.

Harry reluctantly met her gaze. "We went to the kitchen, to warm our hands at the hearth. The…the fire in the hall had gone out."

"Did you leave the bag there?" Conall asked, though he already knew the answer. "By the kitchen hearth?"

Mairi's eyes blazed brighter than the fire. "Well, did ye?"

Harry looked at Dougal, then at her, and shrugged stupidly. "I…I dunno. I canna remember."

Both scouts fixed their eyes on the body of their kinsman, John, who lay charred and broken on the rock below them. Gerald the piper knelt beside the body and covered it reverently with a plaid. All three wept.

"This is your fault," Mairi said to Conall between gritted teeth. "Ye allow youths barely off their mother's teat to swill ale the whole night long while ye're out debauching women. Is it a wonder to ye, Conall Mackintosh, what happened?"

He stared lamely at John's draped body. She was right, and her words, backed by the rueful sounds of his men weeping, seared him like a hot brand.

He should have been here. He was responsible.

Not Harry, not Dougal. Him.

Water hissed on burning timbers, raising a waft of steam skyward, choking the acrid air with a damp closeness that made him want to retch. He felt a hand light firmly on his shoulder, and turned to see Rob's sweat-drenched face looking up at him.

"The fire's nearly out," Rob said. "There's just one wee bit we've yet to quench. Alwin Dunbar's chamber at the back o' the house, the one ye sleep in now."

"Let it burn," Mairi said, and turned her back on them.

A living, swirling mist rolled across the surface of the loch, imparting a ghostly pall to the chill dawn. Mairi stood before the smoking ruins of what had been her father's kitchen and breathed in a heady draft of damp air tinged with sulfur and wood smoke.

Against her wishes, Conall and his men had saved the house, and in the light of day the damage did not appear nearly as bad as it had last night. The kitchen was destroyed, as was her father's old chamber, but the great hall stood intact. Part of the roof would need replacing, and there was smoke damage everywhere.

She skirted the smoldering pile of timbers and thatch, and made her way around to the back of the house. Nearly all of the east wall was gone. No matter. No one had lived here for months, save the Chattan, and after they'd gone no one would likely live here again.

She glanced down the hill toward the camp. All was quiet. The Chattan warriors slept. *He* slept. And all would wake with the sun—all but one. The one they called John. She could see his body, draped in plaids, lying stiff near the center of the camp.

It could have been Kip, or any of her kinsmen.

It could have been Conall.

She gritted her teeth against the bitter taste soiling her mouth. When first she saw the house ablaze, from the lake house window, she'd thought not of Kip, or of any of her own.

She'd thought of *him*. How could she?

She kicked at a live coal with her bare foot and swore silently under her breath.

Idiots, all of them, to have left the fireworks on the hearth. Who in their right mind...but they weren't in their right minds. They were drunk, the lot of them.

She glanced briefly at her father's grave in the garden. Men were all alike. Useless. Irresponsible. She fisted her hands and looked for something to hit.

Then it struck her.

Harry had not been drunk. Nor had Dougal. Aye, Rob had been soused as the traveling priest on feast days, but not the two scouts. She'd seen enough drink-

ing in her day—she glanced again at Alwin's grave—
to know when a man was in his cups.

Her toes dug into the damp, cool earth. What's this?
Hoofprints?

Hoofprints at the back of the house. She knelt and
ran a finger along the impression. She knew little of
horses, but knew a fresh hoofprint when she saw it.
Her gaze was drawn along the cinder pile that had
been the rear wall of the house.

All the mounts were tethered in the camp below
them. No one had reason to ride along the back of the
house. The hill was steep here—aye, nearly a cliff. Her
father had designed it that way on purpose, to dis-
courage surprise visits.

She followed the trail of hoofprints until they
stopped at the place where there had once been a window, the window of her father's chamber.

And then she saw it. A footprint. Plain as day.

Something about it troubled her. She knelt for a
closer look. 'Twas odd. It couldn't have been made
by any of her clan. They all went barefoot till winter
set in, and this was not the print of a barefoot man.
The Chattan warriors favored boots, and they were big
men, all but Rob. Nay, this was not a boot print. 'Twas
more like—

"A slipper!"

Her stomach tightened into a hard ball. She knew
what this was—it had to be. Her eyes darted up the
craggy hillside, following what she thought would be
the most likely path. Rocks, downed limbs, a chute of
earth and loose leaves. Higher, higher still, until—

Her breath caught. A lone rider sat motionless at the

top of the ridge, wisps of morning mist swirling about him like a sorcerer's spent magic.

He looked right through her.

"Tang," she mouthed, and sucked in the lingering fetor of sulfur.

Chapter Ten

The ceremony was mercifully brief.

Conall stood shoulder to shoulder with his kinsmen in a silent circle around John's draped body. Mist coiled at their feet and swirled and eddied over the warrior's corpse like a living, breathing shroud. The last bittersweet notes of Gerald's tribute warbled from the ridge above the camp.

They wept to a man, all save Conall.

He longed to, but held himself in check. His eyes burned dry with a throbbing rawness. He watched as Harry and Dougal and two others lifted John's body and carried it toward the drummer's waiting mount.

"'Tis time," Rob said, and nudged Conall forward.

He wasn't good at this, not like his brothers were. For the first time, men's lives depended on the decisions he would make, on decisions he'd already made.

He closed his eyes and a blaze of color seared his lids. Last night he'd ne'er forget. The star-flecked sky, rough timbers grazing bare legs, chill air raked with the stench of burning sulfur, Mairi's soft and yielding lips. Why in God's name had he allowed the fireworks?

"They're ready," Rob said, and Conall opened his eyes to the flat and somber light of midmorning.

Harry was already mounted. Gerald appeared out of the mist, stowed his pipes in a saddlebag and pulled himself onto his horse.

"Two more shall ride with you," Conall said to them, "as far as the forest camp. After that, 'tis but a day and a night to Monadhliath. 'Tis Chattan land. You'll be safe enough. Tell Gilchrist what has happened."

Harry nodded silently. Gerald's eyes, glassed from weeping, fixed on the body of his friend. Conall slapped the piper's mount and the gelding shot forward.

"Godspeed," he called after them, as the mist sucked them into its cold gray camouflage.

"Come," Rob said. "We've work to do."

They peered up through the trees at what remained of Dunbar's house. "Aye," he said, and followed Rob up the hill. 'Twould be good to break a sweat, busy his hands and his mind.

Together they began to clear away the rubble where the kitchen once stood. One by one, the rest of the Chattan joined them, as did the Dunbars. All but Mairi.

"'Tis no' your fault, ye know," Rob said as they hefted a charred timber and half dragged it down onto the beach. "'Twas an accident, plain and simple."

"One I might have prevented, had I been thinking clearly."

They heaved the timber onto a pile of rubble from the fire, which would be burned to ash later, on the safety of the beach.

"Aye, well I was no' thinkin' too clearly myself."

Conall didn't want to talk about it. They jogged back up the hill to the house in silence, and he threw himself into the work at hand.

Kip directed a group of children who were busy sweeping piles of ash and small debris into buckets. He'd be grown in no time, Conall thought, as he watched him teach one of the younger lads how to use a broom.

He should have kept an eye on Kip last night. Damn it! He'd purposefully avoided him, and had tried of late to put distance between them so their parting in under a fortnight would be less difficult.

Difficult for whom? He'd miss the lad more than he wanted to admit.

If only he'd joined the celebration sooner, perhaps he might have circumvented Kip's journey into the wood and the chance meeting with the Chinese. Had there been no fireworks, there would have been no accident and John would still be alive.

"No accident," he breathed, and hefted another timber onto his shoulder.

Tang had just happened upon Kip on the forest path? Perhaps. Perhaps not. Conall dropped the timber, nearly on Rob's foot, and ducked under a charred beam into what remained of his sleeping chamber.

"Kip," he said. "Where exactly did you meet Tang in the wood last night?"

The boy looked up from his work, sifting through ashes for usable items. "At my hunting spot, just south and east o' the forest camp."

"Hunting spot?" Kip had never mentioned such a place to him before.

"Aye, where I set my rabbit snares." He wiped a

streak of soot across his brow and grinned. "I check them each evening."

"Ah, I see."

Kip's eyes widened. "But dinna tell Mairi. She'll skin me alive. She doesna take to me venturing so far on my own."

"Aye, I suspect she doesn't." It seemed innocuous enough. Still, something about the incident did not ring true to him. "This Tang," he said. "Does he know where you set your snares?"

"Oh, aye."

"And that you go there each eve?"

Kip nodded.

"Symon," Rob said from behind him.

Conall glanced back at his friend. "Perhaps." He wanted to believe it, more than anything. That it was no accident, that Geoffrey Symon was responsible.

Nay. *He* was responsible, and blaming another for his negligence was a coward's way out. And yet...

"Kip, where's Mairi?"

The boy shrugged. "Sleeping, methinks."

"Sleeping? At this hour?" He narrowed his eyes toward the light in the east, but the sun was too obscured by fog to tell exactly what part of the morning it was. They had all overslept after last night's disaster.

"I saw her this morning, early," Kip said. "She told me to stay put, here in the village, and that she was likely to sleep all day since she'd got nary a wink last night."

"I must speak with her." Conall stepped over a heap of charred rubble and started down the hill.

"Where are ye goin'?" Rob called after him.

"To the lake house."

He hurried down the hill into the village and met

Dora coming up the path from the beach. She met his gaze but didn't speak.

"Have you seen Mairi today?" he asked her.

Dora frowned. "Come to think of it, nay." They both looked out across the water to the lake house, which floated in a sea of thinning mist. "'Tis no' like her to sleep the day away."

The skin on the back of his neck pricked. "Aye," he breathed. "'Tis not."

In a half-dozen strides he was on the beach. The sun burned a ragged hole through the fog, drenching him in an eerie white light. He hit the pier at a full run, and the floating timbers rolled under his weight.

'Twas no accident.

Symon was behind it. He felt it, knew it, and so did Mairi. He flung wide the door and stepped inside. The *crannog* was empty, Mairi's bed unmade. He ran his hand over the fur bedcover—cold as ice.

"Damn her!"

Footfalls sounded on the pier behind him. He whirled toward the sound as Dora skidded to a stop, breathless and rosy-cheeked, in the doorway.

"Her boat's gone," she said.

Mairi stepped into the shallows and beached the rowboat next to the standing stone marking the path to the hunter's camp. If the weather held, she'd be back here by late afternoon and home by supper.

She'd been lucky. The thick ground fog had masked her departure, and now fingers of sunlight burned the morning's mist from the steely surface of the loch.

She ran a hand over a cool, mossy crevice in the ancient standing stone. Conall had kissed her here, and she recalled the warm taste of him, his passion and his strength.

Better to recall the humiliation she had felt in his arms last night on the pier. Not to mention his derelict and careless behavior. One man was dead, and others injured, though she knew in her heart someone else was to blame.

Geoffrey.

She was certain of it, and took off on foot northwest toward Falmar Castle. The wood was thick here, and what little light penetrated the dark canopy of trees did naught to quell the shroud of fog blanketing the damp ground.

She kept to the path as best she could, watching for odd trees and rock formations, and other landmarks she recognized. She'd made the trip from Loch Drurie to Falmar countless times, since she'd been old enough to walk, and had no fear of losing her way.

Geoffrey would be surprised to see her. Aye, and he'd best have a good explanation for what Tang was doing in the wood last night and this morn.

The path split, one fork heading north toward Chattan land, the other west toward Falmar. She lifted her skirts and quickened her pace. Her feet were cold, so damp was the ground. 'Twas time to dig out her winter slippers. Soon the snows would come, as would the trade boats. And then she would be free. Free of Geoffrey, and of Conall. 'Twas as much his fault as Geoffrey's. He'd provoked him, and Geoffrey was not a man to back down.

Geoffrey wanted the land, and her, and he wanted Conall dead. She'd seen it in his eyes that day in the wood when he'd caught them kissing.

Conall was certain Geoffrey and his men had been

watching them, watching the village and the construction. Things had gone missing, and now someone was dead.

That someone could have been Conall.

She stopped in her tracks. "Of course! Why didn't I see it before?"

It *should* have been Conall. He slept in her father's chamber with his men scattered about the rest of the house. If Geoffrey had been watching them, he'd have known that. He also knew that none of the Dunbars, save Walter, frequented the house.

She gripped her skirts tighter and picked up the pace. This was too much. If Geoffrey wanted Conall dead, let him wait and do it somewhere else. 'Twould suit her just fine. Let the both of them kill each other. But for him to have put her clan in danger was unforgivable.

Her blood pumped faster, more from anger than the ridge she now scaled overlooking the Symon demesne. The trees thinned, and with them the mist. She broke out onto a barren, windswept crag and stopped to catch her breath.

Falmar Castle lay in the red-gold valley below, nestled between the bare slate arms of a bluff. The setting afforded the Symons protection on three sides, and a view that stretched for leagues on the fourth.

She started down the hill and knew they'd see her coming long before she arrived.

Dora would have a fit if she knew Mairi had come alone. Dora didn't trust Geoffrey, perhaps with good reason. Nonetheless, Mairi would see him alone and settle this once and for all. The last thing she needed was someone else's meddling.

The Symons and the Dunbars had lived in a fragile

sort of peace since long before her birth, and regardless of what had happened last night, she was loath to disrupt that. Her clan was in no position to defend itself against enemies. She would not make one now of Geoffrey, yet she could not allow this incident to pass undenounced.

By the time she reached the valley floor, a half-dozen mounted warriors thundered toward her down the path leading from the castle. She expected no less, and slowed her pace. In minutes they reached her. She smiled at the men she knew, and nodded politely to the others.

"Mairi Dunbar! What brings ye alone to Falmar?"

"Good morrow," she said to the young warrior who leaned down to help her mount behind him.

"Are ye hurt? Is something amiss?"

She settled onto the gelding's back and wrapped her arms around the warrior. "Nay, I'm well, thank ye. But I would see your laird on some business."

He turned in the saddle and grinned at her. "Ah, business is it? I had hoped ye were here on more gentle matters."

He was not the only Symon who favored a match between her and Geoffrey. In fact, she was well liked by all the Symons. She respected them and liked them as well. They'd always treated her as one of their own.

It only made her situation more difficult. She wanted Geoffrey as an ally, a friend, but she'd not wed him. Neither would she tolerate his threats or his attacks.

She was in a precarious position, and even as they trotted across the land bridge to the stone-and-timber keep, she wondered what exactly she would say to him.

He'd been her father's ally, and his only friend at the end of his short life. Though how a friend could sit by and encourage her father to drink himself to death, she could not comprehend.

She recalled Conall's outwardly jovial demeanor at the celebration last night. Rob had been in his cups, but not nearly as drunk as she'd seen her father on numerous occasions. Conall had kept an eye on Rob's consumption, and that of the others, as well, and she recalled that she'd not seen him take a drink for himself.

"Mairi, lass!" an old woman called out to her from one of the cottages flanking the keep.

Mairi smiled and waved. The woman had been a friend of her mother's when Gladys Dunbar was alive.

The warrior guided their mount across the bailey, which teemed with activity, and around to the side of the keep.

"Where is he?" she asked.

"Just in from a hunt. Back there." He reined the gelding to a halt and helped her down.

She smoothed her hair and straightened her skirts, then followed the warrior around a small grouping of outbuildings beside the stable. The stench of newly butchered meat assailed her senses and lent the air a tepid closeness.

Geoffrey was there, kneeling beside the carcass of a red stag, his hands dripping blood. He looked up and cracked a brilliant smile. "Mairi," he said. "I knew ye'd come."

Conall threw his saddle over the black's sleek back and cinched it tight.

"Where d'ye think ye're going?" Rob said.

"After her."

"Fine. I'll go, too."

"And me, as well," Kip said. He bolted toward Rob's white gelding.

Jupiter barked and ran in circles around their mounts.

"Nay, you won't," Conall said. "You're to stay here." He eyed Rob. "All of you."

"Wait for me!" They turned at the sound of Dora's voice. She ran toward them with two bundles of what Conall suspected was food. "I'm going, too."

"We're all going," Dougal said, and waved the rest of the men toward their mounts.

"Hold!" Conall cried, and his men stopped in their tracks. "None of you are going." He snatched the sacks of food from Dora's hands and stowed them in a saddlebag. "I'll go alone."

Rob snorted. "Oh, aye, and be killed the second he sees ye?"

"Think you so little of my battle skills?"

"Nay, 'tis just that—"

"The Symons are nearly a hundred," Dora said. "'Twould be folly to go alone."

Conall made a mental inventory of his weapons—broadsword, two dirks, and a small battle-ax that hung from a loop on his saddle. "'Twould be folly to go otherwise." He mounted the black.

"Conall's right," Dougal said. "Twenty of us appear and there's sure to be trouble. A score against a hundred, we'd have no chance. But a lone man under the cover of night…"

"Exactly." Conall nudged the black toward the wood.

Rob grabbed the bridle. "I willna let ye do it, laddie. Besides, how d'ye know that's where she's gone?''

He knew, all right. He knew in his gut Mairi had gone to Symon, and he was rarely wrong about such feelings. He glanced at Dora, and her sober expression confirmed his hunch.

"She's there," he said. "And of all the stupid, headstrong—" He recalled his first day at Loch Drurie when he'd watched Symon kiss her in the lake house. His anger surged, and he pushed the thought from his mind. "The little fool has no idea of the danger she's in."

"That's the God's truth," Dora said. "And ye canna tell her, neither. She's underestimated Geoffrey from the beginning. I tried to tell her, but naaay…''

"'Tis settled, then," he said. "I'll get her and bring her back." He turned his mount toward the path.

Rob vaulted onto the white gelding's back. "And I'll go with ye." Conall frowned. "I'm small. If 'tis stealth and surprise ye're after, there's no one better."

Dora untethered another horse from the pack and pulled herself onto its back. "And ye canna go without me, neither."

This was getting tiresome. "Why the devil not?" Conall said.

Dora grinned. "Well, how else will ye be able to find the secret entrance to the keep?" She spurred her mount forward.

"Wait! Dora," he called after her as she trotted into the wood. "What secret entrance?"

"Come on," she called back. "The day's half-done. I'll show ye when we get there."

Rob goaded his mount into the wood after her.

Conall held back and met Dougal's dark, serious

eyes. "Did ye send someone to catch up with Harry as I asked?"

"Aye, and when they reach Monadhliath they're to beg your brother Gilchrist for a hundred men."

"Good." He should have called for reinforcements earlier. Damn his own stupid pride.

"Ye could wait till they arrive," Dougal said. "Then go after her."

He could, but he wouldn't. Gilchrist's men wouldn't reach Loch Drurie for another three days and, by God, he'd have Mairi Dunbar home safe by the morrow.

"Nay," he said. "There's no time. Besides, I'll not march a hundred Chattan onto Symon's lands. There's one dead already. Would you have others?"

"But—"

"I'll not engage the alliance in a war over this. Iain would have my head. Besides, 'tis my fault John is dead." He met the steely gazes of his men, one by one. "Mine alone."

He thought it best not to tell them of his true suspicions. They were proud men, and fearless. If they had but an inkling the explosion was Symon's doing, he wouldn't be able to stop them from taking their vengeance.

Dougal nodded. "And 'twould no' be just the Symons. As soon as Fraser heard we were in it...well, 'twould be a nasty affair."

"Exactly." Dougal was smart for his years. "I'm off, then." He turned to Kip, who waited patiently with Jupiter for instructions. "Kip, I want you to stay here and help Dougal."

"But I—"

"Keep Jupiter with you, and do exactly as Dougal says, do you hear?"

"But I want to come with you."

He leaned down and whispered into Kip's ear, "Dougal's a scout, not a warrior. He'll need a good man to help him keep watch over the new docks. 'Twould be a big favor to me if you stayed and helped him."

Kip glanced at Dougal, then the docks, and finally he smiled. "All right, then. I'll do it." Jupiter barked and wagged his thick tail. "Jupiter can stand watch with me."

"Aye, that's the spirit." He shot Dougal a loaded look, and the scout nodded. Conall didn't have to worry; Dougal wouldn't let Kip out of his sight until they returned.

He kicked lightly, and the black shot forward into the wood. Dougal raised a hand in farewell. If all went well, they'd be back before dawn tomorrow.

Conall shook his head and swore under his breath. "Mairi Dunbar, you're more trouble than you're worth."

"That she is." Dora's mount sprang from a thicket on his left, nearly unseating him.

"Christ, woman, dinna sneak up on me like that!"

"We was just waitin' for ye," Rob said as he flanked him on the right.

"Let's ride." He spurred the black into a gallop, and his comrades' answering hoofbeats sounded behind him.

Hours later, they climbed out of the highland wood onto a long, low ridge. Dora bade them stop before the summit and tether their mounts in a dense copse.

"We should go on foot from here," she said. "And

we'll have to wait till nightfall if ye dinna wish to be seen.''

"Are we near, then?" Conall asked.

"Aye. No more than a league." She nodded toward the summit. "Falmar Castle rests in a valley just beyond this ridge."

"Can we no' ride farther?" Rob asked.

"No' without being seen. Unless ye want to go around and approach from the north. There's a craggy knob o' shale that juts out just before the keep."

"We'll have to wait until nightfall all the same. We might as well go around, and tether our mounts closer."

They agreed and were about to remount when something on the ground caught Conall's eye. He stooped and picked it up.

"What's that?" Rob said.

"Dunno, but it seems familiar." He turned the tortoiseshell comb over in his hand. Sunlight glinted fiery copper off the single strand of hair caught in its teeth.

"'Tis Mairi's," Dora said. "She must have dropped it."

"So she did come this way," Rob said.

Conall's hand closed over the comb. He told himself he was going after her simply to make certain she was safe. Any man in his position would do the same. After all, they had a bargain, one that the Chattan depended on, and he'd not allow Symon to jeopardize that. He'd not allow Symon to touch her. By God, if he had...

"D'ye care that much for her, then?" Rob's question jolted him from his stupor.

"Care for whom? What do you mean?"

"Mairi. Ye fear for her. I can see it in your eyes."

Dora saw it, too. He ignored them both and his own confused emotions, untethered the black and vaulted into the saddle. "Come on. Let's find that craggy knob of shale."

The days were short now and, for once, Conall was grateful for the early sunset. Dora led them north back into the wood, then west again, and as daylight waned they came upon a black craggy promontory, dividing the thinning forest from whatever it was that lay on the other side.

"This is it," Dora said, and dismounted. She tied her borrowed steed to a larch.

Conall and Rob did the same. They left their mounts and began to scale the rocky, broken outcrop. Loose scree and twilight made for unsteady footing. They used their hands in places to negotiate what looked like an ancient trail.

Rob reached the summit first. "So, Conall laddie," he whispered down to them, "how determined are ye to get her back?"

He was damned determined.

He grunted and pulled himself up the last few feet onto a flat rock. Falmar Castle lay below them to the south. They looked out across the murky, fetid water surrounding the keep.

"Good God," he breathed, and swallowed hard against the sick feeling rising in his gullet.

"Oh, aye," Dora said, and eyed him apprehensively. "I forgot to tell ye—there's a moat."

Chapter Eleven

He had expected her.

That, and his far too casual attitude, fueled Mairi's suspicions.

"Won't ye sit?" Geoffrey said, and indicated an upholstered bench by the window.

Mairi ignored him and continued to study the finely appointed chamber. She'd been in this part of Falmar Castle only once before, some years ago when she was a girl.

A pine bed, heaped with furs and plaids, rested opposite the hearth. The walls were adorned with all manner of weaponry. That was handy. If what she suspected were true, she might wish to slit his throat later.

"D'ye like this chamber?" Geoffrey said. "The view from the window spans the whole of my valley."

"I've no' come to see the view." She met his gaze and held it. "A man is dead."

"What?" The surprise on his face seemed so genuine, it unnerved her for a moment. "When did this happen?"

"Last night. My father's house was blown to bits." She paused to watch his reaction.

"What in God's—"

"Fireworks."

His blue eyes widened. They reminded her of a child's. "An accident?"

She snorted. "So it appears. But I'm no' so certain. Kip acquired some fire sticks last eve from Tang."

"Ah. They can be dangerous if no' used properly." Geoffrey grasped her shoulders gently and affected the most sickly sweet of expressions. "Thank Christ ye're all right. I dinna know what I'd have done had ye—"

"A man is dead." She shrugged his hands away, and they floated lamely to his sides.

"But Mairi, we should thank Christ only Mackintosh was killed."

A chill curled along her spine. "Mackintosh? Ye mean Conall?"

"Aye. 'Tis a pity, but these things happen." He read her astonishment before she had the presence of mind to hide it, and quickly grasped her arms. "He's dead, is he no'?"

Mairi's thoughts raced. "'Tis your doing," she said finally. "Let go of me!" She wrenched out of his grasp and turned to the window.

"Mairi, what d'ye mean? How could it be?"

She felt his breath on her hair and her pulse quickened. Perhaps she'd been a fool to come alone, after all. She'd never said who'd been killed, yet Geoffrey expected it had been Conall.

She whirled on him. "Where's Tang? He was there in the wood this morn, above my father's house."

Geoffrey frowned.

"He gave Kip the fire sticks. He was there last night. Where is he?"

"I...I know not. I've no' seen him today."

He was telling the truth. Had he seen Tang, he would know Conall was alive and well. Tang would have seen the Chattan sleeping in the camp this morning from his vantage point above the house. She didn't know what to believe.

"Ye were hunting, last night and this morn." She wrinkled her nose at the lingering odor of blood on his person. "Where?"

"Why, north, where I always hunt. 'Tis where the best game is, ye know that."

He was lying. She knew it, felt it, and yet...

"Mairi," he said, and took her hand. "Why on earth would I do such a terrible thing?"

She shot him a look that said she knew very well why.

"Lass, d'ye think I'm a complete fool?" He ran a finger lazily along her palm. She allowed it, though she knew not why. "D'ye think I'd kill a man aligned with so powerful a clan as the Chattan?"

He had a point. Still...

"Did he harm ye, Mairi?"

"Conall?" She drew her hand from his and turned away so he would not see the heat rising in her face. She knew what Geoffrey meant by *harm*.

Conall hadn't, yet he could have.

"Nay," she said. "'Tis no' like that between us."

"I'm relieved to hear it." He turned her toward him. "Because if anything had—oh, Mairi, ye must let me help ye now."

The concern in his face chiseled away at her confidence. What if it was an accident, after all?

"Your docks are built, the trade will come. I can help ye with it—I *must* help ye. Your father would have wished it so."

She bristled. "Aye, of that I've no doubt. But I need no help, Geoffrey, from you or anyone."

"Come now." He touched her face, and she batted his hand away.

"Kip might have been killed last night. Did ye ever think o' that?"

"Well, I—"

"Ye havena even asked about him."

"Mairi," he said, and affected that annoying smile again. "I'm certain the boy is fine, or ye wouldna be here. Besides, we'll have children of our own one day, sons proud to bear the name Symon. No' like that orphaned ragamuffin."

Blood heated her face to near molten temperatures. For a split second she considered hefting a battle-ax from the wall over the hearth and cleaving his head in two.

She bolted toward the door. Geoffrey grabbed her arm and yanked her backward, nearly off her feet.

"Mairi," he said between gritted teeth, "ye had many chances to come to me willing. Now ye're finally here, and here ye'll stay."

She'd never truly feared him before, though most of their encounters had been on her land, not his. A chilling apprehension gripped her now, and she fought to maintain her composure.

"N-nay, I won't."

He pulled her toward the bed, fumbled open a wooden box that sat on the night table, and drew forth a length of shimmering black cord.

"Aye," he said, and slid closer. "Ye will."

Night settled on Falmar Castle like a dark bird of prey, swallowing it whole and digesting it in its midnight gloom. The churr of a nightjar raised the hairs on Conall's neck. 'Twas time.

He divested himself of his weapons, unbelted his plaid and let it slide from his body. "I'm going in."

Rob scrambled down from his vantage point on the craggy ridge overlooking Falmar's moat and the land bridge that spanned it. "Ye should wait another hour or so," he said. "She may come out on her own."

"Nay," Dora said. "Mairi would ne'er rest at Falmar past dark. Something's amiss."

"He keeps her," Conall said, as he tied the tails of his shirt between his legs. He donned his weapons and started over the ridge top.

"I can go with ye," Dora called after him. "I'm a good swimmer, and I know the castle as well as any."

He looked back at her in the dark. "Nay, stay here with Rob. And remember, if I'm not back before sunrise, ride to Loch Drurie and wait there for Gilchrist and his men. My brother will know what to do."

"I dinna like this," Rob said. "Ye willna change your mind?"

He laughed. "Have you ever known me to do so?"

"Nay, ye thickheaded lout."

"Remember what I told ye," Dora said. "About the hatch."

"Aye, I'll find it—and I'll bring her back." Before they could say more, he scrambled down the opposite side of the ridge toward the black, stinking water.

Falmar rose up out of it, a smooth, nearly windowless citadel. Torchlights blazed in the village below the keep and from the cottages ringing the bailey. But the keep itself was dark, save for a pale-copper glow illuminating one of the few windows on this, the north side.

There were no sentries. Symon didn't need them. 'Twas impossible to breach the keep from this direction, unless one knew of the secret hatch Mairi Dunbar had used as a child.

He stared across the inky water toward the spot where Dora had said he'd find it. The stench was near overpowering. He drew a shallow breath and his stomach roiled.

"Bloody hell," he breathed, and dipped a toe. Christ, the water was freezing. When he did find Mairi, he had a mind to take her over his knee and wallop her backside till it shone.

The thought stirred him in a way that was completely inappropriate given his current situation. He adjusted his shirt over his groin. Aye, well, there was one way to cure it...

He jumped.

The shock of the frigid water sucked the breath out of him. He flailed for a moment under the foul, greasy water, his weapons knocking him about, then shot to the surface the way Kip had taught him, and gulped in air.

"I'll kill her," he choked, and began to swim across the reeking pond.

He glanced at the bridge, and though 'twas lit, no one was about. A repeat of the morning's mist would have been most welcome, but the night was clear, the stars brilliant. The only thing in his favor was the absence of the moon. 'Twould rise in an hour or so. He kicked faster.

How in God's name had he gotten himself involved in this? Involved with *her*. Swimming in the black of night toward a secret entrance to the castle of some lessor chieftain who'd likely kill him on sight were he to catch him. He must be daft. His teeth chattered uncontrollably.

He told himself he had to get her back to ensure the integrity of their agreement. The Chattan were counting on him. His brothers were counting on him. Och, 'twas a load of shite.

The Dunbars were all but extinct. He could have taken the land from the very start—and her. So why hadn't he? Even now, why did he risk his life to bring her back to Loch Drurie? He didn't need her, not for the trade agreement.

For all he knew she could have come here seeking Symon's company. She could be here willing. He treaded water for a moment, catching his breath, and gazed up at the coppery glow radiating from the narrow castle window far above him.

Her kisses still burned on his lips. Her flesh still seared his hands. Nay, she might have come willing, but Dora was right, she'd not stay here past dark of her own volition. Symon kept her, and by God, if he'd so much as touched her…

He kicked forward with renewed strength, and fixed his eyes on the sheer rock walls and timbered battlements of Falmar Castle. Finally, after what seemed a lifetime in the frigid water, his hand scraped along the slimy stone foundation. He turned in the water to get his bearings. This was exactly the spot to which Dora had pointed. He felt along the sheer wall. Nothing. No opening of any kind. Where in bloody hell was it? He kicked out with his foot and connected with—

That's it!

An iron grate, three or four feet below the surface.

He felt along the moss-covered grating with his foot. A handle of some kind protruded from the bottom. The water in the moat must have risen since Mairi had last braved this route. Dora had said nothing about the hatch being submerged. Aye, and she'd said naught about the moat, either.

But he'd not come this far only to turn back. He sucked in a breath and somersaulted under the water. The hatch was rusted shut, from what he could feel. He came up for air and unsheathed his dirk. "Christ, I canna believe I'm doing this."

On the third try he finally pried it loose. The hatch cover flew up and he propelled himself into the black opening. 'Twas narrow and angled upward, and there was no way, once in it, to turn 'round. Panic seized him. His lungs were bursting. He kicked for all he was worth and shot unexpectedly to the surface on the other side of the wall.

Where in the hell—?

Why, 'twas a kitchen! Just as Dora had said. He'd swum up into some kind of a drain. Bits of cabbage and vegetable peelings floated 'round him. The stink was not so bad here. He pulled himself out onto the stone floor and adjusted his weapons.

No one was about. He'd been damned lucky. His dirk was still in his hand, and he redoubled his grip on it. Voices carried from somewhere else, down the corridor to his left. He moved into it cautiously, dripping wet, leaving a telltale trail of rank water in his wake. It couldn't be helped.

He had to move, and move fast. Dora had described the castle's basic layout, and he knew that Symon's private chambers were on the second floor. If Mairi was here, he'd wager that's where he'd find her.

He crept along the corridor past a number of closed doors. The great hall was just ahead off to the right, radiating a warm fire glow. A cacophony of voices, music and laughter echoed off the corridor's stone walls. One of the voices he recognized.

Symon's.

He itched to kill him and be done with it.

To his left were steps leading to the second level. He pressed himself against the rough, cool wall and listened for a moment. Perhaps Mairi was in the hall with Symon. From the smell of it, supper had just been laid. Any second, someone was sure to enter the corridor and discover him. He'd be dead before the next course was served.

He had to choose.

A minute later he was stealing along the dark second-floor corridor, listening at each closed door for some sign that Mairi was within. He felt his way to the end of the hallway until his hand closed over the latch of an intricately carved wooden door. He tripped it and waited.

The only sounds were the pounding of his heart and the echoes of the diners in the hall below. Water dripped from his nose, and he wiped it away. He swung the door inward and froze.

"Conall!"

Mairi lay sprawled across a huge pinewood bed heaped with the furs of every kind of forest animal he'd e'er seen. Her hands were tethered above her head to a stout bedpost.

"What are ye doing here?" she cried.

"The question is," he said as he moved quickly to her side, "what are *you* doing here?" His eyes roved over her, instinctively checking her for injury. "Are you all right, Mairi? Did he...did he harm you?"

She struggled against her tethers and shot him a

nasty look that he was wholly unprepared for. "That's all the both o' ye have on your minds, isn't it? Whether or no' the other one's *harmed* me." She struggled harder. "Dinna stand there like a fool! Cut me loose." Her freckled nose wrinkled. "Lord! Ye stink like one o' Walter's hogs."

"Aye, and so will you before the night's out."

"Ye're wet. How the devil did ye get in here without Geoffrey catching ye?"

"The moat," he said. "Your secret entrance, though I dinna think much of it. Dora showed me. She and Rob are waiting for us just outside."

"What? What are ye doing here? Are ye mad?"

"Aye, I must be." This was not the welcome he had hoped for. But with Mairi Dunbar, nothing ever turned out as expected.

"Cut me loose!"

He decided to let her struggle a while longer. She looked damned lovely all helpless and trussed up like a game bird, her breasts straining at the fabric of her gown. Her eyes blazed murder. God, she was beautiful.

"Ye have no business coming here like a thief in the night!"

"So," he said, and ran a finger along her thigh. "You don't want my help?"

"I dinna need your help. I never asked ye for it, and I dinna want it."

He sheathed his dirk. "Fine, then. I'll leave." He turned on his heel.

"Dinna toy with me, Conall Mackintosh!"

He choked back a smile, and reminded himself they were both in a damned dangerous situation. He leaned over the bed and, with one quick jerk, freed her from the tether. The black cording came away in his hand. "Hmm, silk."

She looked at him, her mouth gaping.

"I told you I was good with knots."

She glared at him and scooted off the bed, rubbing her wrists.

"Come on," he said. "We've not much time. They're still at supper. If we're quick we can get out the same way I got in."

"What d'ye mean? I'm no' going anywhere."

Now 'twas his turn to gape. His face grew hot, and it wasn't just the hearth fire that was responsible. Steam rose from his dripping hair. "Are ye mad? I've just risked my life to save ye, and now ye dinna want to go?"

"Ye're doin' it again," she said, and smirked at him. "Your speech."

He fisted his hands at his sides for fear of grabbing her, and a litany of silent curses spewed from his clenched teeth.

"My business with Geoffrey is no' yet finished," she said, and tipped her chin at him in a manner that made him want to slap her.

"Aye, and by the look of things here—" he glanced around what was obviously Symon's bedchamber "—his business with you is not finished, either." He arched a brow at her and she swore under her breath. "Come on," he said, and grabbed her hand. "Let's get out of here."

Mairi gawked at the greasy-looking water filling the drainage chute and shook her head. "I'm no' going that way."

"Aye, you are." Before she could protest, Conall lifted her off her feet and dropped her into it.

"Och, 'tis foul!"

"Aye, and cold as the devil." His powerful hands lit on her shoulders. "Now take a breath and I'll push you down."

"But—" She went under and scrambled a few feet down the narrow chute before her skirts tangled around her torso. She shot to the surface and picked a soggy cabbage leaf from her dripping hair.

"What's wrong?" Conall whispered. In the dim light she could barely make out his features.

"We must go headfirst."

He pulled her out of the water and steadied her on her feet. Voices and laughter carried from the great hall not twenty paces along the dark corridor off the kitchen.

"Be quick about it," he said.

"You first."

"Do you think I'm a complete fool?"

Well, 'twas worth a try. She took a deep breath and, ignoring the debris floating in the water, scrambled headfirst into the drainage chute. 'Twas smaller than she remembered it. Then again, she'd been a child the last time she'd used it. It amazed her that Conall had negotiated it at all.

The water grew colder the deeper she swam. Just as her lungs began to protest, she felt the walls of the chute fall away and the icy water of the moat.

She broke the surface and drew the chill night air into her lungs. A moment later Conall surfaced beside her, gasping for breath.

"This is insane!" she hissed, and immediately started to shiver. "Where's the boat?"

"W-what boat?" His teeth chattered.

She spun around in the rank, black water, searching for Rob and Dora. "Where are they? They're no' here!"

"Nay, they're waiting for us on that ridge over there." He pointed across the water into the blackness. She could just discern the outline of the craggy promontory.

Suddenly it dawned on her. "Ye swam out? All this way?" He was treading water remarkably well.

"Aye." He propelled himself forward. "Now c-come on, before we f-freeze to death."

She tried to keep up with him, but her woolen gown weighed her down. He had to stop and tread water several times, and wait for her to catch up. Finally she slipped below the surface and wrestled out of the garment altogether. She retained her light shift for modesty's sake, but would have preferred to jettison it as well.

They swam for shore—'twasn't far now. Thank God, for the moat stank and chilled her to her very soul. She was amazed by Conall's skill in the frigid water. Long, powerful strokes. Easy, measured breaths.

"Ye've practiced," she said between strokes.

"Aye."

Her foot grazed the rocky bottom. "We're here." She scrambled onto a flat rock and began to wring the water from her shift, which clung to her like an icy shroud.

"Mairi!" a voice called down to her from above.

She squinted into the darkness. "Dora? Is that you?"

"Aye, 'tis us," Rob's voice carried on the light breeze. "Hurry up!"

Conall grabbed her arm and together they scaled the craggy promontory, both of them dripping wet and shivering uncontrollably. When they reached the top, Dora threw a dry plaid 'round her shoulders.

"Christ, ye stink to high heaven," Rob said.

Conall snorted. "Aye, and the next time that bloody moat's to be crossed, I'm sending *you*."

"There willna be a next time," Dora said. "What in God's name were ye thinkin', Mairi?"

Mairi pulled the plaid tight around herself and ignored the question.

"I know exactly what she was thinking," Conall said. "Why didn't you come to me, Mairi?"

She ignored Conall's question, as well, and turned to look back across the moat. Pale light glimmered silver off its dark, fetid surface. No one had followed them. Apparently Geoffrey had not yet discovered her absence.

"Come on," Rob said. "Our steeds await in the wood below."

They scrambled down the ridge into the thin stand of trees. 'Twas black as midnight, but a soft whinny and the comforting smell of lathered horse told her where their mounts waited.

"There are only three of them," she said, once her eyes adjusted to the darkness.

"Aye," Conall said. "You'll ride with me."

She'd do nothing of the kind. While he was busy adjusting his plaid and his weapons over his soaking shirt, she pulled herself onto the black's saddle. The horse reared.

"Oh, Jes—" She threw her arms around the beast's neck and clung for dear life.

"Mairi!" Conall grabbed the reins.

Her heart pounded in her throat. She took a couple of deep, calming breaths as the horse quieted under Conall's sharp command.

The next thing she knew, he had mounted behind her and pulled her practically onto his lap. She was squashed between the pommel and his hard thighs. Water seeped through their newly donned garments. Both of them were soaked to the skin.

"Let's away," he said, and snapped the black's reins.

They rode for a time in silence, and all the while she wondered exactly how much Conall knew. She would never reveal her suspicions about the explosion. The last thing her clan needed now was more trouble.

If Conall thought for an instant that Geoffrey was behind it, there'd be wholesale carnage for certain. Nay, she couldn't allow that to happen. The Symons were good people. 'Twasn't their fault Geoffrey was a reckless fool.

Nay, she'd not tell him. And what he didn't know, wouldn't hurt him.

"Did you think I wouldna have figured it out?" he whispered in her ear, startling her. "Or that no one would notice you'd gone?" His arm tightened around her waist.

"W-what d'ye mean?" What was he, a mind reader?

"The explosion, Mairi—the *accident.*"

She gripped the pommel tighter and started to shiver. "What about it? Had ye and your men no' been out o' your heads with drink, 'twould ne'er have happened. 'Twas your fault a man is dead—yours alone.''

Her words frosted the chill night air, and he stiffened behind her. Remorse washed over her. Shame heated her face. Why had she said that?

"I had nary a drop and you know it," he said. "As for Harry and Dougal..." He leaned closer so that his lips brushed her ear. "'Twas no accident, Mairi. 'Twas not their fault."

She jerked away from him. The obvious question hung there between them, unasked and unanswered. He knew. Or if he didn't know, he suspected.

"What will ye do?" she breathed, afraid of his answer.

The sounds of the forest around them intensified—crickets, the hoot of an owl, wind rustling autumn's crisped leaves in the trees overhead.

She repeated her question, and he goaded the black faster along the forest path.

Finally he said, "Symon shall be dealt with later."

A chill fingered its way up her spine. Then something else occurred to her. "Why did ye come, then?"

He didn't answer.

"Ye came for me, alone in the dead o' night, one man against a hundred. Why?"

The path before them opened onto the lonely northwest shore of Loch Drurie. A silvered moon floated above its glassy surface. Water lapped gently along the beach. The standing stone was just ahead and loomed up like some ancient pearly sentinel in the eerie light.

He drew her close, both arms fitting snugly around her waist, as if they were always meant to be there.

She felt his breath hot on her face and she knew why he had come.

She'd always known it.

"Mairi," he breathed, and grazed her cheek with his lips.

Nay, this wasn't happening. It couldn't happen. His hands on her body, his warmth, his strength. 'Twould be so easy to succumb. So easy.

She grabbed the black's reins and jerked to a stop beside the standing stone. Her boat lay beached beside it, and before Conall could stop her, she threw her leg over the horse's withers and dropped to the ground.

"What are you doing?" he said. "I'll send someone back for the boat on the morrow."

"Nay, I'll row it back now. Besides, 'tis faster." Her heart beat erratically, her palms sweating even though she was wet to the skin and cold as ice.

"I'll come with you."

"Nay, I—"

In a flash he was beside her in the boat, wresting the oars from her hands. "Rob, Dora," he called to their companions. "Take my mount, we're rowing back."

Mairi could barely make out their shapes in the dark, but she heard their soft laughter and Rob's intimate whispers. The boat sliced through the water, and their silhouettes faded into the night.

In no time Conall had rowed them nearly halfway across. He did not speak, but she could see the set of his jaw and the moonlight reflected in his eyes.

He'd come for her.

When she could finally discern the rounded lines of the lake house, she threw off the plaid Dora had given her and jumped from the boat in her soaking shift.

Icy water shocked the breath from her. Ah, but 'twas clean and washed away the stink of Geoffrey's moat. She made for the lake house in long, easy strokes. Just before she reached the pier, she heard a splash.

Conall was right behind her.

She pulled herself onto the floating timbers as he swam up beside her. What was he doing? Surely, he didn't think to—

Dripping wet and chilled to the bone, she raced to the safety of the lake house and slammed the heavy door behind her. Her breath escaped in a long, trembling sigh. Too tired to make a fire, she shuffled in the dark toward her pallet, then nearly jumped out of her skin as the door crashed wide.

Conall loomed in the doorway, breathing hard, water sluicing from his body—a silver shadow in the moon's pale light. "You forgot to bolt your door," he said, and shut it silently behind him.

Chapter Twelve

He'd have her and be done with it.

Perhaps then he'd come to his senses. Conall unbelted his weapons and set them on the table. As he felt his way to the hearth he heard her scramble toward the pallet in the corner.

"What d'ye think ye're doing?" she asked in the dark.

"Building a fire." The peat was already laid. His hand closed over the flint she kept on the crude stone mantel.

"Methinks we've had enough fires for a while. Get out of my house."

He ignored her. One spark and the loamy peat crackled to life, tiny flames dancing amidst thin curls of smoke. Christ, he was iced to the bone and dripping all over the hearth. He pulled at the knot between his legs and his sopping shirt hung free.

"I said get out."

Finally he looked at her. She might have covered herself with one of the plaids or furs on the pallet behind her. But she did not. She just stood there, glaring at him, her wet shift clinging to the lithe curves of her body. 'Twas a challenge if e'er he'd seen one, and everyone knew Conall Mackintosh loved a challenge.

"Take off your clothes," he said.

Mairi snorted. "Ye'd like that, wouldn't ye?"

He'd like nothing better. God's truth, he couldn't remember ever wanting a woman as much as he wanted her. Here, now. His loins burned fire and ice.

"Suit yourself," he said with as much nonchalance as he could muster. "But I'll not stand here and freeze to death."

He shrugged out of his soaking shirt, spraying droplets of water, hissing and spitting, onto the fire. He rubbed his legs and arms vigorously and felt the life return to them. All the while her eyes were on him, widening just a bit as he turned to face her.

Her cheeks blazed against her will, and he knew she'd rather cut out her tongue than show the slightest bit of shock or fear. She tipped her chin higher and looked him in the eye. God, she was beautiful, and his body responded.

"Here," she said, and tossed him a dry plaid, never taking her eyes from his. The woman was pure Scot, but damned if she didn't have nerves of Spanish steel.

He wrapped the plaid 'round his waist and couldn't help the smile curling at the edges of his mouth. "Now you," he said.

Her eyes widened almost imperceptibly. "In your dreams, perhaps."

He did laugh, then, and turned his back on her to afford her some privacy. "I was merely concerned for your health."

"Aye, my health, is it?"

He heard her struggling with her wet shift and was tempted to turn 'round and offer his assistance.

"All right," she said after a moment. "We're both dry and in fine—what was it? Health? Ye can go now."

He turned and was mildly startled to find her dressed neither in gown nor shift, but wrapped in a plaid the same as he. She'd told him to go, twice now, yet her actions begged him to stay.

He moved toward her, fascinated by the play of firelight in her hair and the challenge in her eyes. Eyes as deep and as blue as Loch Drurie in autumn.

"Why didn't you come to me, Mairi?" he asked her again. He admired her courage, her independence, yet her lone journey to Symon hurt his pride in a way he couldn't explain. "Why didn't you trust me?"

"Trust you? To do what? Murder a whole people for one man's actions? The Symons are gentle, good."

"Not all of them." A vision of Mairi lashed to Symon's bed still burned in his mind's eye.

"Besides, I trust no one. Especially men like you." She pulled the plaid tighter around herself. "What good are they, tell me? Look 'round the village. Where are our men when most we need them?"

He couldn't argue with that. Nor could he promote his own loyalty. He'd drifted for years from place to place and from woman to woman. The places, the women—they were all alike to him.

Until now.

The thought unsettled him, and he pushed it from his mind.

"Take my father, for example," she said. "Now there was a man." She grunted mockingly. "A man a woman could depend on."

"Mairi," he whispered, and reached for her.

She slapped his hand away. "Have ye heard the tale? Have ye?" Her eyes blazed with a hatred he'd not seen in her before. "He left my mother to be butchered before my eyes. Didna lift a single weapon in her defense."

A film of tears glassed her eyes, yet she continued to glare at him, clutching the plaid until her knuckles turned white. Her pain was raw, palpable, and cut him to the quick as if he, himself, was the guilty one, and not Alwin Dunbar.

"Mairi, please let me—"

"Dinna touch me!" She backed away from him. "Ye're all alike, the lot o' ye."

"Nay. Nay, we are not." He grabbed her shoulders and pulled her to him. "I came for you, did I not? Did you think I'd let Symon keep you?"

She was trembling, and he knew it wasn't from the cold.

"Wouldn't you?" she breathed.

"Nay." He kissed her forehead. "Never."

She looked into his eyes, and he felt himself—the man he knew—slipping away.

"Why did ye come for me?" she whispered against his lips, tears shimmering in her eyes. "Why?"

Somewhere deep inside of him he knew why, though he didn't want to believe it.

He kissed her and hot tears spilled across her cheeks, searing his lips as he possessed her mouth again and again. She threw her arms around him and in that moment of shared, unguarded passion, he knew his life would never be the same.

"Conall," she breathed.

Her plaid slipped to the floor and she felt his hands

rove her bare skin. He crushed her to him, kneading her buttocks, and she gave up her weight to him, reveling in his strength.

"I want you, lass," he whispered between kisses, then whisked her off her feet and bore her back onto the pallet.

He ripped the plaid from his own body and settled atop her, naked. She gasped at the weight of him, the intense heat shimmering through the coolness of his damp skin. Oh, she wanted him, too. She'd deny it no longer.

"Conall," she breathed again, and instinctively opened her legs to him. He groaned and thrust against her. "Nay, wait. Dinna—"

"Shh, 'tis all right," he whispered against her lips. "We've all the time in the world." He kissed her, gently this time, and pushed a few damp tendrils of hair from her forehead.

Mairi ran a finger over his lips, and he smiled. His eyes flashed green-gold in the fire's coppery glow. There was something in his expression she'd ne'er seen before. Not lust or even desire.

'Twas…joy.

"Kiss me," she breathed, and closed her eyes as his mouth devoured hers.

His hands moved over her body with skilled precision, touching her in places no one had touched her, places even she had rarely touched herself.

"Ah!" Her hips rose involuntarily as his fingers grazed her most intimate of places.

"Do you like that?" he whispered, willing her gaze to his.

"Aye." She trembled under his touch.

He stroked her there again, and again she gasped in wonder. "W-what are ye doin'?"

"You'll see," he said, and kissed her again.

His tongue mated with hers in hot, glassy inquisition as his fingers worked some secret magic driving her to a near desperation she couldn't comprehend.

Her body stiffened and she clutched at him, frantic for...for what? His mouth moved to her breast and, as he began to suckle, she came off the bed in a jolt of pure sensation. Another, and another. And then she was gasping for breath, begging him to stop.

He was sweating now, and his slick, heated body settled again over hers. She nuzzled his face, his neck, reveling in his scent. He lifted her buttocks, and she instinctively wrapped her legs 'round his hips.

"Look at me," he breathed.

She opened her eyes, washed ashore in a near dream-state. New emotions, sharp yet unfathomable, swept her into a vortex. He entered her in one powerful thrust. The shock of it knocked the breath from her.

"Ah, Mairi!"

She clung to him, trembling, battling an elemental urge to push him away.

"Hold me," he said, and tightened his grip on her. "Dinna move." He trembled, as well, and it eased her brief moment of fear.

She kissed him and he responded with a slow caution, as if he worked to control his passion. She didn't want him to control it. Nor would she be controlled. Not now. Not ever.

She moved against him and he groaned in an exquisite pleasure that shimmered in his face and glassed his eyes. Firelight danced in his hair. Gazes locked, they began to move together, and her own passion surged.

They kissed with a fierceness she'd felt all along in his presence. His thrusts grew more powerful, and her own increasingly wild. Her anger, her fear, all the confusion of the past weeks sought vengeance in the frenzy of their lovemaking.

This was what she wanted, what she needed. To be possessed, consumed, driven to the brink of madness. Aye, she was nearly there.

He moved his hand between their bodies. She cried his name, and he pushed her over the edge. In the bliss that followed, she heard him cry hers as he found his own release.

They lay there entwined, bathed in a silk of perspiration, and he whispered words of sweet affection in her ear. When she could finally make a coherent thought, only one came to mind.

What had she done?

The pearly light of dawn seeped under the door of the lake house and played at the edges of the deerskin window-covering.

"Are you awake?" Conall whispered, though he was half-asleep himself.

Mairi did not stir.

He kissed her lightly on the temple and drew the fur bedclothes up around them. She was warm and soft, and he could not get close enough to her. He burrowed deeper into the furs and fitted the curves of her body tightly against his.

She let out a tiny, catlike groan and undulated against him. 'Twas all the encouragement he needed.

They made love again, slowly this time, drifting somewhere between sleep and awareness.

Touching, tasting, he moved over every inch of her body, taking pleasure in her ardent whispers and dreamy, passionate response.

When he slid inside her, she jolted awake.

"Nay," she breathed, and pushed against his chest.

"Do I hurt you?"

"Nay, but—" He kissed her and thrust again. "Conall, I—" And again. "But—" And again. "Ohh," she breathed, and moved against him.

"Aye, that's it. Let me pleasure you, Mairi."

And pleasure her he did.

Afterward, she drifted back to sleep, and he lay there looking at her face in the growing light. She'd wanted him again, as he'd wanted her, yet she'd resisted. Her battle, he knew, was not with him, but inside herself, and raged on for reasons he was just beginning to fully comprehend.

For he was at war, as well. He'd wanted her, desperately. Now he'd had her and should be sated.

But he was not.

He told himself he could enjoy her, if she agreed, until the time came for him to leave. 'Twould not be long now. A fortnight at most. He smiled bitterly in the half-light.

He didn't want to leave.

He entwined his fingers in a long curl of her hair and wondered what would happen if he didn't. 'Twas foolish, unthinkable.

She'd grow tired of him, or he of her. It had always been like that with him. He raised the red-gold lock to his nose and breathed in the scent of her. Nay, he'd never grow tired of her. He knew it as surely as he knew the sun would rise and set each day. For him, the sun now rose and set with her.

"Saint Columba," he breathed, and let the silken tendril slip from his fingers.

And what of Kip? He must consider the boy as well. Careening toward manhood with naught but women and old men to guide him down that reckless path. Could he be father to a lad who was not his own? His uncle and his brothers had been as one to him after his own father had died so untimely young.

Father. Husband.

He swallowed hard and mouthed the words. Nay, 'twas not for him. He was not suited to it. One got too involved, too close. He smoothed the fur covering over Mairi's shoulder and smiled at the freckles peeking out at him.

"Conall!" Rob's urgent whisper sounded at the door, startling him.

Conall hadn't even heard him approach. He slipped from the bed and padded to the door. Light blinded him as he cracked it open, narrowing his eyes at his diminutive friend.

"Harry's back from Monadhliath with Gilchrist's men," Rob said.

"So soon?"

"Aye, they must have ridden like the devil himself."

"And my brother?"

Rob shook his head. "Not with them. He's away on some other business."

He wiped the sleep from his eyes and squinted toward the beach. "All right. Give me a minute."

Rob glanced at the pallet where Mairi still slept. "Take two," he said, and grinned.

Conall shut the door quietly and hunted around for a suitable garment. His shirt lay in a wet heap on the floor. He kicked it aside and donned the plaid Mairi had given him last night. 'Twould do.

He sat on the bed lightly, careful not to wake her, and brushed a kiss across her lips. "If I could love," he whispered, "'twould be you, Mairi Dunbar, who'd steal my heart."

He gathered up his weapons and closed the door silently behind him as he left.

Splashing. Kip's high-pitched yelp.

Mairi felt blindly for her pillow and pulled it over her head. What on earth was the boy doing up so early? Perhaps it wasn't so early after all. She drew a breath.

Then she remembered.

"Conall?" Her eyes flew open, but she knew he was gone even before she glanced around the darkened room. A brilliant finger of light streamed from under the lake house door. She'd overslept, and for once she didn't care.

Her hand moved over the place where Conall had slept. Still warm. She stretched out languidly on the furs and breathed in the scent of him still lingering on her pillow.

A thousand emotions welled inside her. Joy, disbelief, apprehension, regret. And something else. Something so powerful, so overwhelming, it shook the very fabric of her convictions.

"Nay," she breathed. "'Tis folly."

She scrambled to her feet and dressed quickly. The sunlight nearly blinded her when she opened the door on a chill autumn day. A light breeze eddied over the surface of the loch. She pulled a plaid 'round her shoulders and looked back at the rumpled bedclothes.

Conall's wet shirt lay on the floor near her pallet. A wave of tenderness washed over her. She smiled bitterly and stepped out onto the lake house pier.

Kip waved from the beach where he played fetch with Jupiter. The mastiff was soaking wet. That explained the splashing and gleeful shouts she'd heard earlier. Kip flung his stick into the water and Jupiter bounded after it.

Only then did she see them. Warriors.

Fifty at the least. Milling around the camp above the beach. Conall stood amidst a small group of men, most of whom she didn't recognize.

Kip waved again. She hurried down the pier and joined him on the beach. "Who are they? Why did ye no' wake me?"

"Conall said not to." Kip patted Jupiter's muscled shoulder and the dog shook, spraying them both with water.

"Go on," she said to the mastiff, and thumped him on his soggy head. "Go drench someone else."

"They're Chattan warriors," Kip said, and beamed a smile in their direction. "Davidsons and Mackintoshes. From Monadhliath, two days' north."

Conall's brother's men. She remembered he'd spoken briefly of Gilchrist Mackintosh, one of his two elder brothers. A tall, lean warrior with dark hair pulled Conall aside as if to speak to him in private.

"Is that his brother?" Mairi asked.

Kip shook his head. "I dinna think he's here. That one's called Hugh. He's got a bonny horse, and said he'd let me ride her later."

What in God's name were they doing here? She

took Kip by the arm and pointed him toward the village. "Ye'll do no such thing, d'ye hear?"

"But he said I could."

"Go on, now. Take Jupiter up to Dora's and see if she needs any help. It seems we'll be feeding an army tonight. Let's hope they've brought some food."

She stilled Kip's protests with a hard look, and he ambled toward the village, dragging his bare feet in the sand, Jupiter dogging every step.

She eyed the warriors and a spark of fear ignited a wariness in her gut. She and Conall hadn't spoken of Geoffrey's involvement in the explosion. But he knew. The question was, what would he do?

Cool sand scrunched between her toes as she walked toward Conall and the warrior Kip had called Hugh. The other Chattan clansmen paused to look at her. She ignored them and fixed her eyes on Conall. Ten paces from where he stood in whispered conversation, she stopped and waited for him to notice her.

Hugh glanced in her direction and cast her a brief but warm smile, then turned his attention back to Conall. She continued to stand there, her patience waning, and after what seemed an eternity, Conall met her gaze.

He didn't smile, nor did he speak. He merely looked at her, his eyes strangely cool, his expression blank.

She felt her cheeks warm and pulled her plaid tighter around herself. Then, as if he hadn't even seen her, Conall took Hugh's arm and led him up the hill into the camp.

She drew a breath and swallowed hard. What had she expected? That after their night of intimacy and lovemaking, the likes of which she could never have imagined, he'd rush into her arms and shower her with kisses and whispered endearments?

Aye, she had expected that. Had wanted it. Nay, craved it.

But he hadn't.

Perhaps it meant nothing to him. Oh, he'd wanted her, that was clear. And she'd wanted him. But now 'twas over. What had he called it when they'd happened upon Rob and Dora together?

Sport.

The word stabbed at her, and she felt suddenly sick. Tears stung the corners of her eyes. She'd be damned if she'd cry. Over what? She wiped them away with a rough hand, turned on her heel, and made for the village.

Five minutes later she stood in Dora's cottage, her teeth clenched.

"Are ye all right?" Dora handed her a cup of strong broth and gestured for her to sit.

She collapsed on a stool by the hearth. "I'm fine. Why wouldn't I be?"

"Well, I just thought—"

"I'm fine."

Dora arched a wispy brow. "I can see that."

Mairi thought it best to change the subject. "Yesterday morn I saw Tang in the wood above the house." That should get a reaction.

"What? I suspected as much." Dora pulled up another stool and settled in to hear the details. "That's why ye went to Geoffrey's."

She nodded. "A lot o' good that did."

"Ye were foolish, Mairi. Ye should have told Conall."

"Aye, well, it seems I didna have to. He's called

half an army to Loch Drurie, and for what, can ye guess?''

Dora frowned. "Nay, I dinna think he plans retribution, at least no' yet. He sent for them the minute he suspected ye'd gone to Falmar.''

Now this surprised her. "Did he?''

"He was frantic, Mairi. The man loves you.''

She snorted. "Aye, and if I look out in the garden my father will be risen from the dead, standin' there just like Christ.''

"Oh, stop. Drink your broth and let me do the talking.''

She took a sip of the hot, fragrant liquid and felt instantly warm. "Fine, talk then.''

"He's leavin', ye know. Conall.''

She choked on the broth. Dora's words registered, but Mairi couldn't believe them.

"Tomorrow. His brother's called him home.''

"Gilchrist?'' was all she could manage to say.

"Nay, the other one, the eldest.''

"Iain.''

"Aye, that's him. Lives far north at a place called Findhorn.''

"Conall was born there.''

"That's the place, all right.''

She set her cup on the hearth and stared into the dying embers. She'd been right about Conall all along. He was a drifter, an adventurer. Aye, he'd had his little adventure and now he was going home.

"Good,'' she said. "I'm glad he's leaving.''

Dora's eyes narrowed, but she refused to meet them. "Ye love him.''

"Bollocks.''

"Admit it, Mairi.''

She did look at her, then, and mustered her nastiest expression. "I dinna love him. I'd sooner wed Geoffrey Symon than a man like him."

"Och, now ye're talkin' soft."

"I dinna love him," she repeated.

"Your one chance at happiness, and ye'd throw it all away?"

"Happiness? Ye mean like you and Rob?"

"Look at me, Mairi."

After a moment, she reluctantly met Dora's gaze.

"Exactly like me and Rob."

A twinge of remorse skewered her. She hadn't meant to belittle Dora's relationship with the small but steadfast warrior.

"Conall's a good man and ye know it," Dora said.

"He's not."

"Mairi, ye dinna—"

"It doesna matter if I love him or nay. Don't ye see?" She gripped Dora's hand. "He'll no' stay here, and I'll no' go traipsing around the world after him."

"Why not?"

"Why not, she says. Because I'd ne'er leave you and the clan, ye ninny."

"Oh, posh!" Dora collected the cups and set them on the table against the far wall of the cottage. "Ye're afraid."

"What d'ye mean? I am not." She rose and started toward the door. The sounds of children playing drifted through the window from the small garden outside. She could hear Kip, and Jupiter's deep bellow. "I dinna love him, and I dinna need him."

'Twas the truth, wasn't it?

"The sooner he's gone, the better," she added.

Dora shook the rag at her that she used to clean the teacups. "Ye're the most stubborn, pigheaded—"

"They're all alike, Dora. Ye told me so yourself. Remember?"

"Aye, well I was wrong."

"About Rob, perhaps."

They *were* all alike. Her father, Geoffrey, Conall. She meant nothing to any of them. She was but a prize, an added bonus that came with the land. Conall's business was finished here. The first trade boats would arrive before the snows began. He probably thought he could drop in now and again between travels and slip between the furs with her for an evening of pleasure.

"All alike," she whispered.

Nay, we're not.

I came for you.

The memory of his words cut her to the quick. Jesu, she didn't know what to believe anymore. The rough-hewn timbers of the cottage door cut into her back as she pressed herself against it. Her eyes began to film and she gritted her teeth against the wave of raw emotion engulfing her.

"Oh, lass," Dora said, and started toward her.

"Nay!" She held her hand up to keep her friend at bay. "I…I want naught to do with him, d'ye hear?"

Dora's expression softened. She fisted her hands on ample hips. "Foolish pride will make ye a lonely old woman, Mairi Dunbar."

"Perhaps." She nodded, more to herself than to Dora. "Perhaps not," she breathed, then tripped the door latch and slipped out into the comforting bustle of the village.

Chapter Thirteen

He'd tell her and get it over with.

Conall brushed a stray hank of hair out of his eyes and hefted another bucket of stones from off the beach. The damage to Alwin Dunbar's house was nearly repaired.

'Twas the last task he could think of to delay his departure from Loch Drurie. Tomorrow he'd ride for Findhorn Castle in response to Iain's summons. 'Twas timely, and for the best.

"So ye mean to go, then," Rob said as they huffed up the hill to the house.

He didn't answer.

"Ye'd best tell her, then, laddie. Women dinna take kindly to surprises."

He had meant to tell her that morning, as soon as she awoke, but something stopped him. When he saw her on the beach, staring at him—her cheeks flushed from the stubble of his beard, her lips swollen from his kisses, her hair in disarray—he just couldn't.

He must.

The bucket grew heavy. He jogged the last few feet up the hill, rounded the house, heading for the garden, and stopped dead. She was there, on her knees, gathering stones off her father's grave.

"What are you doing?" he asked her, and set the bucket down.

"We need more rocks for the foundation." She didn't even turn to look at him.

"Aye, but there's plenty on the beach."

"These are closer."

Her indifference to him and the casual attitude with which she desecrated her father's resting place unnerved him.

"Besides, he willna need them where he rests, will he? Methinks there are plenty o' stones in that evil place."

"Mairi," he said, and knelt beside her.

She did turn, then, but only to cast him a look that could freeze the whole of Loch Drurie. "What?"

"I…" What would he say to her? He didn't know anymore.

She continued collecting stones as he tried to order his thoughts. He had to break it off, here and now. Not only for his sake, but for hers and Kip's.

"Mairi, about last night. I didna mean—"

"Your brother's men, what are they doing here?" She sat back on her heels and arched a brow at him.

He didn't expect this hard-edged behavior, but it made what he had to say to her easier. "Aye, well… they're here to protect the docks."

'Twas a partial truth, at least. He didn't know what Symon would do next, but he was certain they'd not heard the last of him. And though he was determined to go, he'd be damned if he'd leave Mairi unprotected.

"I see." She reached for another rock, and he grabbed her wrist. Her eyes flashed a warning.

"We must talk." 'Twas a mistake to hold her hand, but he did it anyway and she allowed it. He searched for the right words. "When we first met," he began, "you told me that you would never marry."

"Aye. What of it?"

Her palm was warm in his hand, and where his finger rested against her wrist he could feel her pulse, strong and steady.

"I told you I felt the same."

An icy silence frosted the air between them and he felt her pulse quicken.

"And now?" she breathed.

He held her piercing gaze and forced himself not to answer. God's truth, he didn't know what he felt. 'Twas all so new, so unexpected. He'd been wholly unprepared for the emotions their coupling had stirred in him.

Oh, he'd had his share of women, but never had lovemaking been so intimate, so personal. Never had he felt so…vulnerable.

Her hand slipped from his, her question burning between them unanswered. Her face was expressionless, her eyes an unreadable deep blue.

A blast of wind from off the loch caught them unaware, and a shower of crisped, dead leaves blustered down on them from the canopy of near-naked trees above. A golden leaf caught in her hair. He reached for it unconsciously.

"Conall!"

Jupiter skidded to a halt in a pile of leaves flanking Alwin Dunbar's grave. Kip collapsed breathless beside him. "Come watch me ride Hugh's horse." The boy pulled on his arm. "Come on!"

"Kip," Mairi said, "I thought I told ye no' to—"

"Come on, Conall, watch me!" Kip tugged again.

"Did ye tell him he could ride that horse?" Mairi said. "I specifically told him he couldn't."

Conall's head began to throb. Kip tugged, Mairi railed, and the sky grew black above them. "Shut it, the both o' ye!" He pushed Kip away, more roughly than he'd intended, and shot to his feet. "Go on, leave me alone, boy. Can't ye see I'm busy?"

His heart hammered in his chest, his gut roiled. Conall closed his eyes for a moment to get a grip on himself, and felt the first smattering of raindrops cool his heated face. Thunder rumbled low in the distance.

Kip lay where he'd fallen, looking up at him, eyes bugged and tinged with hurt. Jupiter's dour expression echoed Conall's remorse.

"Ah, damn," he breathed. He offered his hand to Kip, but the boy ignored it.

He was suddenly aware of Mairi beside him, rising slowly to her feet. Too slowly, as if she worked to control her movements. Her eyes blazed with the same hate he'd seen in her expression last night, when she'd told him of her father's negligence and her mother's murder.

Kip saw it, too, and scrambled to his feet. Conall nodded in the direction of the village, and Kip tore off down the hill. Jupiter remained.

"If...ye...ever—" Mairi stepped toward him, her fists clenched at her sides "—ever...touch Kip like that again—" she stopped and glared up at him, trembling "—I'll slit your bluidy throat."

He stood there, at a loss for words, his feet rooted in the damp ground. The sky opened and a biting rain pummeled them with a rushing that filled his ears.

Mairi tore down the hill, then paused to look back at him. The rage in her eyes had dulled. All he saw there now was pain.

No one could hurt her. No one.

Mairi stood in the downpour, her face tipped sky-ward, mud oozing between her toes. It had rained all night, and for all she cared it could rain forever. She was soaked to the skin, chilled to the bone, and embraced every sensation.

Conall was leaving today, and he hadn't even had the decency or the courage to tell her. She'd heard it from everyone but him. It didn't matter. She didn't care. She didn't want him and certainly didn't need him.

She'd never needed anyone.

The scents of the forest sharpened in the downpour. She drew a breath and felt instantly stronger. Clean, pure, absolved. She'd burned her bedclothes at dawn after a sleepless night of unbidden memories sparked by the lingering scent of him on her furs and pillows.

What she needed now was work, hard labor to drive all thoughts from her mind. She hefted the ax and poised it over the downed tree.

"Are ye daft, woman?" A voice sounded behind her. "What are ye doin' out in this weather?"

She lowered the ax and turned to see Rob standing behind her, his small hands fisted on narrow hips. "Go away," she said, and poised the ax again. She swung but never hit the tree.

Rob swiped the weapon from her hands before she realized he was beside her. His strength startled her. "Come on," he said, "let's find some shelter."

"Nay. Go back to the village. I'm busy here."

"Oh, aye, busy killin' yourself. Ye'll catch your

death.'' He grabbed her arm and jerked her toward a thick stand of pines, evergreens whose year-round foliage provided a bit of shelter against the rain.

Rob unpinned his plaid from his shoulder, and spread part of it on a flat rock. ''Here, sit.''

She obeyed, not knowing why. She supposed she liked him, and knew he meant well. He sat beside her and pulled his bonnet low over his forehead. Rain continued to stream down his face all the same.

''What d'ye want?'' she said, and met his gaze.

''I want to talk to ye.''

''About what?'' She could guess, but she was not inclined to make this easy for him.

''About him—Conall.''

Aye, well, he could talk all he wanted. What difference would it make?

''If ye'd but ask him, he'd stay. I'm sure of it,'' Rob said. ''Ye must tell him how ye feel, lass.''

She narrowed her eyes at him and swiped a soaking hank of hair from her cheek. ''And just what d'ye know, Rob Mackintosh, about my feelings?''

''I ken that ye lo—''

''What makes ye think I have any feelings one way or t'other?'' His presumption was outrageous and she'd put a stop to it now. ''If ye've been listening to Dora's prattle, ye're a fool.''

He arched a brow at her. ''Methinks there are a couple o' fools here, all right, but they're no' me and Dora.''

She started to her feet. Rob grabbed the skirt of her gown and yanked her back onto the rock.

''Ow! Let go of me!''

''Nay. I'll turn ye loose when I'm ready. But now, ye'll listen, d'ye hear?''

He deserved a thumping, right on that wet little head of his. Her cheeks burned, and she felt the life returning to her hands and feet. She sighed in compliance.

"All right, then," he said, and nodded. He let go her gown, and she stayed put.

Why, she didn't know. He wished to talk? Fine, she'd listen. But she'd not change her mind about a thing. Conall didn't want her. What of it? She'd never wished for any of this to happen. She had her own plans. Responsibilities. There was no room in her life for a man, especially one who didn't know the meaning of the word.

"He lost them all, ye know," Rob said. "His da, mam, uncle and aunt—all o' them. And at a fair tender age."

Mairi frowned. "Aye, well I'll be sure to offer him a fine, warm welcome to the club."

"Come now, dinna be so hard. I'm tryin' to tell ye why he's so…so…"

"What? Spit it out."

"I dunno. Like he is. Afeared."

She snorted. She could think of a number of colorful expressions to describe him—callous pig came to mind—but "afeared" was not one of them.

"He was a loner from the start," Rob continued. "Aye, he had his brothers, but they were older and self-absorbed. Iain and Gilchrist had their own problems, suffered their own losses, while Conall watched and learned. And then there was the fire."

"What fire?"

"At Braedûn Lodge, when Conall was barely of age. His uncle and aunt burned to death, and his brother Gilchrist nearly so. 'Twas the breaking point for Conall. He couldna take no more. When we thought Gilchrist would die, Conall left the Highlands. I went with him.''

"Aye, well, we've all had our share o' problems, now haven't we?''

"He's rarely been back since then—home, I mean. Gilchrist healed, then married and built Monadhliath amidst the ashes of Braedûn Lodge. Iain lives with his own family at Findhorn.''

"Their ancestral home,'' she said.

"Aye.''

"Conall doesn't see them, then?''

Rob shook his head. ''We journeyed to Findhorn in late summer. That's when Iain asked Conall to come here to Loch Drurie. Aye, the Chattan e'en offered him a reward—lands and livestock and—''

"And what?''

"A…well…'' Rob shot her an almost fearful glance. ''A bride, but he didna want her,'' he added quickly.

"Hmph,'' was all she could manage to say, and steered the conversation back to the topic that most interested her. ''Doesn't he miss them? His brothers and the rest of his clan?''

"Methinks he must, but ye wouldna know it.''

The rain let up, and they listened for a moment to the water dripping from the trees. Anger and confusion simmered inside her, and she worked to control them.

"What kind of a man abandons his own family when most they need him?'' She already knew the answer.

A man like her father. A man like Conall Mackintosh.

Her gaze drifted over the greens and golds of the wet autumn forest. Something caught her eye and she froze, but was careful not to look directly at it. Whatever it was—a deer or a wolf—she didn't want it to know she'd seen it.

But 'twas neither deer nor wolf. 'Twas a man. 'Twas Conall.

She felt him more than saw him, lurking there behind a gnarled larch, not a dozen paces to her left. She didn't think he'd been there long. Rob seemed lost in thought, and she was certain he didn't notice him.

She was glad he was there, for she had things she wished him to hear.

"I've been thinking," she said to Rob, in a voice loud enough to carry. "My clan needs a leader—a man. Perhaps I shall marry Geoffrey after all."

A branch snapped in the wood to her left.

"What?" Rob croaked. "Are ye a bluidy idiot?"

"At least he's a man of honor, who would no' abandon my clan. He'd fight for us, and for what he believes in. Geoffrey's no' some frivolous adventurer, a rogue who cares for nothing and no one save himself."

The words wrenched her gut as they rolled off her lips, but she didn't care. She wanted Conall to hear, and believe. She wanted to hurt him, though a man like him—a man with no heart—couldn't be hurt.

Rob muttered something incomprehensible, then stood. "Up with ye, lass. I'll have my plaid back."

She rose and shook out her soaking gown. "Go back to the village. Our talk is finished."

Rob shook his head at her but did not answer. After a long moment, he ambled off in the direction of the loch.

Mairi picked up the ax and poised it once again over the felled pine. Her chopping echoed in the wood, and the sweat she broke began to warm her frigid limbs. After a time, she looked up and fixed her eyes on the gnarled larch.

Conall was gone.

He waited at the camp till near midday, but she never came. What did he expect? Her feelings about him were made clear in the wood that morn. He was relieved, in a way, that she loathed him. It made his departure easier. Or so it should.

Conall positioned the well-worn saddle across the black's wet back and cinched it tight. Rain sluiced off the horse's withers. "I'm sorry, laddie," he said. "'Tis not a day for traveling, but we shall go all the same."

The black stamped a hoof, splashing mud onto Conall's soggy boots. Jupiter sat in a puddle nearby, looking miserable. All of them were soaked. The smell of wet wool, wet dog, and wet horse assailed his senses.

He pulled himself into the saddle and adjusted his weapons.

"Rob'll be vexed ye didna wait for him," Dougal said. He and Harry stood in the rain, waiting for their orders.

"I told Rob, and I'll tell you," Conall said to them. "I want every man here at Loch Drurie. At least until the trade boats arrive. When I reach Monadhliath I'll send wagons back for the goods. Harry, you know what to do after that."

The scout nodded. "Aye, I'm to cut out part of the Dunbars' share and see it safe to Falmar Castle in payment of their debt."

"Take Rob and fifty men, and if Symon willna accept it, you're to—"

"Aye, I know," Harry said, and patted the bulge underneath his plaid and next to his heart. "Offer the silver."

Conall had given it to him that morning. Aye, well...Iain had told him to use it in his dealings as he saw fit, and this was the best use of it he could imagine. "Remember," he said to both of them, "you're not to let Mairi go with you to Falmar. If you have to tie her to a bloody tree—" and likely they would "—you're to keep her here at all costs." Safe, he thought to himself. "Do you understand?"

Harry and Dougal nodded.

"Send the rest of the goods to Monadhliath for distribution to the clans."

"Aye," Dougal said. "Ye can count on us."

Conall nodded, then took a last look around the camp and over the newly built docks floating on the slate waters of Loch Drurie. He'd done what he'd set out to do. His brothers would be pleased. At least that was something.

But he felt neither accomplishment nor satisfaction, only an emptiness that gnawed at his gut. His gaze drifted to the lake house and a torrent of raw emotion welled inside him.

"Did she no' return?"

He turned his mount in the direction of the feminine voice and was surprised to see Dora standing in the rain, a plaid draped over her head and shoulders. He should unfurl his own and do the same, but there was something about being soaked to the skin and iced to the bone that he liked.

'Twas a penance of sorts, he guessed. Not much of one, when he considered the magnitude of his sins. His kinsman John's untimely death—or murder, he reminded himself—lay heavy on his heart. He'd make certain the warrior's widow and children were well provided for. 'Twas the least he could do, and another reason not to delay his departure for Findhorn.

And then there was Kip, whom he'd allowed against all better judgment to get close to him. The boy looked on him as a son would a father. Conall knew the feeling, for he'd felt much the same about his uncle, Alistair Davidson.

Dora spoke again, snapping him out of his thoughts.

"Nay," he said. "I havena seen her." Mairi was probably still in the wood, and for a moment he considered going after her. He didn't want to leave things this way between them. He'd tried to explain himself yesterday in the garden, but had not gotten very far.

Perhaps 'twas because he didn't really know how he felt about her. How could he explain his departure to her if he, himself, didn't understand his own feelings? He knew that Iain's summons was enough of a reason to leave.

But it wasn't the real reason.

He smiled at Dora and turned the black north, toward the forest path leading from the camp. Jupiter, who normally ran ahead, anxious to be the first to break trail, plodded beside him, eyes dulled and head down.

"Wait!" a small voice cried from the village behind them. "Conall, wait!"

Jupiter was the first to turn, and his eyes lit up. He barked, nearly spooking some of the Chattan mounts tethered nearby at the edge of the camp.

Kip tore across the beach at a full run. Jupiter bounded toward him and the two collided in a muddy and exuberant embrace. The mastiff licked the raindrops from Kip's face while the boy hugged him fiercely.

Conall dismounted. He at least owed the lad a proper farewell.

Kip saw him and wrenched himself from Jupiter's affections. "Conall!" he cried, and raced toward him.

Conall knelt on the wet sand, and Kip tackled him. The boy's arms went 'round his neck like a vise. Conall embraced him and all at once felt the tears.

He choked back a strangled sound—for Kip, for Mairi, for John the drummer and for all of those he'd hurt—and battled the confused emotions raging within him. His love for the boy was a bitter and cruel confirmation of why he must leave, and leave now.

"Keep Jupiter with you, lad," he whispered in Kip's ear, clutching him tightly so the boy wouldn't see his tears.

"Nay, I canna," Kip said. "He...he'd remind me too much o' ye."

Conall squeezed his eyes shut and his tears broke hot on his face. The sheeting rain would mask them from the others who stood nearby, watching, waiting, he knew, to see if he'd have a change of heart.

Conall clutched the boy tighter and wept.

He had no heart.

It had turned to stone long years ago, and had grown dangerously brittle with Mairi Dunbar's love and loathing.

He pushed Kip away and, before the boy could protest, vaulted onto the black's waiting saddle. One light kick and the stallion responded, lurching toward the path that would lead them from Loch Drurie. Jupiter followed reluctantly.

At the edge of the camp, a flash of color caught his

eye on the wooded hillside. He felt her before he saw her, and pulled his mount up short just inside the cover of the trees.

Mairi stood on the hillside, soaked to the skin, her hair plastered to her face, fists balled at her sides, and simply stared at him.

His heart beat erratically in his chest as he fought the overwhelming urge to leap from his horse, scramble up the hillside and sweep her into his arms. He held her gaze and willed her speak.

One word. One move toward him. One sign, and he'd damn his convictions to hell.

The black stirred beneath him, anxious. Jupiter barked. He was aware that all eyes were on them— Dougal, Harry, Dora and Kip.

He begged her with his eyes to stop him, but she did not.

He was trembling now, and gripped the reins tighter to still his hands from shaking. She hated him, and he couldn't blame her. She was right—he was a rogue who cared for nothing and no one. Her eyes confirmed it.

The black whinnied, and Conall kicked him forward, sharply this time. They lurched into the wood, and he felt Mairi's eyes burn into him.

He swallowed hard and didn't look back.

Two hours later, on the ridge top above the standing stone near Loch Drurie's northern shore, Conall reined the black west toward Falmar and Geoffrey Symon's hunting place.

His timing could not have been better. Weekly, on the day following the Sabbath, Symon hunted alone in the wood north of his demesne. Conall knew today was no exception.

The detour would cost him but an hour. There was unfinished business yet between them, and Conall was determined to settle it before moving on. The memory of Mairi bound to Symon's bed still burned in his mind. 'Twas a vision he'd ne'er forget.

Conall's dirk was already in his hand when he at last found the chieftain in a stream-cut ravine, kneeling beside a rushing tumble of water over rock, slaking his thirst.

Rain beat down in sheets as he signaled Jupiter to stay, slipped from the black's saddle and approached Symon on foot, the downpour masking the sound of his footfalls across a sodden blanket of autumn leaves.

At the last moment Symon turned.

Too late.

Conall's arm was already 'round him, his blade under Symon's white throat.

Chapter Fourteen

It rained all afternoon.

Mairi didn't bother to lift her skirts as she slogged through streams of muddy water snaking between village cottages shut tight against the weather. The Dunbars and most of the Chattan had taken shelter against the weather. No one was about, save the odd warrior patrolling the docks and the beachside camp.

Loch Drurie's choppy waters darkened to a mottled slate. Even in foul weather Mairi had always loved the loch. But not today. When she looked out across its austere surface, all she saw was the presage of a cold, harsh winter.

All she felt was alone.

Her gaze drifted along the fine, straight lines of the newly built piers and floating docks. Their tightly lashed timbers swelled and rolled gently on the water's surface.

She wished her father could see it. What she'd done. What they'd all done together. She was glad he was dead, but all the same, a part of her wished that Alwin Dunbar could have seen, and been proud.

Rain pummeled the slate roofs of the village cottages, but she knew those within were dry and warm. She had Conall to thank for that, she supposed. Over the past weeks, he and his men had repaired and fortified every croft. Every family had a proper home, every child a safe place to sleep.

The changes in the village were subtle, yet taken as a whole she could not deny the marked improvement. Everywhere she looked, she saw signs of Conall's intervention and the Chattan's handiwork.

He didn't have to do it, but he had. Why?

She started aimlessly up the hill toward her father's house and pondered the question. It had been but a couple of hours since Conall Mackintosh had ridden out of her life, and during that eternity of time she'd refused to think of him.

But she thought of him now, and couldn't stop the tumult of emotions brewing inside her, overwhelming her mental sobriety. When she closed her eyes all she saw was his face, his eyes mirroring the colors of the forest and glassed with tears as he crushed a weeping Kip to his chest.

It had taken all of her strength, a fierce and unforgiving will and the fear she clung to so desperately to harden her heart and stop herself from rushing into his arms.

Her bare feet trudged along the slippery path. She moved in a trance and paid no heed to the ankle-deep mud peppered with twigs and sharp stones, and the bitter wind whipping at her hair.

She felt what she wanted to feel—Conall's hands on her body, his lips on her mouth. Their lovemaking that second time in the half-light of dawn had been tender and fraught with untested emotion. Nothing like the frantic desperation of their first coupling.

Dora was right. He might have taken her at any time, could have taken her right there on the pier at their first turbulent meeting. But he hadn't. He'd waited until she was willing, until her desire had matched his own.

Why?

She tripped on a half-buried stone and was wrenched from her stupor. Her father's stripped and muddy grave peered up at her through the rain. How had she come upon this place?

Perhaps Alwin Dunbar held in death answers to questions she was too afraid to ask. She stared at where the headstone or at least a cross should have been, and imagined his rotting corpse beneath.

"Does he speak to ye ever?"

Mairi whirled in the direction of the voice. "Walter!"

The old man smiled and pulled his ragged plaid over his head and shoulders as protection from the rain. "He talks to me sometimes, ye know."

Mairi snorted. "Oh does he? And what does my *esteemed* father say?"

Walter stepped closer and offered her part of his soaking plaid. She shook her head. He shrugged and wrapped it tightly around himself. "He says that sometimes a man must do things that are misunderstood by others. Especially by children and women."

The old man was daft, but Mairi loved him all the same. "He says all that, does he?"

"Aye. Well, the first part anyway. The last bit is mine."

"About the children and women, ye mean?"

He nodded.

"So what are ye telling me, old man? That there are things I dinna understand?"

Rain trickled into the deeply etched lines of Walter's craggy face. "That's exactly what I'm tellin' ye. Alwin never forgave himself for your mother's death, ye know."

"Ye mean my mother's murder? What, d'ye think he should have? The bluidy coward stood there and watched while those heathens butchered her."

She ground her feet into the mud and willed the old man to challenge her. Mairi had been there, and she remembered. She'd been a child, but all the same she knew exactly what her father had and had not done.

"Aye, he let it happen." Walter nodded slowly. "But ye dinna ken why."

"Because he was a coward, a drunkard. A man who cared naught for his family or his clan." She knew this well. 'Twas burned into her every day of the ten years following her mother's murder.

"Nay, lass," Walter said. "A coward he was not. And he didna take to drink till after Gladys was killed. Ye know I'm right."

"Hmph." Perhaps he was right, but only about the drinking. "What does it matter? He watched her die and he did nothing."

"He had a choice to make, and he made it."

Mairi frowned. "What choice? What d'ye mean?"

This talk of her father made her uneasy. Walter, and others, had tried in the past to broach the topic with her, but she'd have none of it. Nor would her father ever discuss it.

"'Twas a blood feud between a nomadic clan and ours. That day they outnumbered us two to one. Alwin dragged ye to the house and we surrounded it, protected ye both the best we could.''

"Aye, I remember it.'' But she didn't want to remember. She turned to leave, and Walter grabbed her arm.

"Ye shall hear what I've got to say, lass.''

"Nay.'' The old man's grip was a vise. "I know what happened, and there's no changing what I feel.'' This was madness. She didn't want to hear. She tried to think of something else, of Conall or of Kip, but could not.

"'Twas either Gladys or ye, lass.'' He willed her to his gaze. "She lay on the beach, wounded, and couldna walk. We were fighting up the hill to keep the nomads from the house.''

"Aye, I went to her. I tried to get her up, but I couldna.'' A wave of sickness gripped her. "I couldna,'' she breathed.

"Nay, and neither could Alwin, lest he carry her and leave ye behind.''

Tears stung her eyes as, all at once, she remembered how it was. She shook her head, not wanting to believe. "He could have saved her! I could have run!''

"Nay, lass. Nay.'' Walter loosened his grip on her. "Nomad warriors were already on the beach. Ye were but a child. They'd have caught ye and cut ye down— or worse—had Alwin done different.''

Mairi sank to her knees in the mud and made fists of her hands. "Nay, nay, he could have saved her!'' She didn't want to believe it. She couldn't believe it. Her tears broke as she choked back a sob.

"Alwin swept ye into his arms and ran for the house. And there we could protect ye. After a time, we drove them off.''

"They...killed...her," she sobbed, and felt Walter's gnarly hand light on her shoulder. "He...we... watched them."

"He had a choice, lass. And he chose you."

She plunged her hands into the cool mud of the grave and wept. Not for her mother, or for herself, but for her father, Alwin Sedgewick Dunbar.

He'd had a choice. He'd chosen *her*.

Perhaps somewhere deep inside herself she'd known it all along. Mairi tilted her face skyward and let the rain wash the tears from her eyes. Walter stroked her wet head, as one might a child's, then turned to leave.

"Th-thank ye," she said.

The old man nodded, then disappeared behind the house.

Mairi sucked in a breath and willed herself to stop shaking.

Sometimes a man must do things that are misunderstood by others.

She closed her eyes and saw Conall's tortured expression as they stood there that morn, just hours ago in the rain. Something snapped inside her.

Mairi shot to her feet.

Dora stopped dead as she rounded the house and saw her. "What the devil are ye doin' out here? Look at ye! Why, ye're covered with mud."

Mairi gripped her arm. "Did Rob go with him?"

"What? Ow, let go!"

Her thoughts raced, her emotions tumbled in a fever of confusion. But one thing was clear. She must find him. "Which way did Conall go? Is Rob with him, or did he stay—"

"North, toward Findhorn," Dora said. "And nay, Rob is here. The crazy fool rode off alone."

She could catch him up. Aye, she must.

Mairi knocked Dora nearly off her feet as she flew by her. "Och, sorry!" she called back over her shoulder.

"Where are ye goin' now? What are ye doin'?"

"Nowhere. Nothing. I'll be back in a—" She tripped over a branch, but quickly recovered her footing. "I'll be back."

Minutes later she burst into the camp and eyed the sixty or so Chattan mounts tethered just inside the wood. A small one would do. She spotted Rob's white gelding and started toward it.

"Ho, what are ye up to?" a voice called after her.

She froze. A Chattan warrior, one of the new arrivals she didn't know, moved toward her. Mairi cleared her throat, put on her most innocent expression and waited.

"Ye should no' be out in this weather," the warrior said.

How many times would she have to hear that today? 'Twas just a bloody rainstorm, after all. Fine Scottish weather. She smiled and ignored his comment. "I need to borrow a mount, just for a minute or two."

The warrior frowned. "Why?"

Why, indeed. "Um..." She racked her brain for a reasonable excuse, then her eyes lit on an empty basket next to the flooded fire ring. "That basket," she said, and picked it up. "Each day I collect downed acorns on the hill." She glanced at the ridge above the camp. "Just there. 'Tis no' far, but I can make better time in this foul weather if I ride instead of walk."

'Twas a ridiculous request, but 'twas all she could think of. She forced another smile and prayed the warrior would relent.

His expression softened, and she knew she'd won. "All right, but be quick about it. Ye'll catch your death."

She gave a brief curtsy and bolted toward Rob's gelding.

"Ho, wait!" the warrior called after her. "No' that one. He's the gentlest nag o' the bunch."

Aye, that's exactly why she'd chosen the diminutive white beast.

"Take mine. She's more surefooted, and willna slip on that muddy hillside."

She would waste no time arguing with him. He saddled the mare and gave her a boost into the saddle.

"On second thought," he said, "I could go with ye." The warrior's hand rested lightly on her ankle. His dark eyes flashed a hint of desire.

"Nay," she said quickly, and spurred the mare to action. "Ye mustna leave your post."

The warrior frowned.

"I'll be right back," she lied. "Perhaps then…" Lord, what could she say that would appease him? Wait, she had it. "Perhaps then I could fix ye a bowl of broth? At my lake house," she added.

He grinned and arched a brow. "Hurry back, lass. 'Tis been weeks since I had any…*broth.*"

Mairi slapped the mare's rump and they shot into the wood. She'd keep to the forest path and, with luck, she'd overtake Conall before the day was out. He'd slow the black to a walk in this weather, she was sure of it. Conall loved that horse. And she intended to drive her own mount hard, as fast as it would go.

"B-bluidy hell," she stuttered as the mare picked up speed and she bounced along in the saddle. "I h-hate horses!"

Clan war be damned.

Conall should have killed the bloody whoreson in the wood when he'd had the chance. He'd burned to do it. But for once in his life he'd put his clan's interests above his own. His interaction with the chieftain had been brief. After threatening to geld him with a dull blade should he ever touch Mairi again, Conall had let Geoffrey Symon live.

Now, not an hour later, he regretted his decision.

Near to the place where he'd first made his detour to intercept Symon, Conall dismounted and guided the black under a mossy overhang jutting from the cliff flanking the road. The weather had not let up, and he, Jupiter and the stallion could all use a brief respite from the rain.

He wasn't hungry, but he knew he should eat. He couldn't remember when he'd last had a meal. Yesterday sometime, he supposed. The black's leather saddlebags were nearly soaked through. He fished around inside one of them and found what he sought.

There was nowhere dry to sit, so he crouched on a flat rock and propped his back against the cliff. Jupiter plunked down in the mud beside him. Dora had prepared a sack of food for his journey. He opened it and smiled bitterly.

Smoked ham.

Exactly like the one Mairi had belted him with the first time he'd seen her. The first time he'd kissed her.

A flood of memories washed over him like an icy river, and just this once he let himself remember.

He closed his eyes and conjured the feel of her beneath him. That fearless innocence, those challenging eyes, a will of tempered steel. A man could lose himself, heart and body and soul, to a woman like her.

"Ah, Mairi," he breathed, and tossed the shank of ham to the mastiff.

What could he possibly offer her? He had neither lands nor livestock nor gold. 'Twas true, the Chattan had offered him payment for his work at Loch Drurie. But what Mairi Dunbar needed, what she deserved, was not a thing that could be bought.

The love of a good man.

A man who'd stand by her, protect her and her clan. A man she could count on.

He ran a hand through his tangled hair, wringing the water from it. Could he be that man? Could he love her the way she was meant to be loved?

He crushed the sack in his hand and something sharp poked him. Reaching inside, his fingers closed around it and he knew what it was. Mairi's tortoiseshell comb.

"Bloody Dora."

Conall sprang from the rock, and Jupiter followed, tail wagging, the half-eaten ham shank clamped between slobbery jaws. "We're going back, lads," he said to his animal companions as he stuffed the comb into his sporran and the food sack back into the saddlebag.

He mounted and reined the stallion south, back the way they'd come. Jupiter broke into a trot beside them. If he pushed, they'd reach Loch Drurie by dark. The sky was near black as it was, and the rain looked as if it would ne'er stop.

"Damn," he breathed, and kicked the stallion faster.

His head spun with a thousand disconnected thoughts, pummeling him from all directions as did the rain.

Would Mairi even have him? She'd likely toss him out on his ear. But he had to try. What she'd said that morning in the wood, about marrying Symon, she couldn't have meant it. She couldn't have, could she? Nay, not after what they'd shared.

He urged the stallion faster still and, as they rounded a blind corner where the trees were particularly dense, the horse collided with—

"God's blood!"

The black reared, as did the horse coming from the opposite direction. Jupiter bounded from the path as Conall and the other rider hit the mud in concert with a dull splat.

"What the—?"

"Conall!" the rider cried.

Conall blinked the mud from his eyes and recognized the warrior as one of his brother's kinsmen. "What are you doing, man? Trying to kill me?"

The warrior laughed. "Your brother would no' take kindly to that, methinks."

The two of them scrambled to their feet and did their best to wipe the mud from their already drenched garments.

"Ah, hell," Conall said, and gave up the impossible task. "The rain will clean us up well enough."

They recovered their mounts and checked to make sure neither of the horses was injured. Jupiter watched them with what Conall knew was amusement.

"Dinna say a word," he cautioned the dog.

Jupiter cocked his head.

The warrior's name was Alfred, and Conall had met him once or twice at Findhorn. He was surprised that a lone Chattan warrior was so far afield, and wondered what Alfred's business could be.

"Where are you headed?" he asked him.

"I was about to ask ye the same thing. I've just come from Monadhliath—a shortcut through the wood. I'm to carry these herbs—" he patted his saddlebag "—from one o' your sisters-in-law to the other."

The warrior's story made sense. Gilchrist's wife, Rachel, was a healer, the best among all of the Chattan clans. And Iain's wife was with child again.

They remounted, and Conall took a moment to adjust his weapons. "My brother's summoned me home," he said.

"To Findhorn?" Alfred asked. "Aye, well that's where I'm headed. We can ride together, then."

Conall shook his head. "Nay, I've a change of plan."

"Oh?"

"Tell Iain I'm not coming home, not yet, at any rate. I've something I must set right first."

Conall knew Alfred was puzzled by the message, but he had no intention of going into details. He didn't have any details to give. He knew not what he was doing, himself. How the devil could he explain it to others?

Alfred nodded, and Conall gripped the warrior's gauntleted hand in a gesture of camaraderie and farewell.

"Godspeed," Alfred said.

"And to you."

Jupiter barked, impatient as always, and Conall spurred the black south toward Loch Drurie.

The confusion of hoofprints ended abruptly just off the road near a moss-covered cliff. The rain had stopped some time ago, though the sky grew ever darker. Daylight waned, and, with it, Mairi's hope of overtaking Conall.

She had driven the mare as hard as she'd dared, but the steed had a mind of its own, slowing the pace on a whim, and stopping for minutes at a time to munch at the occasional roadside carpet of grass.

Mairi rubbed her backside and winced. "Bluidy horses and bluidy saddles."

They both could do with a rest, and as the mare was already grazing, she decided this was as good a spot as any. She eased herself off the saddle and cursed the stiffness in her legs and the tiny shooting pains on the outsides of her knees.

If God had meant for men to ride, he would have— "Ow!" She landed badly in a mud hole and cursed again. He would not have made it so bloody uncomfortable!

A smooth, flat rock just under the mossy cliff beckoned her. She glanced briefly at the mare and, satisfied the beast would not run off, sat down as gingerly as possible.

The smells of the forest were heightened by the wet weather. Bay laurel and loamy soil, made rich by an abundance of decomposed autumn leaves, filled her senses. Mairi drew a breath and tried to collect her thoughts.

"Where in God's name is he?" She shot the mare a nasty expression. "I suppose ye'll be no help at all."

Even if Conall had driven the black at a brisk pace, she still should have caught him by now. She studied the jumble of hoof- and boot prints under the rocky overhang.

Perhaps he didn't wish to be caught.

The thought hung there, taunting her. A flurry of doubt and anxiety gnawed at her confidence. Until now, she'd pushed all thoughts aside and had focused her energy on the ride. But as the short autumn day drew to a dreary close, she had to face the truth of things.

Conall was gone. Most likely for good.

He didn't want her, and that was that.

If he'd cared for her, even the tiniest bit, he'd not have left Loch Drurie without so much as a farewell. She'd been foolish to think he...he might have loved her.

Mairi looked down at her bare, mud-caked feet and tattered gown. Water dripped from her tangled hair. "D'ye blame him?"

Her gaze drifted again to the place on the road where the hoofprints stopped. She was no scout, but it seemed to her that he hadn't continued along the road. In fact, for some time now, she'd seen hoofprints going in both directions—north and south.

Perhaps he took to the wood at some point. After all, he was alone, and who knew what evil things there were in this part of the forest that might prey upon a man.

Or a woman.

She wrapped her arms around herself protectively and peered into the thick stands of trees flanking the road. 'Twas cold, and she shivered as she strained to see in the fast-approaching twilight.

What had she been thinking to ride all this way alone? And for naught. "Fool," she breathed, and rose stiffly to her feet. The mare was still eating. Mairi grabbed the reins and jerked the beast's head up. "Come on, we're going back."

She mounted carefully and settled into the saddle with a groan. The next time she had such a bright idea, she'd force herself to think it through before acting on it.

The mare turned easily and clipped along at a brisk pace, as if it were eager to return to Loch Drurie. Mairi held on to the pommel and let the horse do the navigating.

After a time, they came to a point in the road that she had noticed earlier but had not wanted to stop to examine. In the half-light of dusk she could barely make out the chaos of hoof- and boot prints in the soft mud.

She'd passed another spot just like it, a half league or so back, but she didn't have the same feeling of foreboding about it that she felt here.

Strange. She leaned from the mare and strained her eyes to see, but couldn't make sense of what had happened here in the mud. No matter. Conall probably just met up with someone he knew.

The mare trotted on, and at one point Mairi caught herself drifting off. She stiffened in the saddle and widened her eyes against sleep. She was exhausted, and hadn't kept a close watch on her bearings. How much farther could it possibly be?

"Saints preserve us, there she is!"

Mairi snapped to attention and strained to see ahead in the near dark. "Rob?" she called out, certain the voice belonged to the small warrior.

"Mairi!" another voice called. "It *is* her."

Relief washed over her. A moment later, the riders reined their wheezing and lathered mounts to a halt beside her. 'Twas indeed Rob, and Dougal, too.

"Thank Christ," Rob said, and snatched the reins from her hands. "What the devil were ye thinkin'?"

"What are ye doing here?" she demanded.

"The question is," Rob said in as stern a voice as she'd e'er heard from him, "what in bluidy hell are *ye* doin' here? And on your own. Are ye daft, woman?"

"Aye," she said. "I am, indeed. But I've recently come to my senses."

"Well, good." Rob threw the mare's reins back to her. "Let's away. 'Twill be full dark soon, and there's no moon tonight to speak of. Christ, 'twill be the middle o' the night by the time we get back to the village."

Rob and Dougal turned their mounts and, flanking her, the three of them trotted south toward Loch Drurie. Mairi was glad they'd come after her and doubly glad they'd found her. She didn't relish the idea of riding back in the dark all alone.

"How did ye know where I'd gone?" she asked, curious as to how they'd found her.

Rob snorted. "I'm no' an idiot. Besides, I knew for a fact that ye werena pickin' acorns off the hillside."

She cringed in the dark. It had been a ridiculous ploy and she was embarrassed about it now.

"Aye," Dougal said. "And there's someone waiting for ye at home."

Her heart leaped to her throat and she involuntarily jerked the mare's reins. "Conall? Is he—"

"Nay," Dougal said. "One of his brother's men. A

warrior who says ye owe him…what did he call it? Oh, aye…some *broth.*''

Mairi thanked God the two of them couldn't see the disappointment and humiliation that blazed on her face. She spurred the mare forward. Rob and Dougal fell into step beside her.

The night grew frigid, and black as Conall's stallion. By the time they reached the hunter's camp and the ancient standing stone marking the path skirting the loch, the clouds had all but disappeared, and with them her foolish dreams.

Mairi tilted her head back and gazed at the brilliant field of stars twinkling through the canopy of trees overhead. She was glad Conall was gone. 'Twas for the best. She had a clan to build, an adopted son to nurture. In less than a fortnight the trade boats would come.

And with them her freedom.

Chapter Fifteen

Three months later

Mairi clutched the timbers of the lake house pier and retched over the side into the water.

"Here," Dora said, handing her a damp rag.

"Ye're a saint."

"That's the third time this week. How long, Mairi?"

Mairi blocked out the vision of Dora kneeling beside her. Her head spun like a drunken dervish, her stomach roiled. The last thing she needed was Dora's mothering.

"Go away," she said, and shot her a miserable look.

"How long," the older woman repeated, "since ye've bled?"

Mairi closed her eyes and curled into a ball. The rough timbers of the pier jabbed at her side, but the discomfort kept her mind off her queasiness. She didn't want to think about Dora's question, but knew she must. Soon the whole clan would be able to tell.

She might as well get it out in the open and have done with it.

"Since well before Christmas," she said, and opened her eyes. A brilliant winter sky came into focus.

Dora smiled and brushed a damp lock of hair from Mairi's forehead. "I suspected as much. Why did ye no' tell me before?"

Why, indeed? "I didna want to believe it." She stretched like a cat and ran her hand along the soft curve of her abdomen. "But methinks I canna hide it much longer."

"Come on," Dora said, and grasped her hand to help her up. "Let's go inside. There are things we must settle."

Mairi obeyed and followed her into the lake house. Dora closed the door behind them, then bade her sit on one of the two stools flanking the table. The day was icy. Mairi warmed her hands gratefully over the peat fire blazing in the hearth.

Dora dragged the other stool up beside her and settled in for what Mairi was afraid was to be a long and uncomfortable conversation. "Ye'll have to tell him, ye know."

"Tell who? What are ye talking about?"

"Rob can send word, or go himself if need be."

What Dora proposed was unthinkable. Mairi shot to her feet and felt the blood rush from her head. Another wave of nausea gripped her, stronger this time than before.

Dora saw it in her face, which Mairi was certain was green as a gillfish in midsummer, and pulled her back down onto the stool.

"Conall must know, Mairi."

"Know what?" She knew perfectly well what.

"That ye carry his babe."

"Nay!" She clutched her stomach protectively and scowled at her. "I'll ne'er tell him and neither will you—nor anyone else," she added, remembering Rob and Dougal and Harry, and the rest of the Chattan who'd been with them these past months. "D'ye hear?"

Dora swore under her breath. "Ye are so pigheaded! Ye dinna deserve this blessing."

"Ha! A blessing is it? For who?"

"For the both o' ye!" Dora rose in a huff and set the kettle on the fire to boil.

Oh, now 'twould start. Dora would have her drinking every kind of foul tea imaginable until the babe was born. Just the thought of it caused her stomach to lurch.

"If he knew," Dora said as she set a cup on the table and filled it with something awful she'd plucked from the pocket of her gown, "he might feel different about things."

"Aye, he might, and that's exactly what I dinna want."

Dora stopped what she was doing and frowned at her. "Why not?"

"Why not?" Mairi couldn't believe she had to ask that. She met her friend's puzzled gaze and shook her head. "Because I dinna want his help, nor his pity."

Dora snorted, and finished preparing the cup. "Are ye tellin' me ye wouldna wed the man who's the father of your child?"

"I'm telling ye exactly that." Mairi had thought this through a hundred times since she first suspected she might be pregnant. "I'll no' marry a man who doesna want me. 'Twould be a humiliation too great to bear.''

"Humiliation, my eye. Ye love him—'tis plain as day."

"I don't! He played me for a fool and I got what I deserve.''

"What ye deserve is each other," Dora said. "The both o' ye are idiots. Ye can go on foolin' yerself, Mairi, but ye dinna fool me. Ye love him."

"What does it matter if I do? And I'm no' saying I do, mind ye. 'Tis just that—'' God's blood, she didn't know what she felt anymore.

"And another thing," Dora said, "ye dinna know for certain that he doesna want ye."

But she did know.

Three long months and nary a word from Conall Mackintosh. He hadn't even sent word to his companions, Rob and Harry and Dougal, who'd remained at Loch Drurie to supervise the trade.

In fact, his whereabouts were wholly unknown. 'Twas said he ne'er returned to Findhorn Castle. She wondered, now, if his brother Iain had truly called him home, or if the summons was a fabrication he'd designed to make easy his departure.

"'Tis been a hard winter," Dora said. "More snow than we've seen in years. The roads are thick with it. Except for the packhorses in and out of Monadhliath to meet the boats from the south, no one's come to visit."

Did Dora think to make excuses for the man?

"Geoffrey's visited," she snapped. "Nearly every fortnight since Christmas."

Dora screwed her face up. *"Geoffrey."* The word oozed off her lips like a fetid blister. She handed Mairi the steaming cup of God knows what. "Here, drink this down. 'Twill be good for the babe."

She wrinkled her nose but obeyed, thinking that if she did, Dora might leave and she could get some rest. Mairi was never one to sleep in the day, but of late she'd been so tired. 'Twas the pregnancy. She remembered Dora's last breeding, and how exhausted she'd been. Aye, well, she'd also had five other bairns to care for at the time, and a husband who'd been more trouble than help.

"E'er since Conall left," Dora said, obviously not willing to let the subject go, "Geoffrey's been sniffin' around ye like a dog. I thought ye despised him."

"Nay, 'tis you alone who despises him." And wasn't that the truth. Dora hated him. Mairi now wished she'd never told her of her suspicions about Geoffrey's hand in the explosion.

"'Tis true," she continued, "I've never loved Geoffrey, but he's been an ally to the clan, and now that I understand things better I can see what a true friend he was to my father."

"Oh, posh! He encouraged Alwin to drink himself to death and ye know it."

She didn't know that for a fact, and would not hold it against Geoffrey now. So many things had changed in the past year, in the past few months.

Her clan was thriving again. Because of the lake trade there was plenty of food, wool for clothing, and household crafts the likes of which she'd ne'er seen before. Come spring, Rob said the traders would bring livestock. Aye, life was good. Better than it had been in years.

She had paid her father's debt with the very first shipment of goods, though the boats had arrived late after having met with some unexplained misfortune. She'd been surprised when Rob and Harry returned from Falmar with more than half of what she'd offered.

"I still canna believe Geoffrey accepted those few goods in payment," Dora said, again reading her mind. The woman was almost scary.

"Aye, well, he likely had a change of heart."

"Hmph. The man has no heart." Dora snatched the empty cup from her, swabbed it out with a rag and put it back on the shelf by the hearth.

All at once, the lake house rolled under the weight of something moving across the pier. Footfalls. Both women looked to the closed door. Mairi got to her feet. "Someone's coming."

The door crashed open and Kip burst across the threshold, gasping, his warm breath frosting the chill air.

"Kip!" Dora guided the wet boy toward the hearth while Mairi shut the door. "Why in God's name are ye running?"

"Look!" he said, and fished a tiny cloth bag out of the child-size badger sporran Rob had made for him last month. "'Tis for ye." He pressed the bag into Mairi's hand.

"What is it?" she said, as she tested the weight of it in her palm.

"Geoffrey brought it," Kip said. "And he told me to tell ye—"

"Geoffrey is here?" Dora said. "Where? Where is he?" She moved to the window, peeled back a corner of the deerskin covering and looked out toward the beach.

"Och, nay, he's gone home," Kip said. "He wanted

to see ye, Mairi, but I told him ye werena feelin' so good—on account o' the babe.''

"What!" both women shouted in unison.

"Ye know," Kip said, and pointed matter-of-factly to Mairi's slightly rounded stomach. "The babe."

Mairi felt her eyes widen and her mouth gape. "But how on earth did ye know?"

"Rob told me. 'Tis Conall's babe, aye?" Kip grinned at both of them, and Mairi shot Dora a murderous look.

The older woman shrugged her shoulders and cracked a sheepish smile. "I didna ken for certain."

"Ye told Rob?" Mairi shouted at her, incredulous. "How could ye do such a thing?"

"I didna think he'd tell anyone." Dora looked to Kip for help.

"Oh, aye, the whole clan knows of it," Kip said.

Mairi was tempted to wipe the grin off Kip's face with the back of her hand. And she'd have words with Rob before the day was out. "Geoffrey knows, too?" she asked.

Kip nodded. "Are ye no' gonna open your gift?"

She was so astounded by Kip's revelation, she'd forgotten about the tiny cloth bag, clutched so tight in her hand the hard object inside nearly cut into her flesh. She loosened the string at the top and dumped the contents into her palm.

"A brooch!" Kip said. "'Tis bonny."

'Twas bonny, and finely crafted. It surprised Mairi that Geoffrey could be so thoughtful. And yet, 'twas not the first time in the past few months he'd given her such a gift. She felt badly he'd had to learn of her condition from aught than her own lips. She'd meant to tell him herself, but it seemed that plan was already foiled.

Mairi knelt before Kip and clutched his narrow shoulders. "What did Geoffrey say when ye told him?"

"No' much. Only that he was sorry ye was sick, but such is the way o' things when a woman's breedin'. Whatever that means." Kip shrugged. "He said he was happy for ye."

"He did?" she and Dora echoed together.

"Aye, and that the child would need a father."

Dora sucked a gasp, but Mairi took the words in stride. She reminded herself she was a practical woman and had more than just herself to think of now. She'd not have her child live with the scourge of being a bastard. He *would* need a father. One who'd be loyal, who'd protect her clan and her babe as if they were his own.

"A father like Geoffrey Symon," she whispered.

Two and a half months' forced labor in the hold of a foreign ship was more than enough to break a man. Or make him stronger. In Conall's case, it simply afforded him time to dream up new ways of killing the man who'd put him there.

But that's not what he was thinking about as he liberated Jupiter from the wharf-side beast circus in Wick to which Geoffrey Symon's men had sold him before turning Conall over to a Nordic slave trader bound for the Shetlands.

He was thinking of Mairi Dunbar, as he had every day of his captivity, praying to God she was well and safe.

He thought, too, about his brothers. Iain would think

Conall had simply ignored his request to return to Findhorn. In the past Conall might have most certainly ignored the summons, much as he'd managed to avoid nearly all familial responsibilities.

But he was a changed man, and that had not been his intention when he'd turned the black 'round that day in the wood, retracing his path back to Loch Drurie, back to Mairi.

"Come on, boy. Let's away." He returned the mastiff's slobbery licks of joy with a squeeze and a head pat, noticing in the moonlight that the dog was fat and newly groomed. He'd evidently fared a damned sight better than Conall had these past weeks.

What Geoffrey Symon didn't know when he sent a dozen men out after him the day Conall threatened his life in the wood north of Falmar, was that a Nordic slave trader bound for the Shetlands was the poorest choice he might have made had he wished to rid himself of Conall for good.

Symon had been too much of a coward to directly order his murder. He knew 'twould have brought the whole of the Chattan down on him. Instead, he'd opted for the slave trader.

It had proved to be the wrong move.

The Mackintoshes had allies in the Shetlands on Fair Isle, where, a fortnight ago on its return trip, the slave trader had landed to take on provisions. George Grant, cousin to Iain's wife, Alena, had married a Viking maiden from that very shore—Ulrika, daughter of Rollo. Her brother Gunnar was chieftain there now, and had bought Conall's freedom for a mere ten kegs of Viking mead.

He would not forget this kindness.

Conall had spent nearly a sennight on the remote

windswept isle, regaining his strength. Not long enough, but 'twas all he could abide. Vengeance burned like fire in his gut and would not be quenched till his hands slid 'round Geoffrey Symon's neck and squeezed.

The coin Gunnar had advanced him had purchased a decent enough mount once he'd reached the mainland. Symon had kept the black and, by God, Conall would have him back. That, and other things he'd come to think of as his.

"Soon," he whispered to himself as he mounted. "Soon."

As Jupiter fell into step beside him, Conall urged the purchased mare south toward Falmar Castle, the memory of Mairi Dunbar's kiss and Geoffrey Symon's treachery driving him on.

"Four days' hence, ye'll be in that man's bed."

Mairi glanced out the half-opened door of Dora's cottage and shivered. "'Twill be fine."

Dora kicked the door shut and handed her a steaming cup. "Drink this, and I dinna want to hear any whining about it."

"Ugh." For the past week, e'er since the clan had discovered Mairi's pregnancy, Dora had plied her with a half-dozen different concoctions, most of them as noxious as the water in Falmar's moat.

"Ye'd wed a man ye dinna love." 'Twas a statement, not a question.

"Why not?" Mairi said. "You did."

"Aye, but I was young and stupid. Ye're a grown woman, Mairi, and a smart one."

"That's precisely why I accepted Geoffrey's offer."

She'd had Kip go after him the day he delivered the

brooch to her. She'd met Geoffrey at the edge of the village and, after sending Kip home, she'd told him of her decision. At that moment, in Geoffrey's eyes she'd read not joy, but triumph. His hands on her had been overbold, his kisses hard and possessive.

Mairi pushed the memory from her mind, refusing to dwell on how wrong it all felt. If she did, she might change her mind, and that was not an option. She had her child to think of now.

She shook off her melancholy and forced a smile as Rob burst into the cottage, his cheeks red as apples, carrying an armload of new-cut peat for the fire.

"Christ, 'tis cold." He glanced around the dimly lit room and frowned. "Where are the bairns?"

"At the house," Mairi said, "with Kip. I had things to discuss with Dora."

"Things." Rob shot them both a loaded glance. Mairi noticed a bit of frost clinging to his short, tawny beard.

"Aye," Dora said. "She's hell-bent on it."

"Still?" he said.

"Still."

Rob shook his head, then knelt and stoked the hearth fire until the smoke died down and bright flames danced. "Weddin' Geoffrey Symon." He snorted, then pulled a dirk from his belt and skewered a block of peat. "I dinna like the man."

"Nor does she," Dora said.

Rob glanced over his shoulder at them, the peat hanging like a slab of meat from his blade. "Then why, lass? What's your hurry?"

Would they not let up? Dora had spent days trying to talk her out of it, and now Rob was starting in.

Bloody nuisance. Her mind was made up, and that was that.

"My babe needs a father. Ye know I'm right."

Dora snorted. "Mine did well enough these past two years without one."

"Aye, but they've got one now, don't they, love?" Rob said.

Dora blushed, and Rob grinned at her. Their eyes shone with a mutual adoration that tugged at Mairi's heart. She quickly crushed the emotion and crossed her arms over her chest. "My babe needs a father and that's that."

Rob turned his attention back to the fire. "I'll no' argue with ye."

"Ye won't?" Now this surprised her. She cast Dora a smug smile.

"The babe does need a father." Rob sheathed his dirk and rose stiffly to face her. "His own."

Mairi bristled.

Dora joined him in front of the hearth, and he wrapped an arm 'round her waist. "I wish ye'd let Rob set out to find him."

"Or at least send word to Findhorn," Rob said, "on the off chance he's returned there. Conall has a right to know."

"He has no rights!" She whirled toward the door, biting back a litany of curses.

"Aye," Dora said. "She loves him, plain as day."

Mairi swore.

She didn't love him. She didn't!

She yanked the cottage door wide and sucked in a breath of icy air. "Geoffrey's sending an escort. I ride for Falmar today."

"Ye're with child!" Dora cried.

"Aye, and the whole bluidy world knows thanks to the both o' ye." She glared at them.

"The man's no' comin' to fetch ye, himself?" Rob said.

"'Tis Geoffrey's hunting day today. He'll meet me at the forest camp near the standing stone at the north end o' the loch. Ye know the place."

"Near the crossroad," Dora said.

"Aye."

"I'm going with ye," Rob said, and grabbed a saddlebag off a hook on the wall.

"Me, as well," Dora said.

"Nay, I'll go to him on my own." She relieved Rob of the saddlebag and placed it firmly back on its hook. "But ye're to join us the day of the celebration. The whole clan's to come."

Ignoring their protests, Mairi pulled her shawl tightly around her shoulders and took her leave of them. She stepped onto the floating timbers anchoring the lake house to the shore as if in a trance.

One thought consumed her. After they married, Geoffrey would expect her to…oh, she'd tried, but she couldn't bear the thought of his hands on her. True, Geoffrey had held her before, kissed her before, and she'd found it tolerable, pleasant even.

But things were different now. She was different. A hot shiver raced along her spine as she recalled the feel of Conall's arms around her, their tongues melding like molten glass.

"Ye must be strong now. Smart."

Hers had never been a world of frivolous emotion. And this was certainly no time to succumb to it. If her submission to Geoffrey ensured her child a name and a future, so be it. Her mind was made up.

Closing the lake house door behind her, she threw off her shawl and knelt beside her pallet before the pine chest that had once belonged to her mother.

For years she'd held on to the gown that had been her mother's favorite. 'Twas the finest thing Gladys Dunbar had owned, and Mairi would look her best when she went to Geoffrey.

"Where on earth could it be?"

Her fingertips brushed the edge of something familiar, and she gasped in recognition. Slowly she drew the coarsely woven garment from the chest. 'Twas Conall's shirt, the one he'd left behind after their night of lovemaking so long ago. A wave of raw emotion welled inside her.

For months she'd fought it, denied it to herself and to the world, would have ripped her own heart out if she thought 'twould have eased her pain. She clutched the shirt to her breast and focused on one lucid truth.

She loved Conall Mackintosh.

All the same, less than an hour later, she placed a slipper-clad foot on the knee of one of Geoffrey's warriors and mounted a saddled mare. Surrounded by armed men, Mairi guided her mount onto the lakeside trail leading north toward Falmar Castle.

Chapter Sixteen

On the journey south from Wick, Conall had avoided both Findhorn and Monadhliath. He could think of no good reason to involve his brothers or his clan in the business at hand.

'Twas between him and Geoffrey Symon.

He would have satisfaction. He would have blood. He would have his damned horse back, and then he would ride to Loch Drurie and ask Mairi Dunbar to be his wife.

Only then would he go home and explain it all to Iain and Gilchrist. They would be angry he hadn't asked for their help, but they would understand his reasons. They always did. They always would. They were his brothers, family. He didn't realize how much he'd missed them till now.

For the first time in his life Conall knew what he wanted, what would make him truly happy. And contrary to what his brothers suspected, 'twasn't a life of carefree adventure and endless conquest. Though he had a feeling life with Mairi Dunbar, if she'd have him, might offer a bit of both. And so much more.

The night they'd made love in the lake house he'd

looked into her eyes and realized how much more there was, how much more there could be for the two of them. He'd never felt that way with any woman in his life.

He'd had a long time to think about it, shut up in the foul hold of that rotting slaver. He was certain now, about himself and about her.

When Jupiter stopped at the crossroad near a familiar ridge above an even more familiar loch, Conall pulled his mount up short and drew a breath of frigid air. Winter sun glittered off icy water.

He recalled his swimming lessons with Kip and smiled. He conjured up the color of Mairi's eyes, her touch, the willful arch of her fiery brows when he asked her to do something she didn't wish to do.

An overpowering urge to ride east toward her village gripped him. Jupiter must have felt it, too, for he trotted off in that very direction. Conall hardened his heart and called him back.

"Not today, boy," he said, and gestured for the mastiff to follow him down the hill toward the forest camp and the standing stone marking the path leading west to Falmar Castle. "Tomorrow we shall see her, and the lad."

As they picked their way down the heavily wooded hillside, Conall considered his next move. 'Twas dead on winter, and he'd no intention of swimming that fetid moat again. But neither did he wish to announce his presence at Geoffrey Symon's front door. This presented a problem.

He wanted the chieftain alone, and once he had him, he intended to kill him. Not by treacherous means, but in a fair fight. Just the two of them. He didn't wish to engage their clans in an all-out war. Nor would Symon, if he were smart. One word to Conall's brothers about his abduction, and they'd see Falmar leveled, stone by stone if need be.

Nay, 'twas not the kind of vengeance Conall burned for.

The unmistakable sound of livery carried up the hill from the forest camp. Jupiter froze in place, ears pricked. Conall stilled his mount, drew his broadsword and narrowed his eyes on an opening in the trees twenty yards below him.

What he did burn for was the opportunity unfolding before him.

Geoffrey Symon, dressed in leather breeks and a fur tunic, stepped into the cold circle of light between two naked larch trees and a smattering of pines.

There were others with him, but not many from what Conall could hear. Silently he slid from his mount and tethered the mare to a tree. Using hand signals well-known to his companion, he ordered Jupiter, now shielded by a thicket of gorse, to stay.

'Twas hard to tell from this vantage how many men accompanied the chieftain. In his mind, Conall counted the days since he'd left Wick. Of course! 'Twas one day beyond the Sabbath—Symon's hunting day. What a stroke of luck. He'd not have to breach Falmar at all.

Conall stole down the hill, sword in hand, recalling that Symon preferred to hunt alone. There were men with him now, but likely he'd send them away or ride off alone, as he had that day three months ago when last they met.

"I should have killed you then," he breathed.

A flash of red-gold hair caught the light as a white mare trotted into view. Conall's heart stopped. Symon reached up to help a woman—a vision—from the mount.

Mairi!

She placed her hands on Symon's broad shoulders and smiled at him as he set her lightly on her feet.

Conall could barely breathe.

He'd ne'er before seen her look so lovely. Under her cloak she wore a gown of pale fabric that, if he didn't know her to be poor as a church mouse, he would swear was silk. And slippers. For the briefest moment he recalled her slender feet, those long legs, and how they'd felt entwined 'round his hips as he made love to her. *Oh, Mairi.*

Her hair was long and loose and a bit wild, as was its wont. He longed to touch it. Atop her head she wore a wreath of dried flowers that set off the color in her cheeks.

Crouched in the stinking hold of that Norse ship day after day after day, the memory of Mairi Dunbar the only thing keeping him alive, Conall at last had embraced the magnitude of his love for her. But now, seeing her in the flesh, hearing her voice, her lilting laugh, feeling the warmth of her smile inside himself—'twas almost more than his heart could bear.

Only her smile was not for him. 'Twas for Geoffrey Symon.

Conall edged closer, unable to stop himself. Though well hidden by the dense foliage, his footfalls masked by the sounds of other horses and other men—more than a dozen, he realized, as he quickly scanned the camp—he risked discovery at any moment.

"Won't ye sit, love," Symon said to her.

Love.

Conall waited for some smart retort to slip from Mairi's lips, but she merely smiled at the endearment.

"Nay," she said. "I'm weary of sitting. 'Tis a long ride 'round the loch."

Symon moved closer, his face edged with what seemed to Conall to be genuine concern. "Are ye well?" He took her hands in his and gazed into her eyes.

Conall redoubled his grip on his sword.

"Oh, aye. Just a bit tired."

Symon smiled. "'Tis natural for a woman in your condition."

What condition? Oh, God, was she ill? Conall slipped behind a stout pine as Geoffrey led her away from his men to the very edge of the clearing, not a dozen feet from where Conall stood concealed.

His heart beat wildly. He worked to control his breathing as he imagined every terrible illness she might be plagued with. It occurred to him that he should simply snatch her up, here and now, and bear her away to Monadhliath. His brother Gilchrist's wife was a healer, the most skilled Conall had e'er known. Perhaps she might help if—

Symon placed his hand on Mairi's stomach, and Conall held his breath, waiting for her to slap it away. To his amazement, she did not.

"I pray each night 'twill be a son." Symon stroked the soft curve of her body, and the joy and pain Conall read in her face told him more than words could e'er reveal.

A...son? A child?

The truth hit him like a hundredweight stone.

"I shall be an ideal father," Symon said, and brushed a kiss across her forehead. "And husband."

Good God, she carried Geoffrey Symon's child!

Conall gripped the pine for support as he felt his knees give way beneath him. Recovering his balance, he tightened the death grip he had on his sword.

"Aye, and I'll hold ye to both promises for as long as ye draw breath, Geoffrey Symon." Mairi removed his hand from her body, and Symon used the opportunity to pull her close.

"Kiss me," he said.

Conall didn't want to watch anymore. He didn't want to hear what words she might say to him, but he was powerless to move without revealing himself.

"I'm tired." Mairi tried to turn away from him, but Symon was persistent.

"One kiss."

Conall squeezed his eyes shut, only to see the vision of Symon kissing her, and Mairi kissing him back, emblazoned on the backs of his eyelids.

When he dared look at them again, Mairi was turned away from him, her body rigid, her head down. "I'd have some time alone e'er we continue on to Falmar."

"Why, love?" Symon asked.

Mairi cast a look toward the trees, so near to where Conall stood he thought she might see him.

"Ah, I understand." Symon smiled at her. "Verra well. Take all the time ye need."

When Symon brushed another kiss across her cheek, Conall could swear she flinched. 'Twas naught but his imagination, his wishing it were so. He simply couldn't believe what he'd just witnessed.

She'd married Geoffrey Symon. She'd…shared his bed.

Conall stood motionless for what seemed an eternity, staring at her, his mouth dry as ash, trying to fathom how she could have done this thing. 'Twas not so very long ago she'd shared *his* bed, and had looked upon him with what he'd known in his heart—but had denied—was love.

This marriage made no sense to him. She'd gotten what, all along, she'd made clear she wanted. Conall had helped her get it. Deliverance from her father's debt, her independence, a means of keeping her land and her clan intact. Why, then, had she done it? Why had she given herself to Symon?

Conall pressed his forehead into the rough bark of the pine as if 'twould stop the dull pounding in his head. All plans of retribution threatened to slip away on the icy breeze that lifted Mairi's hair away from her face like gentle fingers. Would he make her a widow, her child an orphan, to satisfy his bloodlust?

Why, Mairi? Why?

As if in answer, she looked up and her gaze collided with his.

Mairi thought she would faint dead away.

But she didn't. She stood there in shock, unable to move, unable to take her eyes off him for fear he'd vanish like an apparition. Aye, one conjured from her most secret yearnings.

Clad in the same garments she'd last seen him in nigh on three months ago—a dark hunting plaid and leather boots, a homespun shirt she recalled the feel of—he looked leaner than she remembered him.

In his eyes she read an almost painful confusion— one she knew well, one she, herself, had felt throbbing inside her like a dull ache these past months.

"Conall," she whispered, simply to hear his name

on her lips, a name she hadn't uttered since last they were together.

He took an awkward step backward, and her feet moved of their own accord in response. His gaze flashed briefly to the clearing where Geoffrey stood with his men in a tight circle, sharing oatcakes and passing a wineskin amongst them.

Mairi ignored them and moved into the cover of the trees, drawn to him as if by some force outside her body. When at last she reached him, she fought an overpowering urge to throw herself into his arms.

"Mairi," he breathed, and looked at her, studied every feature, as if seeing her for the first time.

They stood inches apart, yet he did not touch her. She felt his breath on her face as she looked into his eyes, yet he made no move to kiss her.

She thought she might die if he did not.

At last she had the presence of mind to speak. "Why have ye come?"

The question fueled an uneasiness in his expression.

"No reason," he said. "Save to…wish you well. You and…" He nodded toward the clearing. "Symon."

His words caused her stomach to clench. Her hand flew instantly to her abdomen.

"Are you…" He grasped her arm, as if to steady her should she falter. His touch alone was enough to make her want to weep. "Are you unwell?"

"Nay, far from it." She shook off the roil of emotions welling inside her and looked away. "I'm well, quite well."

"And your babe?" He nodded at her hand resting on the soft swell of her stomach.

Her gaze flew to his. "Ye know?" He'd heard what

Geoffrey had said to her a moment ago. How else would he have known?

"Oh, aye." He shrugged and cast her a brief smile. "That's…why I've come, in fact."

Her heart stopped. "Is it?"

How had he known? No one knew, not even Dora until a handful of days ago. But he did know, he had known—she could see it in his face.

"Aye." He stepped back, putting an arm's length between them, his gaze flitting over the foliage, then skyward, then up the hillside where she saw a tethered mount and Jupiter peeking out at her from a bush.

"So then…" She moved toward him and boldly placed a hand on his arm. "Ye dinna mind the idea of the babe?"

"Not if it makes you happy." He met her gaze again. "Does it, Mairi?"

She couldn't believe his answer. Perhaps she'd misjudged him. But if that were the case, why had he stayed away all these months? Why had he left her to begin with?

"Aye," she breathed. "More than I can tell you."

He went stock-still at her words, and said nothing in return. Her momentary joy turned to doubt.

He fixed his gaze on the loamy earth between them and spent what, to her, was an excruciatingly silent moment, nudging a stone with his booted foot. She'd seen him do that once before, the night of the explosion after he laid the dead body of his kinsman John gently upon a rock. 'Twas as if he were searching for words and none would come.

When she thought she could bear it no longer, he at last looked at her. "He shall be a good father—"

his gaze flashed briefly to where Geoffrey stood in the clearing with his men "—and husband."

Her stomach did a slow roll. She felt as if she were weightless, floating, caught in a spectral ether from which there was no escape. "Geoffrey, ye mean?"

"Aye."

"Then…"

"Aye." He drew himself up, redoubling his grip on the broadsword that, oddly, he'd seemed to be using to support himself the last minute or so. "'Tis a good match. You chose wisely, Mairi Dunbar."

Never once in their past association had he used her surname when addressing her. His manner was cool, his eyes distant. She couldn't bear it. She simply couldn't. Emotions she was desperate to conceal flooded her chest, constricted her throat, heating her face to burning.

"I…I must go. G-Geoffrey…" She turned, clutching her stomach, fearing she'd lose what little food she'd managed to force down earlier that day.

"Mairi." He reached out and grasped her wrist. She froze in place, her gaze fixed on the moss clinging to a nearby tree. She feared that if she looked at him, the tears stinging her eyes would flow free, betraying her feelings.

Gathering her resolve, she drew a breath, pretending she didn't feel how warm his hand was, how strong it felt, how right, her blood beneath the skin pulsing warm and fast against his fingers.

"Fare you well," he said, and let her go.

At the break in the trees where the ground leveled off into the clearing, she looked back at him. For the briefest moment something flickered in his eyes, a raw grief that seemed to weigh him down, and that she, too, felt to the core of her bones. Then 'twas gone.

He turned into the wood, and for the second time in her life she wanted to cut out her heart and send it with him.

"Ye are much changed, brother, since last we met." Gilchrist set his ale cup down beside the trencher he shared with his wife, Rachel, and cast Conall a long, measured look across the table.

"Am I?" Conall held his brother's gaze. It had been a long time since they'd all come together here at Findhorn Castle, their birthplace and seat of Clan Mackintosh.

His eldest brother Iain sat at his customary place at the head of the table, his wife Alena on his left, seated next to Conall, Gilchrist and Rachel on his right.

Laughter and high-pitched squeals drew Conall's attention briefly away from them to the hearth, where Jupiter lounged in front of the fire, sated from a heavy meal, busily licking the children who crowded 'round him measuring their hands and feet against his enormous paws.

'Twas good to be home. To share a meal with his brothers and their families. To hear children make merry. To feel, at last, a part of the whole.

He realized he'd always been a part of them. They were one, a family, a clan. 'Twas he, himself, who'd put distance between them in the years since he'd grown into a man. A distance that was measured not only in leagues, but in the casual, often charming indifference he'd spun with purpose into a shield around his heart.

He knew, now, why he'd done it. To protect himself

should he lose them. To be certain such a loss would not break him. And he *had* nearly lost them, both of them. Iain to battle, Gilchrist to fire. He glanced briefly at his brother's burned hand gently cradling Rachel's, and remembered.

Loving Mairi Dunbar had made him see the truth of things. But too late.

There'd been a price to pay for his distance, and 'twas dear, too dear. He knew that now. Love was a gift not to be held in check for fear of its loss, but to be spent lavishly and with abandon, risking all.

Losing Mairi had taught him that. Again, too late.

He smiled wanly at Gilchrist, then looked away, fixing his gaze on the fire as he absently drummed his fingers on the table next to his untouched trencher of food.

A moment later, a serving maid he'd once enjoyed sidled up beside him and refilled his ale cup, and purposely grazed her breast against his arm. Conall ignored her.

"His appetite for food has waned nearly as much as his appetite for women."

His sister-in-law's comment drew much laughter from the men at the far end of the table, though she herself did not laugh. Nor did his brothers.

Alena turned to him. "You love this woman."

'Twas not a question. He felt his brothers' eyes on him but did not return their stares.

When he'd arrived at Findhorn earlier that day, Conall told them what they hadn't already known about the events at Loch Drurie, his departure nearly three months ago, his meeting with Symon in the wood, the abduction, and how he made his way back to Falmar intent on revenge. As predicted, his absence had been credited to his flighty nature. Foul play had ne'er been suspected. Lastly, he'd told them what he'd witnessed between Mairi and Geoffrey Symon in the clearing.

But he hadn't told them everything.

Perhaps now he should.

"Aye," he said quietly, and looked into his sister-in-law's pale eyes.

"Then what the devil are ye doin' here with us?" Iain boomed. "Go after her, man."

"Hear, hear." Gilchrist raised his ale cup and drained it.

"Nay, you dinna understand. She...doesn't love me."

"Are you certain?" Rachel leaned forward, one delicate brow arched in anticipation of his answer.

Alena studied him, as did his brothers. They were all ears.

"Aye, well...reasonably certain. She's married Symon. She carries his babe."

Rachel clucked her tongue. "That means little. What did she say when you told her?"

"When I told her what?"

"That ye love her, ye dolt," Gilchrist said.

Even the men at the far end of the table, men Conall had known all his life, were silent, ears pricked.

Conall shrugged. "Well, I didna exactly tell her. I mean...it could hardly have mattered. She'd made her choice. She was happy about it—about the babe, at least."

More than I can tell you.

Mairi's words burned fresh in his mind, as they had the whole long ride back to Findhorn. The look in her eyes when she'd said them was one he'd ne'er forget.

'Twas a raw fusion of love, sadness and things he couldn't fathom but could feel.

"Conall." Alena placed a gentle hand on his arm, drawing him back to the present, and forced his gaze to hers. "If she does not know you love her, she hasn't made a choice at all."

He hadn't thought of that.

"Do you know—and do not be offended—was it the child came first, or the wedding?"

"I know not." In truth, he couldn't bear to think on it.

Alena exchanged a quick glance with their sister-in-law. "Mayhap the child came first, and who knows how it might have happened. Mayhap she had no choice at all."

Another possibility he hadn't considered. A possibility that enraged him. He felt warm all of a sudden, as if blood rushed to his head. Abruptly he stood.

Rachel followed Alena's lead. "Perhaps Mairi Dunbar has simply done what's best for her child. Any woman would have done the same."

"Aye," Gilchrist said. "Particularly if the man she loved left with no' so much as a word of farewell, and with no firm plans to return."

He hadn't told them how it had been between him and Mairi when he'd left her that rainy day three months ago. But his brothers knew him well—too well—and Gilchrist had guessed rightly.

The sound of Findhorn Castle's great door swinging inward distracted him for only a second before he said, "She doesna know how I feel. I never told her. I was…" He shook his head.

"Ye were a great numbskull, is what ye were!"

The diners turned toward the entrance to the hall.

Rob stood in the vestibule, dwarfed by the half-dozen men who accompanied him, his chubby hands fisted on his hips, his beard nearly frozen, looking as if he'd ridden all night.

The sight of Rob's compact but stalwart features after all these months buoyed Conall's spirit. All the same, he didn't have it in him to argue. "She's married," he said simply.

Rob's tawny brows shot skyward. Likely he wondered how Conall knew. "She's nothing of the kind. But she means to be, day after tomorrow."

"What?" All three brothers spoke at once. Iain was on his feet. Gilchrist, too.

"That's why I've come," Rob said. "To bring ye the news."

Conall's head spun. A dozen times in the past two days he'd thought about what he might have done had Mairi not already wed Symon.

He loved her. More than all the world. More than clan, more than family. Though, thank Christ, he had no such terrible choice to make, as had both his brothers when first they'd met their brides. But he did have another choice, one that might seem impossible to others, but to him was blindingly clear.

"If she's not wed him, there's still time." He whistled for Jupiter, then turned a quick circle in search of his weapons.

The mastiff lumbered to his feet, brown eyes bright, drool hanging from the side of his mouth. The children fell silent as Gilchrist walked calmly toward the hearth where Conall had stowed his few belongings, and handed him the shoulder baldric housing his broadsword.

"Ye'd love a child not your own?" Gilchrist looked hard at him, as did Iain.

"What are ye talkin' about?" Rob plucked a full ale cup from a passing maidservant and began to drink, his eyes on Conall, waiting for his explanation.

For weeks at Loch Drurie, Conall had battled the love he'd felt for the boy, Kip. A love he knew in his heart was as resolute as if the lad were his own blood.

He knew he could love Mairi's child, regardless of who the father was. He did love it already. 'Twas part of her. In time, 'twould be part of him.

"Aye," he said, "as I love her. It matters not to me if the child is Symon's."

Rob sprayed ale over the lot of them. Gilchrist jumped back. Iain swore. Conall didn't know what to think.

"'Tis no' Symon's child, ye dolt." Rob poked him in the chest with the empty ale cup. "'Tis yours!"

Chapter Seventeen

Today was her wedding day.

She should be joyful. At least she might pretend to be for the sake of the good people of Geoffrey's clan that she'd known all her life.

Unable to keep still, Mairi paced the rush-strewn floor of the chamber in which her husband-to-be had installed her for the past two nights. She was unused to lying about with nothing to occupy her time, no enterprise in which to throw herself.

But Geoffrey was insistent. He would not have her working. He would not even allow her out-of-doors for longer than a few minutes at a stretch. The cold was too bitter, he'd say, each time she attempted to step out for a walk about Falmar's busy bailey.

A wife should be pleased that her husband cared so much for her and her unborn child that he would not risk their health. But in the back of her mind, Mairi had a feeling Geoffrey's motives for keeping her indoors had more to do with controlling her than with safeguarding her health.

E'er since the day she'd agreed to be his wife, he'd kept close watch on her. He'd sent Tang to camp out above the village until his escort had come for her two days ago. She'd known, because Rob had seen the Oriental up in the wood watching them. The diminutive warrior had wanted to send him packing, but Mairi had insisted he not.

Now, here at Falmar, she regretted that she'd not allowed Dora and Rob to accompany her that day, as they'd wished. They were to have come today, along with the rest of her clan, to join in the wedding festivities, but Geoffrey sent word just this morn that they were not to come till the morrow.

She felt alone, isolated. Trapped in an odd sort of way, though 'twas ridiculous. Geoffrey had been nothing but kind to her these past months. A new man. A changed man. A man who, at every opportunity, told her he loved her. But 'twas not *his* love she wanted, though she was grateful for it. Grateful that her child would have a father and a name.

"Would that his own father wanted him."

In a fit of anger she grabbed a ceramic ewer off the chest near her bed and dashed it to pieces against the hearthstones.

There. She felt better now.

Her tantrum, she knew, wasn't directed at Conall Mackintosh, but at herself, for being so foolish, so weak. She must be strong now, for her child. For herself and her clan. A new day had dawned, and though 'twas gray and cold, fueling with each hour a nonsensical premonition that winter would never end, she was determined to do now what must be done.

Make peace with herself and get on with her life.

Aye, but if she were to do that, she'd need more freedom than Geoffrey had granted her. The air was stale in the room, and she could use a good stretch of the legs to get her blood pumping, to put some color into her cheeks.

Smoothing the skirt of her mother's one good gown over the softened curve of her abdomen, she readied herself to go below stairs and seek out the man who, in a few short hours, would be her husband.

Geoffrey had summoned one of the traveling priests that serviced the clans in this remote part of the Highlands. He was expected today. Tonight they would say their vows before him, and after that...

Well, at least she knew what to expect.

As she made her way down the staircase and turned into the corridor, she allowed herself to remember, one last time, what she had felt like in Conall Mackintosh's arms that night in the lake house—his mouth on her breast, his hands caressing her, their bodies joined in what, for her at least, had been a coupling of heart and soul and mind, manifested by a pleasure so powerful that the mere memory of it threatened to buckle her knees.

She grabbed hold of a stone archway for support and closed her eyes, banishing the vision from her mind, willing the instinctive response of her body— her quickening pulse, an ache in her breasts, the pooling of heat at her core—to cease.

"What of Fraser?" a familiar voice said, jolting her from her thoughts.

Mairi froze in place in the dimly lit corridor, realizing that the chamber just beyond the archway was Geoffrey's study. He was conversing with Tang.

"He comes today," Tang said. "Our sentries report he is but hours from the demesne."

"Good. I'd have him witness this joining of Dunbar's lands to mine. 'Twill please him, nearly as much as it pleases me.''

Mairi held herself in check. She'd known all along, for more than a year, that Geoffrey lusted for Dunbar land. 'Twas no surprise to her. And why shouldn't he have it? 'Twould make him more powerful in the eyes of the Frasers, to whom, years ago, he'd pledged his allegiance.

The creak of a leather seat and the sound of footfalls muffled by fresh straw told her Geoffrey had risen from the chair that was his favorite and was now pacing the room. Mairi inched closer to the doorway.

She knew 'twas wrong to eavesdrop on Geoffrey's private conversations, but she couldn't help herself. The uneasiness she'd felt since her arrival at Falmar escalated, though for no good reason she could pinpoint.

"Well done, lord," Tang said.

"Some say I should have acted sooner, with force if need be, to secure the lands and the lake trade that now comes with it. Fraser himself backed the idea."

She liked to think the land wasn't the only reason Geoffrey wanted her. He'd professed for months that the land had nothing to do with him desiring her for his own. She knew 'twas a lie, but still, she wanted to believe his affection for her was real.

"Yet you did not." She heard the shuffle of Tang's slippers across the floor.

"'Tis better, I think," Geoffrey continued, "to have my bride willing, than not. See how well it has all turned out. Fraser will be pleased, indeed."

"And the child?" Tang said.

Mairi held her breath.

The only reason she'd agreed to wed Geoffrey was

that he'd been so willing to safeguard her child as his own. To love him, and Kip, as well, as if they were all his family. He'd made her that promise the day she met him at the edge of the village, and 'twas the solitary reason for her compliance.

Geoffrey laughed. 'Twas not the response she'd expected to Tang's question. 'Twas a low, sober laugh, not at all a sound of joy or even amusement. His next words chilled her to her very bones.

"There will be no Mackintosh bastards in my household."

She stifled a sound that was half gasp, half scream. One hand flew to her mouth lest she betray her presence, the other to the soft swell of her abdomen.

"Ye have ways," Geoffrey said, "potions and such, that ye might use to ensure such an outcome."

Mairi felt her knees give way, and struggled to remain upright, grasping for handholds in the rough-hewn stone of the corridor.

"Of course," Tang said.

"If she's otherwise harmed in any way…"

"Nay, she shall survive it well, and go on to breed new sons. Your sons, lord."

Her stomach threatened to empty itself where she stood. Mairi battled the urge to retch, even as she felt a telltale flash of heat consume her and perspiration break across her skin.

"Excellent," Geoffrey said.

She refused to hear more. She clamped her hands to her ears and closed her eyes against the tears welling, hot and terrible, from a place deep inside her that felt, all at once, viciously, violently ravaged.

He'd tricked her! Betrayed her trust. He'd convinced her of his affection and his intent to keep her and hers safe from harm. She should have known he would never have accepted Conall's child. She should have known!

"Mairi."

Geoffrey's voice shocked her back to the moment. Her eyes flew open. Her hands moved protectively to her abdomen. He stood in the corridor, not an arm's length from her, his face half in shadow, his expression grim.

"Are ye no' well?"

"I...I'm f-fine," she breathed.

He stepped closer and gathered her into his arms. His hands were cold on her back, his scent hot and cloying. 'Twas all she could do not to break free of him and run.

"I see ye are not. But dinna worry, love. I'll have Tang prepare something special to soothe your nerves."

A strangled cry escaped her lips. Her knees gave out beneath her. Before she could stop him, Geoffrey lifted her into his arms.

They rode all night.

By late afternoon of the following day, Conall and his brothers had nearly reached the crossroad on the forest trail leading west toward Falmar Castle. Rob, along with forty of Iain's warriors in full battle dress, accompanied them. Jupiter followed faithfully behind. Earlier that morn when they'd passed the diversion to Monadhliath, Gilchrist had sent a man up the hill to muster some of his own men should they need them.

Within days they could raise hundreds more amongst the Chattan clans scattered across the highlands that stretched from Monadhliath to Findhorn and on to Inverness, but Conall thought none of it necessary. Symon was no fool. Even with Fraser to back him, he didn't think the chieftain would dare take up arms against so formidable a force as the alliance.

Besides, 'twas not a clan dispute. 'Twas not a dispute at all. What Conall had to do, what he had to say, was between him and Mairi. Now when he recalled their brief meeting in the wood—her words, her expressions, the few times she'd ventured to touch him—every moment of their time together held new meaning for him.

Are you happy? About the babe, I mean?

More than I can tell you.

"Christ, I was a fool."

Gilchrist shot him a pithy glance as they drove their mounts up the short rise toward the crossroad. Conall ignored him.

"Why didn't you fetch me sooner?" he hissed to Rob, who goaded his short mare into parallel step with Conall's borrowed mount.

"I told ye. Mairi'd have none of it. Dora begged her. I begged her."

None of this surprised him. She was as stubborn as a summer day was long.

"You should have come anyway, when first you discovered she was with child." *My* child. Our child.

'Twas a blessing he didn't deserve. He couldn't wait to see her, touch her, gather her into his arms and tell her his heart, beg for her forgiveness. Would that he had done so two days ago when he'd had the chance. Three months ago, when first he knew he loved her.

Aye, he'd known it then, but had fought it, denied it.

And now, he'd ne'er forgive himself if she married

Symon. He marveled, not for the first time, that the chieftain, proud as he was, was willing to have her, knowing she carried Conall's babe. He'd obviously misjudged Symon's regard for her.

'Twas his own bloody fault all of this had happened. His alone. He shook his head, remembering more of their conversation in the wood. She'd clearly thought he didn't want her, that he didn't want his own child. What else would she think? He'd actually told her he thought Symon would make the babe a good father, and her a good husband.

Conall swore and drove his mount faster.

"'Twas no' much more than a sennight ago she told us," Rob shouted, catching him up. "Besides, I didna truly think ye were at Findhorn. I'd thought to tell your brother in your place. There'd been no word o' ye for months."

On the long ride, Conall had revealed to Rob all the events since last they'd seen each other at Loch Drurie. Rob was as enraged as Iain had been when Conall told him about the ambush in the wood and the Nordic slaver.

"You did right in coming, and I owe you much. Had I been able to get word to you, to anyone, I would have."

"That whoreson will pay." Rob's cheeks blazed with color, and Conall knew it wasn't from the cold.

His brothers shared Rob's view, which is why they took an army with them to Falmar.

"I cannot think on that now," he said. "'Tis the farthest thing from my mind, truth be told."

Besides, what there was to settle with the Symons was between Conall and the chieftain alone. He'd told

Iain that a dozen times in the past twenty hours, but his brother would not be swayed.

"Hold up!" Gilchrist cried as they topped the rise.

"The crossroad," Conall said, and spurred his mount to the head of the pack. Jupiter bounded to his side. The mastiff's fortitude was amazing.

The horses were lathered, the men spent, everyone's breath frosted the icy air. They'd barely rested since leaving Findhorn, and it appeared Iain would now call a break. Conall would have none of it.

"I'll ride on," he said to his brothers. "You can catch me up."

"Nay." Iain nudged his mount alongside him. "We'll all go."

Conall smiled at him, unsurprised. "My thanks for this, brother, even though 'tis not entirely necessary."

"Of course it is," Gilchrist said, edging his way between them. "We're clan. Family."

"Aye." Conall met their steady gazes in turn and nodded. "That we are."

"All right, then," Iain said. "Let's ride."

Dark clouds masked the setting of the sun, when it finally came. There was no twilight to speak of, just a dull, dim gray. A nightingale's song broke the steady thud of hoofbeats on the half-frozen ground, and the sounds of creaking livery as the men rode in silent determination toward their goal.

Halfway to Falmar on the east-west trail, Jupiter stopped short where a narrow path led north, higher along the ridge line flanking the trail.

Conall joined him. "What is it, boy? What do you smell?"

The mastiff nosed a tangle of whortleberry just off

the path. Conall squinted into the half darkness and suddenly recalled where he was. 'Twas the path he and Rob and Dora had taken the night he swam Falmar's moat to retrieve Mairi.

He remembered the narrow path had many cuts along it, affording one opportunities to rejoin the main road, should one wish to.

Jupiter began to whine.

"What's amiss?" he heard Iain shout from the head of their party, which was now stopped to see why Conall tarried.

"I dinna know," he called to his brother.

"'Tis a wee path that parallels the road," Rob said, "in some places no more than a stone's throw from it."

"Ride on," Conall called. "I'll follow the path for a bit, then meet up with you."

Jupiter took off. Conall didn't wait for his brother's response. Driving his mount through the foliage, he followed the mastiff onto the path.

Mairi stared in horror at the cup of steaming liquid in Geoffrey's hand.

"But ye must drink it, love. 'Twill make ye well again."

Her mouth went dry as he eased onto the bed beside her. While Geoffrey hadn't lived the noblest of lives, never in her wildest imaginings had she thought him capable of such evil. The look of triumph in his eyes as she took the cup from him was more chilling, even, than his words.

He meant to kill her unborn child.

"That's it," he said, encouraging her. "Drink it all down. And if ye like, I'll have Tang prepare more."

"A-aye. When it c-cools a bit." With a shaking hand she managed to reach past him and place the cup on the table flanking the bed. The smell of the potion itself made her want to retch. The thought of what it would do to her child made her want to rip Geoffrey's own dagger from its sheath and plunge it into his heart.

She did neither.

Instead, she smiled at him. 'Twas the hardest thing she'd ever done in her life.

"The priest is arrived, is he no'?"

Geoffrey smiled back. "Aye. He waits below stairs. As do my kinsmen from the west."

He meant the Frasers, who'd arrived at Falmar mere moments after Geoffrey had come upon her in the hallway. 'Twas a stroke of luck, for their presence had distracted him for hours. Hours she'd used to prepare a means of escape.

She didn't know for certain if Geoffrey was aware of her eavesdropping, but instinct told her he was not. After he'd carried her up to bed to rest, he'd left her chamber unlocked, and her free to roam about the castle.

"Leave me now, so I might prepare. A bride has much to do."

He leaned in to kiss her, and she forced herself to kiss back. The moment he left the chamber, she washed her mouth out with a slug of fresh water from the ewer, then dashed the foul contents of the cup that Geoffrey had ordered prepared for her into the chamber pot under her bed.

Fleetingly she thought of Conall. Recalling the momentary look of pain in his eyes when she left him in the wood, she cursed herself for not telling him the truth of things. 'Twas foolish pride that had stopped her.

But that was meaningless now, as were her other feelings, and his. All that mattered was the safety of her unborn child. She had no choice. She must get to Findhorn, or at least Monadhliath, and ask the Mackintoshes for help.

She dragged from under the bed the saddlebag she'd packed earlier that afternoon. A bit of food, a full water skin, and a couple of dark hunting plaids were all it contained. 'Twould have to do.

From the small window in her chamber she saw that torches had been lit all along the land bridge leading to Falmar's entrance. The icy water of the moat glittered black. Men came and went, on foot and on horseback, over the bridge. Geoffrey had gone all out to impress the Frasers, and preparations were still under way for the celebration that would follow the speaking of their vows.

'Twas now or never.

Mairi tossed the saddlebag over her shoulder and used one of the hunting plaids as a cloak, covering her telltale red hair and shrouding her features. She was below stairs and out the great front door, which stood wide tonight, in minutes.

No one had noticed her amongst the scores of Frasers and Symons already making merry. She kept her head down and her feet moving as she stepped into the bailey and made for the line of mounts tethered nearby.

A Fraser warrior stood guard over the animals, though at the moment he seemed much engaged with a buxom Symon lass sporting two overflowing ale cups.

Mairi saw her chance and took it.

The mount she chose was small and apparently docile, for it allowed her to lead it away from the rest of the pack and out of sight behind a farrier's cottage.

It took her three tries before she was seated, awkwardly and skirts askew, in the saddle. Riding was not on her shortlist of talents. She swore and grabbed the pommel as the horse took off in response to her digging her heels into its sides.

By the time it shot from the cover of the cottage and into the bailey, which was choked with other riders, revelers on foot and wagons loaded with kegs of ale, she'd managed to grab the reins and find her seat.

No one seemed to pay her any mind. The young warrior charged with guarding the mounts was already kissing the buxom lass. Mairi guessed 'twould be hours before he noticed one of his charges was missing. And one hour was all she needed. Just enough for a head start.

Where the land bridge met the gate at the outer bailey, she turned in the saddle and looked back. The plaid slipped from her head, revealing her fire-bright hair, as her gaze connected with a set of ice-blue eyes.

Geoffrey stood amidst the revelers looking directly at her.

She didn't think, she didn't cry out, she simply turned and rode, thundering across the land bridge toward the wood, driving the stolen mount as fast as it would go. Which proved much faster than she'd expected. 'Twas all she could do to keep her seat.

In seconds she'd made the wood, revelers and other riders scattering before her. A wagon nearly pitched over the edge into the moat as its driver worked frantically to remove it from her path.

She didn't have to look back to know Geoffrey was behind her. By the time she turned onto the tiny, unmarked path flanking the main road—the path she and Conall had used the night he'd come to fetch her—she heard hoofbeats on her tail.

The path was steep and the foliage close. She leaned low over the pommel and urged her mount to fly. When at last they made the ridge line, she saw torches on the road below her streaming out from Falmar's main gate. Geoffrey's men. They'd missed the path! Thank God!

When the trail leveled out, she reined the horse in, slowing their speed. She must think now. The path would join the main road again in little more than a league. She had to get off it and away from the road altogether. But which way? Due west? Northwest? Findhorn and Monadhliath lay due north, and while she knew this bit of the forest like the back of her hand, 'twas dark, and she feared getting lost should she leave the path.

Hoofbeats sounded behind her. Nay, wait, in front of her!

Oh, God.

"Which way?" Her mount burst into a clearing, and she reined him hard left, then right, assessing her options. There *was* someone behind her—and ahead of her.

Before she could make her choice, the rider following close behind caught her up.

Geoffrey! The moon had risen, and cast the hard features of his face in a deathly gray.

In seconds he was on her. "Bitch!"

She fought him, but he was far too strong. Mairi

screamed. Their mounts reared, and Geoffrey tumbled with her to the ground, breaking her fall.

"Think ye to jilt me again?" He rolled on top of her, pinning her beneath him. "With my liege-lord witness to it?"

She struggled to free herself, but 'twas useless. "I'll never wed ye, never!"

Hoofbeats drummed on the path ahead. Others— dozens, hundreds, she couldn't tell how many—thundered on the road below them from both directions.

"Aye, ye will, and willing, too. Or I'll see that orphaned snipe ye call son meets with an accident."

"Kip!" God, no! "Ye'd dare to kill him, and my unborn babe, as well?" She fought violently, pummeling him with her fists, twisting beneath him, desperate to free herself.

A rider, silhouetted against the moon's pale light, burst into the clearing, nearly trampling them. A Fraser? A Symon? 'Twas too dark to tell.

Geoffrey rolled sideways, dragging her with him, paying his kinsman no mind. "Ye think I'd let that bastard spawn live inside ye? Think again!"

She snatched at the dirk belted at his waist, but he was too quick for her. A split second later 'twas in his hand, its point pressed against her abdomen.

"Dinna harm my child!" Mairi cried.

The rider leaped from his mount. His war cry ripped the air. "*My* child!" he roared.

"Conall!"

Chapter Eighteen

Jupiter got to him first.

Symon cried out as the mastiff sank his teeth into a flailing leg. He dropped the dirk, and Mairi scrambled for it. A heartbeat later, Conall jerked him off her, his own blade poised at Symon's throat.

"Get up!" he ordered, dragging the chieftain to his knees.

Symon clutched at his trapped leg. "Devil beast!"

"Jupiter, off." At Conall's command, the mastiff released him but continued to snarl, planting himself squarely between Symon and Mairi.

"'Tis truly you?" Mairi struggled to her feet, brandishing Symon's dirk.

"Are you hurt?"

"Nay." She was breathing hard, and he feared desperately for her welfare. Moonlight flashed off steel as she maneuvered around the dog. Just in time, he read her intent.

"Stay back!"

Symon swore as Conall dragged him backward, away from her, pressing the edge of the blade against his throat.

Men's shouts and hundreds of hoofbeats sounded on the road below them. Torchlight flashed through the trees. Conall's mount nearly reared in the tight surroundings as Geoffrey cried out and began to struggle.

"He gave me poison to drink, to murder my child!"

Conall's gut clenched. He'd heard a moment's worth of the conversation between them when he'd come upon them, but hadn't realized Symon had already acted on his words.

"I poured it out. I fled. I meant to find your brothers, and—"

Symon shrieked out a laugh. "And do what? Tell them ye're a whore?"

Conall nearly slit his throat.

"Get up!" He jerked Symon to his feet and slammed him into a tree. "Draw your sword! Draw it!"

"Sweet God," Mairi breathed, and moved behind him. The feel of her hand lighting briefly on his arm was like a tonic.

"Take my mount," he said to her. "Get ye gone!" He sheathed his dirk and drew his broadsword. Symon did the same.

"Nay, I will no' leave ye."

Hoofbeats sounded closer. Jupiter began to bark. Light flickered from behind them on the path, but Conall would not be turned. Symon whirled on him as another mount burst into the clearing, its rider bearing a torch, flooding their surroundings with golden light.

"Rob!" Conall nodded toward Mairi. "Get her out of here."

"Nay! I will no' go."

Rob reached for her arm, tried to make her mount behind him, but she'd have none of it.

"Nay, I say!"

Geoffrey lunged.

Conall reacted, a rush of raw emotion propelling him forward. Steel clashed with steel. They pushed off and came at each other again.

Mairi cried out.

Symon ducked, parried, and Conall went for him, his rage exploding into a dark, primitive force, fueling a strength and determination he hadn't known he possessed.

Symon would have murdered his child. *Their* child.

He'd heard his brothers speak of bloodlust, that all-consuming maelstrom of passion and pain and rage that would not, could not be quelled without action. He'd not felt it till this night, this moment, when what he cherished most in the world—the stalwart woman behind him, the babe inside her womb—was viciously threatened.

At the edge of his awareness he registered a thunder of hoofbeats, torchlight, his brothers' shouts, clanking livery and steel unleashed. But all his world was Symon, who came at him one more time.

Conall's blade connected, his sword arm rigid as stone. 'Twas met with more resistance than he'd expected as it slid into Symon's gut. In shock, the chieftain's blue eyes widened.

Suddenly men were all around them, on horseback, on foot—his kinsmen, his brothers—weapons drawn. Jupiter barked a greeting.

Symon's body thudded to earth as Conall freed his blade.

Weeping, Mairi rushed to his side. In a daze, he pulled her to him, held her close.

Iain didn't bother to dismount. Grasping the situation, he said, ''See to your woman. The Frasers are below.'' With his sword he pointed toward the road. ''Gilchrist and I will take care of it.''

''Nay. *I* shall take care of it. 'Tis my doing.'' He nodded at the dead chieftain lying at his feet.

His brothers exchanged a glance, surprised, he knew, at this change in him. He *was* changed. Irrevocably. The love of the woman looking up at him was the cause.

''What mean ye to do?'' she said, clutching him desperately. ''They are an army, come to see Geoffrey wed. They will strike ye down, they will—''

''Go with Rob.'' He pressed her into the warrior's arms.

''Nay, I will not! I will stay with ye.''

''Take a dozen men with you,'' he said to Rob. ''Take her to Loch Drurie and stay there.''

Rob nodded and pulled her toward his mount.

''Nay!'' Mairi struggled, but Rob would not be put off. In the end it took two men to seat her behind him on the mare, with her fighting them every move.

'''Twill be all right,'' Conall said, and held her gaze as he sheathed his bloodied sword.

''Will ye come?'' she asked, breathless.

A kinsman steadied his horse so he could mount. ''Aye,'' he said. ''Count on it.''

They were the longest hours of her life.

Mairi paced the worn floorboards of the lake house, taking care not to wake Kip. He'd fallen asleep on her pallet, waiting up with her for Conall to return.

'Twas well past midnight, now, with no sign of him or anyone. In the village all was quiet. The sounds of insects, nocturnal birds, an occasional splash of a fish breaking the still surface of the loch were the only respite from a silence that weighed heavy on her heart.

Count on it, he'd said. And she knew he'd not break his word.

He'd come to claim her and his child. Still, she couldn't believe he hadn't known 'twas his that day in the wood. She'd been so certain. On the ride back from Falmar, Rob convinced her he'd *not* known. He'd thought the babe was Geoffrey's!

That explained much.

Mairi paused, gazed blankly at the fire crackling in the hearth and shook her head, remembering.

The question burning in her mind, the question that kept her from sleep, from any rest at all, was *why?* Why had he come? Did he think to take the child, once born, but not her? Men have done so before. Perhaps he didn't want either of them, but was forced to action by his brothers.

Another possibility filled her mind, her heart, infused her blood with a drug that was part joy, part fear, and that kept her pacing, on edge, ears pricked to every sound.

Perhaps he wanted them both.

"D'ye hear it?" Kip's sleepy voice pulled her from her thoughts.

"Go back to sleep. 'Tis a dream."

"Nay, I hear them." He blinked the sleep from his eyes and threw off the plaid that covered him.

Mairi listened.

"There!" Kip said. "'Tis a dog's bark." Like a

shot he was at the window, ripping the deerskin drape away so both of them could see.

"Good Lord."

Torchlight danced between the trees in the wood above the village, reflecting gold off the dark water.

"Look!" Kip shouted. "He comes!"

A moment later Jupiter burst from the trees onto the beach, instantly grabbed a stick and began to play. Not bothering to slip on his boots, Kip ripped the cottage door wide and shot down the pier toward shore.

"Conall!" he cried. "Conall!"

Mairi's heart twisted tight inside her chest. She gripped the window frame and waited. What if he'd only come to wish her well? To offer gold or goods for her child's maintenance? She couldn't bear to watch him break Kip's heart again.

Could she bear having her own cloven in two?

A rider broke from the trees, and she knew at once 'twas him. He sat tall in the saddle, the golden light of torches borne by his kinsmen illuminating the chiseled features of his face.

Mairi held her breath.

Kip hit the beach at a dead run and nearly collided with the mastiff. The two of them tumbled head over heels over paws onto the sand, Jupiter licking Kip's face with unleashed joy.

Conall dismounted a few feet from where they tangled. Kip looked up at him, his face alight. Conall spoke to him, but 'twas impossible from this distance for Mairi to hear his words.

When he knelt in the sand and opened his arms to the boy, she felt a pressure inside her chest she feared might crush her. Tears welled hot in her eyes as Kip embraced him, and Conall pulled him close.

She moved to the open door and watched as Conall lifted him off his feet and swung him 'round. She heard their laughter, Jupiter's deep bellow, and choked out a sound—half laugh, half joyful cry—herself.

The two disengaged, and Kip and Jupiter scampered off together into the trees to welcome the other riders. Cottage doors opened. Women poked their heads out to see who'd come. Dougal and Rob appeared, taking charge of directing the party to the camp next to the village where they might rest.

All of this Mairi was aware of only peripherally. For her gaze was fixed on the man who now stood at the far end of the pier, still as stone, looking at her.

He approached, and she dared not breathe.

Torchlight silhouetted his shoulders and powerful legs as he moved with purpose toward her, the floating timbers of the pier rolling under his weight.

She backed into the cottage, unable to take her eyes from him. Soft firelight lit up his features, burned golden-green in his eyes as he drew near. What meant he to do? To say?

She watched, rapt, as the muscles of his face strained with emotions she could not fathom. He stepped across the threshold and quietly shut the door.

They stood there for a moment, a lifetime, mute, drinking each other in. At last she said, "Ye've come."

"Aye. Did you think I wouldn't?"

"Nay, I knew ye would." She took stock of his clothing, his hands, the dirk belted at his waist. She saw no blood, nor any outward sign that a battle had ensued after Rob had spirited her away to safety on Conall's order.

Save one thing.

A long black braid of human hair hung from his badger-skin sporran like a trophy. With a shock she realized 'twas Tang's. She knew without asking that Conall had killed him.

"What of Fraser?" she said, fearful to hear the answer. "Shall there be war between ye?"

He cast her a half smile, and the sight of it, the memories it invoked, caused her heart to swell. She worked to keep a rein on her emotions.

"Nay," he said. "There shall be no war."

She was stunned and knew it showed on her face. "How did ye manage to avoid it?" Fraser was a proud man. 'Twas hard to believe he'd allow the killing of one of his chieftains to go unpunished.

Conall's smile broadened. He lifted his shoulders in a casual shrug. "I did what I do best," he said. "I bargained."

She laughed at that. She couldn't help herself, recalling the day they met, when first he proposed the arrangement to build out her docks and deliver the lake trade.

As she continued to look at him, his smile faded. Hers faded, too. She stood her ground and waited for him to speak. He did not. 'Twas almost as if he couldn't speak. The situation reminded her much of that rainy day they had parted three months ago.

It dawned on her that this waiting, this holding back on her part—fueled by pride and fear—'twas, perhaps, the cause of all their trouble to begin with. "Conall," she said, and took a step toward him.

A heartbeat later his arms went 'round her. He crushed her to him, peppered kisses in her hair, across her eyelids, over her face. His mouth, at last, claimed hers and she gave herself up to pure sensation.

"Are you hurt?" he said, pulling back long enough to inspect her for injury. "Did he harm you?" He meant Geoffrey.

"Nay." She looked up at him and was undone by the raw emotion she saw reflected in his eyes. "But he meant to. If ye hadn't come, he might have."

"Mairi, I—" He shook his head, and 'twas clear to her he would say more but couldn't get the words out. "The babe."

"All is well," she said quickly. "There's naught to fear." Dora had examined her closely upon her return and had confirmed it.

"Thank God for that." He ran his hands over her arms, looking at her with unmasked wonder in his eyes, as if seeing her for the first time. "*Our* babe," he said. "Mine and yours."

"Aye."

He pulled her tight against him, burying his face in her hair. She held on to him, reveling in the feel of his arms around her, his scent, his breath hot against her ear.

"Why did you not tell me? Send for me, when first you knew? Nay, dinna answer, for I know why."

"Do ye?"

He pulled away to look at her. "Aye, because I gave you no reason to believe I wanted such a gift. I left you without a word, without a hint of my heart's true feeling."

"I did the same," she admitted. "I let ye go."

They looked at each other, and she read the pain in his eyes. A pain she shared. One that would not be lifted till all that needed saying was finally said.

"I would no' bind ye to me unwilling. Nor will I now." There. 'Twas done.

"Mairi, I—"

"Rob told me of your mishap, of Geoffrey's treachery, the slave ship and the Norseman who offered ye aid." She was babbling now, fearful of what he'd say next.

"I deserved it."

"Dinna say that."

"Aye, well…" He shrugged. "All the same, the time away helped me to see things clear in my mind, in my heart."

She dared to hope the light she saw in his eyes, the half smile edging his lips, meant…

"The day I left here, I had a change of heart and turned 'round. I was on my way back to you when Symon's men overcame me in the wood at the crossroad. Did Rob tell you?"

"Nay." She was stunned. "But…why?"

He smiled, and crushed her so tightly to him she could barely breathe. "Do you not know?"

She tilted her face upward and looked into his eyes. His lips hovered a hairbreadth above hers.

"For the same reason I meant to come for you once I'd learned you were not wed. To win you back, if it were possible."

"Yet ye believed the child inside me belonged to Geoffrey?"

"Aye."

Mairi stopped breathing. "Ye would have done that?"

He kissed her again, gently, with a tenderness she'd ne'er experienced with him before. "In a heartbeat. For I love you, Mairi Dunbar, more than all the world."

At once she felt the weight of her doubts lift off like some wild bird newly freed from long captivity.

"I knew that day I left you long months ago. I knew but wouldn't believe."

He cupped her face in his hands and kissed her again. Then, without warning, he lifted her off her feet and into his arms. She gasped in surprise and delight.

"And what of you, sweetling?" he said as he carried her to the narrow bed heaped with plaids. "Could you love a fool?"

"Nay," she said, and his face fell. "But I could love a rogue, an adventurer."

He laughed and laid her gently on the bed, easing himself beside her. Firelight danced in his eyes. His hair burned gold and red, and colors she'd yet to discover and could not name.

"Methinks there will be adventure enough for me right here." He moved his hand to the soft swell of her abdomen, and his face grew serious. "Will you have me, Mairi? As husband? As father to Kip and to our child?"

She felt the sting of tears and willed them not break for fear her joy would be mistaken. "Aye, I will. With all my heart." She kissed him and the power of their love coursed like fire through her body, awakening every inch of skin, every nerve.

His hand slid downward, his fingers toying with the hem of her gown, easing upward along her leg. "Ye *are* a rogue," she breathed, and giggled against his lips.

He touched her, and she gasped.

"Aye," he said, "*your* rogue." And then he proceeded to prove it.

Epilogue

Six months later

"She's a redhead!" Kip cried, and opened his arms to accept the tiny, swaddled newborn.

"O' course she is." Dora cast Mairi and Conall an amused look. "What did ye expect?"

Conall's arms tightened 'round her, and Mairi gazed up at him, her heart full. "She's as beautiful as her mother," he said, and brushed a kiss across her lips.

"But I wanted a brother!" Kip turned forlorn eyes on him. "Did ye no' want a son?"

Mairi held her breath and awaited her husband's answer.

Conall looked thoughtfully at the boy. "I already have a son. You."

Kip's face lit up, and Mairi's heart swelled with love for their new-made family.

"And the lass's name?" Dora, ever practical, arched a brow at them.

"Gladys, after my mother," Mairi said.

"And Ellen, after mine." Conall lovingly stroked the baby's fire-gold hair.

"Gladys Ellen," Dora said, and nodded satisfaction.

"I shall call her Gladdy." Kip placed the baby in Mairi's arms. "She can play with us!" He ran to the door and yanked it wide. Jupiter pranced into the room, his enormous tail *thwacking* against the furniture.

"Aye, when she's older." Dora shooed them both into the corridor of the fortified house on the hill above the loch. "Now, let's leave your mam and da to themselves and the little one." She stood in the doorway and sighed, her eyes fixed on Gladdy's tiny face.

After Dora closed the door, Mairi said, "She's pregnant, ye know."

"Dora?" Conall nearly came off the bed. "At her age?"

"She's no' so old." Mairi pouted and smoothed the baby's hair.

"Does Rob know?"

"Oh, nay. She's trying to think of a gentle way to break the news."

Conall laughed. "Aye, well, the best way is to hit him right over the head with it. Perhaps 'twill knock some sense into him."

"As it did with ye?" She shot him a mischievous half smile.

"Aye," he breathed, and kissed her again, this time more fervently.

"So, is it worth it to ye?" Mairi whispered against his lips. "The responsibility, the risks?"

"Is what worth it, sweetling?"

She nodded at the sleeping babe in her arms. "Love."

His eyes shone. "Aye, wife. 'Tis a gift and a wonder I know not how I lived without. You taught me that, Mairi. You and Kip, and our babe." He worked a fingertip into Gladdy's tiny, clenched fist. "I shall love and protect you, little one, all the days of my life."

Mairi gazed into her husband's shining eyes, and knew without doubt that he would. In the days since they'd wed, they spoke often of Alwin Dunbar, of the choices he'd made, and the gentle peace Mairi had come to know, at last, in understanding him.

"I was right about ye all along, Conall Mackintosh." She smiled up at him, and he tilted his head in question. "Ye are much like my father, after all."

* * * * *

DEBRA LEE BROWN

Golden Heart winner Debra Lee Brown's ongoing romance with wild and remote locales sparks frequent adventures in the Alps, the Arctic—where she has worked as a geologist—and the Sierra Nevada range of her native California. It's not surprising Debra chooses to set her novels in the rugged highlands of medieval Scotland. An Old English mastiff—the size of a Shetland pony—and a stubborn Scottish husband provide Debra with additional inspiration for her writing. Debra invites readers to visit her Web site at **www.debraleebrown.com** or to write to her care of Harlequin Reader Service, P.O. Box 1325, Buffalo, NY 14269.

HHIBC625

ENJOY THE SPLENDOR OF
Merry Old England

with these spirited stories
from Harlequin Historicals

On Sale November 2002

GIFTS OF THE SEASON
by Miranda Jarrett
Lyn Stone
Anne Gracie
*Three beloved authors come together in this
Regency Christmas collection!*

THE DUMONT BRIDE
by Terri Brisbin
*Will a marriage of convenience between a lovely
English heiress and a dashing French count
blossom into everlasting love?*

On Sale December 2002

NORWYCK'S LADY
by Margo Maguire
*Passion and adventure unfold when an injured
Scottish woman washes up on shore and is
rescued by an embittered lord!*

LORD SEBASTIAN'S WIFE
by Katy Cooper
*Watch the sparks fly when a world-weary nobleman
discovers that his adolescent betrothal to a deceptive
lady from his youth is legal and binding!*

 Harlequin Historicals®
Historical Romantic Adventure!

HHMED27

FALL IN LOVE
THIS WINTER
WITH
HARLEQUIN BOOKS!

In October 2002 look for these special volumes
led by *USA TODAY* bestselling authors,
and receive a MOULIN ROUGE VHS video*!
*Retail value of $14.99 U.S.

See inside books for details.

***This exciting promotion
is available at your
favorite retail outlet.***

Only from

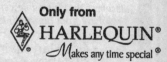

HARLEQUIN®

Makes any time special ®

Visit Harlequin at www.eHarlequin.com   PHNCP02

If you enjoyed what you just read,
then we've got an offer you can't resist!

Take 2 bestselling love stories FREE!

Plus get a FREE surprise gift!

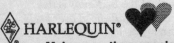